CAROL HIGGINS CLARK

HITCHED

A Regan Reilly Mystery

DOUBLEDAY LARGE PRINT HOME LIBRARY EDITION

SCRIBNER
New York   London   Toronto   Sydney

This Large Print Edition, prepared especially for Doubleday Large Print Home Library, contains the complete, unabridged text of the original Publisher's Edition.

SCRIBNER
1230 Avenue of the Americas
New York, NY 10020

Copyright © 2006 by Carol Higgins Clark

SCRIBNER and design are trademarks of Macmillan Library Reference USA, Inc., used under license by Simon & Schuster, the publisher of this work.

Manufactured in the United States of America

ISBN-13: 978-0-7394-6671-1
ISBN-10: 0-7394-6671-2

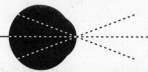

This Large Print Book carries the
Seal of Approval of N.A.V.H.

Acknowledgments

I would like to express my gratitude to the following people who helped get Regan Reilly to the altar!

My editor, Roz Lippel, who's been there since Regan first laid eyes on Jack "No Relation" Reilly.

My agent, Esther Newberg.

My publicist, Lisl Cade.

Associate Director of Copyediting Gypsy da Silva, copy editor Anthony Newfield, proofreaders Barbara Raynor and Jonah Tully.

Art director John Fulbrook III, jacket designer Jason Heuer, photographers Jethro Soudant and Glenn Jussen.

My mother, Mary Higgins Clark, my family, and friends.

My readers who have accompanied Regan along the way, as she went from *Ms.* Reilly to *Mrs.* Reilly.

Thank you one and all!

For Roz Lippel
and
Lisl Cade
—my editor and my publicist—
My good friends
With love and thanks!

HITCHED

Saturday, April 2nd

Regan Reilly descended the staircase from the second floor of her parents' home in Summit, New Jersey, as she had on countless Saturday mornings in the thirty-one years of her life. As usual, she was headed for the kitchen where her mother would be putting out breakfast. But this Saturday was different.

It was her last Saturday as a single.

Regan's hand lightly brushed the banister as she reached the bottom step and turned toward the living room. The presents from her bridal shower, held the night before, were neatly stacked in the corner—everything from the latest and greatest cappuccino machine that Regan was sure she'd never be able to figure out, to a clock radio that blared "Today is the first day of the rest of your life" when the alarm went off. The set of gleaming kitchen knives had intrigued

Regan the most. A private investigator, she had examined them closely. The only other present that could have been considered a deadly weapon was the cookbook, her father, Luke, had remarked.

Luke and Regan's fiancé, Jack "No Relation" Reilly, had escaped to a restaurant in town, and then returned to join the women for an after-dinner drink. All the obligatory oohing and aahing over the household goods and lingerie were mercifully over. Jack's mother, sisters, and aunts were at the shower as well as many of Regan's old family friends. It had been a lively party.

Regan had flown in two days before from Los Angeles where she had her own PI agency. There was now one week left to finalize all the arrangements before she went from Ms. Reilly to Mrs. Reilly. Today she was heading into New York City with her mother, Nora, and her best friend, Kit, to pick up her wedding gown.

Getting married is a lot of work, Regan had thought more than once since she'd gotten engaged six months ago. It was easy to see why women turned into Bridezillas. But all the hassle was worth it. Jack was what she had waited for all her life and they both wanted to celebrate with their friends and family by having a large, festive wedding.

After years of enduring dates with losers, weirdos, and, worst of all, cheapskates, Regan often felt that she would never meet her soul mate. It took her father getting kidnapped for her to find Jack. He was the head of the Major Case Squad in New York City and had worked day and night to get Luke back. In the process, he and Regan had fallen in love.

At the large butcher block table in the kitchen, Nora and Kit were sipping coffee and munching on blueberry muffins.

"Good morning," Regan said cheerily. "Kit, I can't believe you're up. We don't have to head into the city for another fifteen minutes."

"I was sleepless thinking about seeing you in your wedding gown today," Kit said in her usual droll tone. "I never thought the day would arrive. I never thought *my* day would arrive. Yours did. Mine, I'm sure, never will."

Regan laughed as Nora cooed sympathetically. "Of course it will."

"Mom, don't worry about Kit," Regan said

as she poured herself a cup of coffee. "Kit, we'll get through everything that this next week entails, get me married off, and then I'm sure we'll be planning your wedding before . . . before uh . . ."

"Before what?" Kit asked as she spread butter on her muffin. "Before the cows come home?"

"Way before that," Regan answered with a wave of her hand. "Life can change in an instant. I still have a week before I walk down the aisle. Who knows what could happen before then?"

Nora jumped up, an alarmed expression on her face. "Don't even think like that, Regan. Everything is going to be wonderful. Now let's finish our coffee, get in the car, and drive into the city to pick up the gorgeous dress you will wear one week from today. I must say I'm glad it'll be the last time we have to deal with those crazy designers and that drafty loft they have the nerve to call a bridal salon."

Regan and Kit looked at each other and laughed.

"Mom, Charisse and Alfred are a very talented couple and they are starting to make their mark in the fashion world. They're booked a year in advance. I'm glad they were willing to squeeze me in. Pretty soon they're going to be household names."

None of them could have predicted that Charisse and Alfred's quest for fame would be sped up by their appearance on the front page of the following day's *New York Post.*

With Regan at the wheel, Nora's Mercedes-Benz glided into the Holland Tunnel.

"It's a lovely day," Nora sighed as the sunlight disappeared behind them. "I hope it's like this next Saturday."

"I do, too. But it's April. You never know . . ." Regan's voice trailed off.

"A girl in my office scheduled her wedding for late October on Martha's Vineyard. Wouldn't you know a nor'easter hit that very day? When they got to the reception, the restaurant was without power. And the backup generator had gone kaput," Kit remarked from the backseat.

"Thanks, Kit." Regan smiled. "I'll be sure to pray for good weather."

Fifteen minutes later they parked the car in a lot not too far from the heart of Little Italy. Alfred and Charisse's Coutures was located in a loft on the entire third floor of a building that, in Nora's opinion, was in need of a makeover.

"I don't know what the allure is of places like these," Nora muttered as they walked down a side street that looked like the Broadway set for *Cats.*

"People love it down here," Regan commented. "And if you're in fashion, it makes you seem hip to have an address like this. It's where old New York meets the new. The pushcarts of yesteryear have been replaced by trendy boutiques."

"What's wrong with Madison Avenue?" Nora asked as she stepped over a piece of broken glass on the cracked sidewalk. They stopped in front of an old building and caught the door as a young couple was coming out. Regan held the door open as she pushed the buzzer for Alfred and Charisse's loft. There was no answer. She pushed it again, and they waited.

Kit looked at her watch. "It's eleven o'clock."

"I can't imagine where they'd be. They live here and they're expecting us," Regan said.

"We've already made it through security . . ." Nora remarked wryly, glancing around at the empty lobby.

"That we have," Regan agreed. "Let's head upstairs."

The three of them got on a large, battered, groaning elevator, which took its time about everything. The car slowly ascended to the third floor where it stopped with a jerk. A loud click and a mournful moan followed. After an agonizing six seconds, the door opened.

Right away Regan could tell something was wrong. The door to the loft was ajar. Whenever she'd been at the salon, Alfred always made a point to keep the door closed. He was paranoid that his genius might float out the door and people would somehow steal the ideas for his designs. Regan hurried across the hall and pushed the door fully open. There was no one in sight. The dress racks were empty. But one lone gown was in shreds on the floor.

"Charisse?" Regan called. "Alfred?"

There was no answer.

Nora grabbed Regan's arm. "Regan, be careful."

"Charisse?" Regan called again, her voice rising. "Alfred?" She slowly moved farther into the loft and saw that the shredded dress had drops of blood on it. Regan inhaled sharply and hurried to the back of the loft and around the corner to where she knew their bedroom was. Gingerly, Regan opened the door.

"Oh, my God!" Regan cried.

Charisse and Alfred were stretched out on their bed, bound and gagged. Regan hurried over and removed Alfred's gag.

"Regan!" he cried, struggling for breath. "A couple of thieves broke in here in the middle of the night. They tied us up. I thought they were going to kill us. They smashed our safe here in the bedroom and grabbed our cash and jewelry!"

"They did more than that," Regan said quickly as she ran around the bed and untied the cloth around Charisse's mouth. "It looks like all your dresses are gone. Except one that could use a lot of help."

Two screams pierced the air: One belonged to Alfred. The other emanated from the owner of that sorry bridal gown who had just arrived in the next room.

Regan couldn't decide whose scream was worse.

———◆———

Jack had gone to his parents' house in Bed-ford, New York, after Regan's shower. He'd wanted to spend a little time with his family on Saturday. The next week would be hec-tic, and he was burdened with a series of bank robberies that had been taking place around the city since January. The robber always struck when it was raining hard or snowing and everyone was wearing gloves and hats and bulky clothing. The perp would walk into a bank wearing a dark hooded raincoat, dark glasses, and a fake beard or mustache. Most criminals who knew they'd be caught on surveillance cam-eras did their best to disguise their look—this bank robber was no exception.

The banks were always on alert, but this case had them all stymied. They'd studied the surveillance pictures from all eight rob-beries, but so far had no suspect. Whoever it was always managed to escape into the driving rain or snow and disappear.

It was driving Jack crazy. He hoped there'd be a break in the case before he got married and went on his honeymoon. He and Regan would be spending two and a half weeks in Europe. Then, the best part was that after this trip she was coming home with him, not heading back to Los Angeles. The last few weeks she'd sent numerous boxes filled with clothes, pictures, and books to his apartment. It didn't bother her at all to move into his place. She didn't give him any of the I-won't-feel-as-if-it's-our-home. Instead, she'd said, "I love your apartment. Let's see how we feel in a year or two, then we can make a move if we want."

Jack's mother had cooked a late breakfast for the assorted family members who'd come into town for the shower. Most weren't leaving until after the wedding.

"One more week, Jack," his mother had said when she handed him a plate of eggs.

"This time next week Sheila Mullen will be drowning her sorrows," Jack's older sister, Trish, teased.

"I haven't seen her since high school," Jack protested.

"She was always sweet on you," his mother remembered. "But Regan is 'The One.' "

"You've got that right, Mom," Jack said as he salted his eggs. He was about to dig in when his cell phone rang. He glanced at the caller ID: 201. That's Nora's cell phone, he realized. Flipping it open, he answered quickly. "Is everything all right?" he asked.

As he listened, his body relaxed. "Nora, I'll leave now." He closed the phone and looked around at all the inquiring faces of his family members. "Regan's dress was stolen. The designers' studio was broken into last night. That's all I know."

"That's enough!" his mother exclaimed as Jack took off out the back door.

___

"Mommmmmyyyyyyy! Look at my dress!"

Regan finished untying the rope that bound Charisse's delicate wrists and ran back into the front room while Alfred yelled, "I'll call 911!" The scene that greeted Regan was like something out of a Greek tragedy. A red-haired young woman was crumpled on the floor, clutching the shredded blood-ied garment that as of eight hours ago was supposed to make her feel like a princess on the biggest day of her life. Now the sight of its ruination had transformed her into a raving lunatic. "Whyyyyyyy? Why me?"

An older woman, presumably Mommy, was standing over the bride-to-be, weakly attempting to offer comfort with a half-hearted shoulder massage. "I told you you should have worn my wedding dress. You're a little heavier than I was when I married your father, but it could have been let out. I packed that gown up so carefully in the hopes that one day a daughter of mine would want to wear it down the aisle. The pictures of Grandma on her wedding day sixty-two years ago, wearing that very dress are stunning." She shook her head. "Stunning. Too bad you didn't want to continue a family tradition."

A howl erupted from the mass of white fluff as the bride shut her eyes and cradled the gown to her breast. She lifted her head and started to shriek, "But Mom—" The second she saw Regan she stopped short. Wiping her heavily made-up eyes that now resembled a raccoon's, she grunted, "Who are you?"

"Regan Reilly. If misery loves company, then you should know that my wedding dress is among the missing."

"You see?" her mother said. "She's not crying."

"She's probably still in shock," the girl replied as she picked at a piece of black goo that was stuck in the corner of her eye. "And her dress might still be in one piece."

"I happen to be a private investigator," Regan said. "If you don't mind, could you please let go of your dress? I saw there was blood on it. It could be used to gather evidence."

In a dramatic gesture, the girl tossed the dress aside, pushed herself off the floor, and straightened up to her height of five feet nine inches. Regan figured she was probably in her midtwenties. Her short, stylish red hair, freckles, shapely but slightly stocky build, and tough attitude reminded Regan of a girl she'd gone to high school with. That is, until the girl got expelled. But the girl from high school never showed any emotion, even when she was ceremoniously shown the front door by the principal. This one looked like a case of "the bigger they come, the harder they fall."

The girl brushed off her jeans and ran her hands through her hair, which appeared to have been recently cut. All the how-to wedding books told you to get your hair cut at least two weeks before the wedding so it would look natural. Too bad they didn't drive home the fact that you should have your dress safe in your own closet at least a month before the big day.

"I'm Brianne," the girl said somewhat peevishly. "This is my mother, Teresa."

Regan shook both their hands and quickly

introduced them to her mother and Kit who had come into the room. Under different circumstances, there would have been congenial wedding talk, but these weren't different circumstances.

"How did this happen?" Brianne asked. "And where's Alfred and Charisse?"

"Here I am!" Alfred announced, appearing in a burgundy silk robe. Regan had noticed that Alfred never walked into a room. He made an entrance. Just under six feet tall, he had a thin frame, wispy brown hair and ever present facial stubble that always made Regan wonder about his shaving schedule. How could he always look as if he hadn't picked up a razor in at least three days? But he was attractive in a brooding way. "Brianne!" he now cried, sweeping toward the distraught bride-to-be. He took her strong hands, which she kept perfectly manicured—the better to flaunt her rock of an engagement ring—and leaned down to kiss them. He then turned to Teresa who was watching him with a stone face. She had never been impressed by Alfred's airs nor the prices he charged, and now she was more perturbed than ever. Her dyed-blond hair had been teased and sprayed so much it resembled a shellacked helmet. She wore bat's-eyes glasses decorated with rhine-stones, tight brown pants, high heels, and a stretch top that she tugged over her rear end every few seconds.

"Mrs. Barth! I'm so sorry! Thieves broke in last night and tied us up. They stole every-thing."

"Except my dress," Brianne muttered. "I wish they'd stolen it instead of me having to see it in this condition. It's very upsetting."

"We want our money back," Teresa said flatly.

Alfred gulped. "I will make Brianne a new dress."

"I get married *next* Saturday."

Me, too, Regan thought. There's no way they can produce two of these dresses by next week.

"Charisse and I are used to working day and night," Alfred said in a martyred tone. "I called the police. They are on their way."

"I called Regan's fiancé," Nora offered. "He's the head of the Major Case Squad. He was at his parents' house in Westchester but he'll get here as soon as he can."

"Thanks, Mom," Regan said, then turned to Alfred. "This is a crime scene. We have to be careful not to do anything that might contaminate evidence."

"My studio is a crime scene," Alfred repeated, shaking his head in disgust. "I feel violated."

Regan walked over to the front door. "There's no sign of forced entry. Did you lock up last night?"

"We ordered Chinese food because we were too tired to go out. Charisse answered the door and paid the delivery boy. Did you double lock the door, Charisse?"

"I can't be certain," Charisse said quietly. "The bag was heavy and the wonton soup was starting to spill from the container. It was hot."

Oh, great, Regan thought. The door might not have been shut properly and someone could have just pushed it open. If it weren't double locked, they might have been able to open it with a credit card.

"We had dinner in bed and were so exhausted that we just fell asleep with the television on," Alfred continued. "The next thing I knew two figures dressed in black with stocking masks over their faces were in our room tying us up. One of them smashed the safe. It all happened so fast."

"The television was still on?"

"Yes."

"Do you know what time they broke in?"

"It was three o'clock. The repeat of Larry King was coming back on. Those miserable jerks turned off the TV before they left. Just to be mean. We had to lie there in the horrible silence, scared to death until you arrived, Regan. There was nothing to distract us."

"Hello . . ." a male voice called.

They all turned as several police officers came through the door at once. Regan introduced herself. The policemen all knew Jack, and from their comments she could tell they liked and respected him very much. The officers took statements from Alfred and Charisse. A fingerprint specialist dusted the salon and bedroom. Brianne's wedding dress was placed in a special-evidence bag. A handful of reporters showed up, one with a cameraman. Brianne was happy to give them a piece of her mind, before they even had a chance to talk to Alfred, Charisse, or Regan.

When the area was cleared, and several of the police officers had left, Charisse went into the kitchen to make coffee. She opened the refrigerator and screamed. A note was taped to one of the shelves. In black Magic Marker was scrawled a message—YOUR DE-SIGNS STINK. GET OUT OF THE BUSINESS OR ELSE!

Alfred had been through hell for the last nine hours, but when he read the note, it was the worst blow of all. The words on the paper cut into his soul. He screamed and turned to Regan. "You've got to help me find who did this, Regan. I'll never sleep at night again if these vicious, cruel people aren't caught. This must have been a planned attack!"

Regan could feel Nora's body stiffen, even though she wasn't in Regan's sight line. "I'm getting married next week," she said softly. "I've got so much to do and now I have to worry about a dress . . ."

"I promise you, you'll have a fabulous dress. I *promise! Help* me, Regan! *Pleeease!* I have another bride coming to pick up her dress today and I have to tell her it's gone! I'm a little afraid of her. Don't leave me!"

"Okay, Alfred," Regan acquiesced. "My fiancé could be here soon. We'll both help you. Here he is now."

Jack was in the doorway, looking as handsome as ever. He was wearing blue jeans, a crisp white shirt, and a brown suede jacket. When he saw Regan he smiled broadly. She walked over, and as they gave each other a quick hug, Jack said under his breath, "I thought I was going to be the only one fighting crime the week before our wedding. Just promise me you'll make it to the church on time."

"You know I will," Regan said as she felt herself shudder slightly. She didn't want anything to happen to ruin their day and the start of her new life with Jack. So why did this queasy feeling suddenly come over her? She tried to push it away, telling herself, I'll help Alfred but I'm not going to let anything get in the way of my wedding. I've waited too long for someone like Jack to come into my life.

But for Regan, things never turned out to be that simple. The week before she got married would be no exception.

—————◆—————

In a row house in Queens where the planes from LaGuardia Airport roared overhead, old buddies Francis McMann and Marco Fertillo were stretched out on two well-worn couches in the small living room. Twenty-two years earlier they could be seen stretched out side by side on their mats at nap time in kindergarten, usually being told by their long-suffering teacher to stop kicking each other. Their horseplay continued for the next thirteen years, until high school graduation, when Marco took off for points west. Francis stayed close to home and got a job as a construction worker. Every couple of years since, Marco returned to New York for a visit, which never made Francis's mother happy.

"Marco's a bad influence on you," she'd cry. "Stay away from him. Why doesn't he have a job?" she'd ask Francis.

"He works at odd jobs around the country."

"Odd jobs around the country my foot," she snorted. "How long is he going to stay there with you doing nothing?"

It was the same question Francis's girlfriend, Joyce, kept asking, especially since the place where they now laid their heads was her apartment. Joyce worked at the local pet store and had been attracted to Francis because he was named after St. Francis of Assisi, who loved animals. Francis loved animals, but that's about all he and St. Francis had in common.

A parrot in the kitchen called out, "Lazy bums. Ahhhh."

"Shut up, you stupid bird!" Marco yelled impatiently. His wrist was throbbing. He played with the gauze wrapped around the inside of his arm, which he'd accidentally slit when he was shredding Alfred and Charisse's gown with his pocket knife.

"Don't let Joyce hear you talk to Romeo like that," Francis said sleepily.

"That bird drives me nuts."

"Lazy bums! Lazy bums!" Romeo chirped with gusto.

Marco got off the couch, lifted the window shade, and peered out. His beat-up gray sedan was parked out front on the street. Joyce had the bottom floor of a two-family house, and there was no room for visitors' cars in the driveway. Which meant Marco was always having to move his car so he wouldn't be ticketed. He'd been doing this three mornings a week before 8 A.M. since Christmastime when he showed up for what turned out to be his most prolonged visit. It was only because Francis had broken his leg in a construction accident and was stuck at home until it completely healed that Joyce agreed to let Marco stay. He practically set up camp around the Bernadette Castro sofa bed in the living room.

"I'd go out of my mind sitting here by myself day in and day out," Francis explained to Joyce more than once. "He keeps me company." But now that Francis was finally doing well with his physical therapy and hoping to get back to work soon, Marco knew his days at Joyce's pad were numbered. He had no money and no place to go. That's why he'd convinced Francis, who he'd nicknamed Linus back in kindergarten when he caught Francis sniffing a security blanket he'd hidden in his assigned cubby-hole, to pull off the job last night with him.

"Come on, Linus!" he'd urged. "That snob Alfred turned his nose up at us at the craps table, won the money that should have been ours, and then had the nerve to give us his business card in case we were ever in the market for his designer wedding dresses after he'd insulted our sweatshirts. When he dropped his keys and didn't notice, it was a sign from God!"

"I don't think God had robbery in mind when Alfred dropped his keys!"

"Everything happens for a reason," Marco had argued passionately. His lean body paced the floor of the living room all week. He was five feet ten inches tall, with olive skin, brown hair and eyes, and a narrow slit for a mouth. "There was a reason we went down to Atlantic City last weekend."

"To gamble."

Marco ignored him. "There was a reason we picked Gambler's Palace. There was a reason Alfred ended up at the same craps table we were. There was a reason he dropped his keys."

"And the reason he dropped his keys was

because his pocket was overflowing when he pulled out his business card."

"Well, the other reason was so that we could teach him a lesson. He not only gloated about winning all the money that had been ours, but he had the nerve to comment on our clothes."

"All he said was that he never understood the appeal of sweatshirts in social settings."

"That hurt my pride," Marco protested. "He was a pompous jerk."

"You got back at him when you told him that if his green velvet jacket had four more pockets it would look like a pool table."

"I don't feel vindicated. Not only that," Marco paused, "I'm broke."

"You're broke?"

"Practically. If we pull off this job, then I'll be able to leave here."

Francis's ears had perked up. He knew Joyce was getting fed up. He had to get Marco out of her house. But this was resorting to drastic means to hasten his departure. Ultimately swayed by Marco's relentless nagging, Francis had agreed to take the risk. Even though Marco wasn't big in the charm department, he could still get Francis to do what he wanted.

And they'd done what Marco wanted last night in the middle of the night. Caught up in the excitement of robbing the salon, Marco had gotten carried away and decided to slash one of the gowns. In the process he'd cut himself. Although he was pleased with the way the dress looked with the drops of blood all over it, now his wrist was really throbbing, and he thought the cut needed stitches. But he was afraid to go to the hospital because going to the hospital meant having to explain what happened. He couldn't risk it.

"Your car still there?" Francis asked.

"That big old clunker isn't worth stealing," Marco answered.

"Unless someone knew those dresses were in the trunk. If you sold those you could get yourself a new Mercedes."

Marco let go of the shade and turned to look at his friend. They were the same height and weight, but Francis had strawberry blond hair that was starting to recede and the map of Ireland on his face. His pale blue eyes looked a little worried. He'd never done anything like this before. In high school, Marco had convinced him to swipe food from the school cafeteria, and they'd taken a few cars for joyrides, but nothing as serious or premeditated as this. It made Francis wonder what else Marco had pulled off in his travels around the country.

"We have to be careful, Marco," Francis continued. "I don't want to get in trouble."

"You're so chicken! You've been worried about trouble since we were five years old. Thanks to me we have twenty thousand dollars, some gaudy jewelry that we can hock in Atlantic City, and four valuable designer gowns. And we put a man who dishonored us in his place. It was a good night's work."

"If we get caught, Joyce will kill me. Your blood is all over that dress. They can do DNA testing, you know."

"We won't get caught. I've never been arrested so they don't have my DNA on file. I say we go to Atlantic City tonight and celebrate."

"That's too dangerous."

"Dangerous? What are you talking about?"

"If Alfred realizes he lost his keys in Atlantic City, they might start looking for us there. You know, they say criminals often return to the scene of the crime."

"The scene of the crime was his loft in Manhattan."

"But we stole his keys in Atlantic City. And what do I tell Joyce? It's Saturday night again."

"Tell her to go out with her girlfriends."

Marco picked up the remote control off the coffee table and flicked on the television. NY1 reporter Kristen Shaughnessy was at the anchor desk.

"This just in. Spring is wedding season and brides all over the tristate area are making preparations for their big day. But a few brides showed up this morning to pick up their dresses at Alfred and Charisse's Coutures in downtown Manhattan and were shocked to learn that the salon had been broken into and four dresses were stolen . . ."

Francis sat up quickly, clutching the ratty blanket he'd owned since grade school, while Marco stared at the screen.

"The thieves left one dress behind, which they did their best to destroy. The robbers took the time to slash the gown to ribbons, and it appears that one of them may have cut himself. Blood was spilled on the front of the dress. The NYPD Crime Lab will be checking it for DNA. The owner of that dress, Brianne Barth, is *not* happy."

The newscast cut to a clip of Brianne staring into the camera. "Mark my words. If I find out who did this, they'll regret the day they were born."

"Them's fightin' words," Kristen said in a voiceover. "I can't say I blame her. The designers are not happy, either." The image of Alfred and Charisse filled the screen.

"I'm shocked that anyone could stoop so low as to try and deprive our April Brides of their gorgeous gowns. But we won't let them!" Alfred declared. "Regan Reilly is going to help us get them back! Right, Regan?"

The camera turned to Regan. "We're going to do everything we can," Regan replied in a serious tone. "Thieves often make one stupid mistake that trips them up. If that's the case here, we'll find out what it is and make sure the culprits land behind bars. Where they belong."

Marco stared at the screen. "We didn't make any stupid mistakes, Regan Reilly!"

"Oh, my god!" Francis squealed. "We're going to get caught!"

"Did you make a stupid mistake?"

"I don't think so," Francis moaned as he clutched the blanket for comfort, the blanket Joyce wouldn't allow anywhere near her bed. He knew that this was not going to end well. "Maybe getting out of town tonight is a good idea after all."

———◆———

Regan, Jack, Nora, Kit, Brianne, Teresa, Alfred, and Charisse were all seated on the horseshoe-shaped couch in the salon, finishing up the sandwiches and coffee that Charisse had ordered from the local deli. The fact that she was fed and had already appeared on local television had slightly cheered Brianne. But not for long. She wiped her mouth and announced, "Alfred, I want a cash refund. My mother and I are heading over to Kleinfeld."

Teresa nodded in agreement. "This is outrageous."

Kleinfeld was the legendary bridal shop that had provided beautiful wedding gowns to happy brides for generations. It opened its doors in Brooklyn, New York, in 1941 and recently moved to a new location on West 20th Street in Manhattan. Kleinfeld had the largest selection of designer wedding gowns in the world. Women from all over walked through their doors and found the dress of their dreams.

"Cash refund?" Alfred gasped.

"Cash on the barrel," Brianne answered. "Or at least a check. I can't be nervous all week about whether I'm going to have a dress or not next Saturday."

"It's not right," Teresa said mournfully. "Not right at all."

"I wouldn't be able to go to sleep tonight wondering whether I'll have to walk down the aisle in my prom dress."

"I promise we'll get it done for you," Alfred moaned. The thought of handing back the five thousand dollar deposit made him dizzy.

"I'm not willing to take that chance." Brianne shook her head stubbornly and stood. "Nice meeting you all. We're out of here. Alfred, I want my money back. *Now.*"

Alfred threw his hands in the air. Dragging his feet, he went around the corner and into his little office. A moment later he came back and handed Brianne a folded yellow check. "If you don't find anything, just call. I will make you a new dress in time for your wedding. That is, if you let me know by tonight," he added almost snippily.

"Can you fix my wedding dress so that Brianne could wear it?" Teresa asked.

Alfred's face looked aghast. He started to stammer. "Ah, ah . . . most designers are only interested in working on their own . . ."

Teresa's expression was steely. "It wouldn't be very good publicity if you didn't help one of the brides you let down because you either didn't lock the door or you lost your keys."

"I don't know whether I lost them or not," Alfred protested.

"I heard the police ask you. You said you couldn't find them. It's your fault this happened."

Oh, boy, Regan thought. The police had questioned Alfred extensively because there was no sign of forced entry. He said that he couldn't find his keys and had promised to look for them. He couldn't remember the last time he'd used them.

"Charisse is always the one taking care of things like that," he'd explained. "When we go out, she is the one who brings the money and the keys. I rely on her for all those little matters . . ."

Charisse was sitting quietly in the corner. With her delicate features, pale skin, and long, wavy blond hair cascading past her shoulders, Regan thought she looked like she came from a long-ago era—and she certainly dressed the part. She now had on a white lacy blouse and burgundy velvet pants that matched Alfred's silk robe. She had an ethereal quality that made it hard for Regan to believe that she was the one with the practical sense. But, then again, her partner was Alfred. "Even though Alfred leaves that kind of thing to me, I couldn't ask for someone more protective. He double locks the door during the day. I don't think that whoever was in here last night gained access with Alfred's keys."

"Whatever," Brianne said dismissively. She glanced at the check and stuffed it in her front pocket.

You're not so careful either, Regan thought. That check has to be for several thousand dollars. "Brianne, I'd like to talk to you . . ."

Teresa looked at her watch. "We have to go."

"Can I have your number?" Regan asked. "I'd like to call you later. I'm also going to be speaking to the other three brides whose dresses are gone. Will you please think about the times you were here—did you see anyone or anything that seemed suspicious? Also, I'd like to know if there was anyone who knew you were having your gown made here and might have wanted to try and ruin your wedding for you."

"Are you trying to blame this on me?" Brianne asked.

"Of course not," Regan answered. "I just want to explore all the possibilities. It's hard to believe that this was a random crime."

"Everyone makes enemies," Teresa declared.

That's a sweeping statement, Regan thought. Brianne must have more than a few.

"Let me tell you something, Regan," Brianne said. "I've gone out with a lot of jerks. Like everybody else . . ."

Regan noticed that Kit was nodding vigorously and a slight smile came over Jack's face. He'd met a few of Kit's questionable beaus and obviously agreed with her assessment of them.

"But I don't think any of those losers are smart enough or would have had the nerve to pull something like this off."

"That's for sure," Teresa agreed.

"I'd still like to call you."

"Fine." Brianne pulled out a business card from her large purse and handed it to Regan. "I work for a decorator. My cell phone number is on there."

"Thanks."

Brianne leaned down and picked up her other bag that contained everything she needed for her final fitting: brideworthy strapless bra and underwear, control-top panty hose, and her white wedding slippers. "A waste of energy carrying this up here today," she muttered with disgust.

Alfred flinched, ever so slightly, then escorted the mother and daughter out to the elevator. When he returned, he collapsed dramatically onto the couch by the window. "Look at how gloomy it's gotten outside. It's starting to pour. It's a dark, dark day . . ."

Jack's beeper went off. His office was trying to contact him. He quickly called back and Regan watched as a look of frustration came over his face. He hung up the phone and turned to her. "I've got to run. It started raining uptown twenty minutes ago and our rainy day robber struck again."

"We're all doomed," Alfred cried. "Doomed!"

6

Luke Reilly was enjoying his Saturday. He had just played an early round of golf with a couple of his buddies who teased him about being the Father of the Bride. Getting in his car, he knew that he was going home to an empty house. He didn't like that much but smiled at the thought of Regan and Nora picking up Regan's dress and enjoying their day in the city with Kit. It was hard to believe his little girl was getting married. As he drove, a slight feeling of sadness came over him. To be expected, he thought. It's natural at a time like this.

When he pulled into the driveway, he parked the car, hurried up the path, and unlocked the front door. The weather had suddenly taken an ominous turn, clouds had rolled in, and it started to rain.

Luke stepped inside and glanced at the family picture on the table in the front hall that was taken a couple of years ago at Christmastime. She takes after me, he thought. His hair was now silver, but Regan had clearly inherited her Black Irish looks from Luke. His eyes moved to the picture of Regan taken on her first communion day. She'd been so excited about that little white dress and veil, he remembered, and the anklets with the ruffled trim and patent leather shoes that completed the outfit.

She was standing in front of their fireplace with a big smile, clutching her prayer book, one of her front teeth missing.

Who knew? he thought. Who knew that she'd grow up and take on the task of tracking down criminals?

Next to the first communion picture was a photo of Regan and Jack taken right after they got engaged. They both looked so happy. If Luke had had a son, he would have wanted him to be just like Jack—responsible, smart, loving, with a good sense of humor. Now he'd have him as a son-in-law.

Life was good.

Luke had bought himself a new tux and, Luke being Luke, had picked it up two months ago. He didn't know about Regan and Nora but he was ready for the wedding if they wanted to get married tomorrow.

I'll see what I can dig up for lunch, he thought as he headed into the kitchen. There was plenty of food left over from the shower, and he'd put together a plate.

The house seemed so quiet, especially compared to the way it was last night. The phone on the kitchen wall rang. Luke raised his eyebrows. It's never quiet around here for long, he thought. I should have savored the moment.

"Hello."

"Is this the Reilly residence?"

"Yes, it is."

"Is this the home of Regan Reilly, who is getting married next week in New York City?"

Luke frowned. "Who's calling?"

"I'm calling from an engraving company. A friend of hers is sending her a very special present and wanted to have the date and time of the wedding engraved on the gift."

"Wouldn't the friend know that information?" Luke asked skeptically.

"Of course, but we can't reach the friend, and our engraver is here now. We weren't sure whether it was at 9 A.M. or 4 P.M. We can't read the handwriting of the clerk who took the order and we just wanted to be sure of the exact time of the wedding."

"Who's the friend?" Luke asked.

"Ohhh," the male's voice said, sounding uncertain. "She really wanted this to be a surprise. It's such an incredible gift."

"Can I have your name and number?" Luke asked.

"If I could just confirm the time—"

"You can when I call you back."

The person at the other end hung up.

Just as I thought, Luke mused as he replaced the phone in the receiver. Someone finds out about a wedding and figures that the bride's parents' house will be empty for several hours. So they scope out the situation, plan a break in, and hope that there are wedding presents around. If they're lucky, good jewelry has been left out.

Nora got plenty of publicity and was often photographed wearing expensive earrings, necklaces, rings, bracelets, the whole works. She had said they should get someone to stay at the house while they're gone next Saturday. Luke made a mental note to see if Nora had someone lined up for that.

Luke didn't like the feeling that came over

him. I gave this guy enough information even though I didn't confirm the time of the wedding, Luke thought. Whoever was at the other end of the line could tell that this *was* the bride's house. An owner of three funeral homes, Luke had seen plenty of trouble in his day. People often checked the obituary pages and burglarized the home of the be-reaved while the funeral was taking place. You can't get any lower than that, he thought.

Reaching into the refrigerator, Luke pulled out a bowl of what looked like chicken salad. I'll get one of the guys from work to stay here all day on Saturday, he thought as he reached in the bread drawer for a roll. The Reillys had an alarm system, but Luke wanted someone he knew in the house.

The phone rang again. This time it was Nora.

"Hi, honey," he said. "How's it going?" He sat down at the table and listened to a *Reader's Digest* version of what had hap-pened. "That gown was expensive," he joked halfheartedly. It wasn't worth men-tioning the phone call he'd just received. At least not now.

Luke flashed back to the picture of Regan

in her first communion dress. She'd been so happy. Next week she was supposed to wear another beautiful white dress and veil. This time she'd be on Jack's arm, and they'd be smiling together. It wasn't fair that her dress had been stolen. My little girl, he thought.

"Tell Regan that she'll look beautiful no matter what she wears," Luke said, his voice a little husky.

"Jack already told her that. Alfred says he'll make her another dress. But he's in such a state that I don't see how he'll be able to get it done."

"Maybe you should get a backup."

Nora sighed. "It's not that easy. We'll figure it out. I just wanted to let you know what was going on. Regan is taking on this case. I tried to tell her not to when Alfred was out of earshot, but you know Regan. She's determined. And Jack is busy with another bank robbery that happened less than an hour ago."

These things come in threes, Luke thought as he looked around the kitchen and glanced at the back door. "You didn't think it was going to be a typical week before the wedding with those two, did you?"

"No. But I didn't expect this. Well, just as long as everyone is safe. That's all that matters."

"It certainly is," Luke said as he glanced at the back door. He walked over and tested the lock. "It certainly is."

7

"It took you over an hour to go buy ciga-rettes?" Francis asked Marco.

"I was doing some thinking," Marco an-swered.

Francis had been thinking as well. He had planned to spend the winter in hibernation on the living room couch, with his leg up, watching television and collecting work-man's compensation. Joyce would cook him dinner every night. By the time spring rolled around, he'd be back to work. If you had to be laid up, winter was a good time for it.

But then Marco had shown up, and all Francis's plans for a cozy winter's rest were shot.

Marco had gone out immediately after they saw the story on the robbery. Joyce wouldn't let Marco smoke in the house so all winter long he'd disappear for his nicotine fix. Sometimes he'd take a couple puffs in the driveway. When it was raining he'd get in his car and drive off. Francis was allergic to smoke and was grateful that Joyce was so strict with Marco. She said she'd throw him out if she ever caught him smoking in her house.

It was now after two o'clock. "If we're going to Atlantic City, we should hit the road soon," Francis called to Marco who'd gone into the kitchen and helped himself to a can of soda.

"I've been thinking," Marco repeated.

"Good for you, Marco. I think, too."

Marco ignored the remark as he returned to the living room and sat down on the La-Z-Boy recliner. "Francis, where do lots and lots of people get married?"

"Churches and synagogues. Open fields. Parks. Joyce said she wants to get married outside so people can bring their dogs."

"That's beautiful. I mean, in what town?"

Francis frowned. "I don't know. My parents went up to Niagara Falls for their honeymoon."

"I don't mean honeymoon! Forget it. Listen, a lot of people get married in Las Vegas. They have tons of weddings there every day."

"So."

"So brides need wedding gowns. We have wedding gowns."

Francis blanched.

"I have a buddy out in Las Vegas. We can send the gowns to him. He can unload them. I'll give him a call. Plenty of people get married out there on the spur of the moment, and it's too late for the bride to get her hands on a designer gown. We'll make it easy. My pal Marty can go hang around the courthouse steps where they all go to get their licenses." Marco took a sip of his soda. "It'll be what you call an impulse buy. We'll make a few extra bucks."

"Who is this guy?" Francis asked.

"I met him in my travels."

"Can he be trusted to turn over the money to us?"

Marco nodded. "He wouldn't mess with me."

I wonder what that means, Francis thought. "It's Saturday," he said quickly. "The post office is already closed."

"So we'll do it Monday. I want to get rid of those gowns. I don't like riding around with them in the trunk. If we ever got stopped, and they checked the trunk, we're dead meat."

Francis waved his hands forcefully. "Why don't we just throw them in a Dumpster and be rid of them?"

"Too dangerous. And not profitable. Did you call Joyce and tell her we're going out of town tonight?"

"Not yet."

Francis's cell phone rang. His body twitched. I'm not cut out for this, he thought. I'm turning into a wreck. He looked at the caller ID. "It's my mother."

Marco rolled his eyes.

"Hi, Ma."

Francis's mother, Janice, lived out on Long Island with his father, who was an electrician. Janice worked part time as a waitress at the local diner. She was a sturdy woman with strong opinions that she never kept to herself.

"How's your leg?" she asked. "With this rain I thought it might be bothering you."

"I'm all right."

"You don't sound all right. Is Marco there?"

"Yes." Francis glanced over at his friend who could tell that he was about to be disparaged.

"Hmm," Janice grunted dismissively. "Joyce at work?"

"Yes."

"I made a nice lasagna. Why don't you and Joyce take a drive out when she gets home? I suppose you can bring Marco if you have to."

"Thanks, Mom. But we can't."

"Why not? What are you doing?"

"Marco and I are . . . we're . . . we're going to Atlantic City."

"Again? Weren't you there last week?"

"Yes. We had a great time. I need to get out again and get some fresh air."

"We've got fresh air out on the Island. What about Joyce?"

"I don't think she'll be joining us."

"You just got off the crutches. Do you really think you should be walking around the casinos?"

"I'll be fine."

"When are you and Joyce getting married?"

"What?" Francis asked, astonished.

"You heard me. I don't approve of living together before marriage. You know that."

"I have to get back to work first," Francis

said evasively. He paused and licked his lips. "What made you ask that now?"

"I just got home from work. Right before I left the diner it came over the radio that a bridal salon in Manhattan had been broken into and the dresses were stolen. Everyone started talking about the poor brides who were left in the lurch. They have to scramble to get new dresses. Whoever did that must have been a real louse. A real louse! They broke into a safe and made off with money and jewelry. So why did they have to steal the dresses? They couldn't have been raised well."

"I guess not. Mom, I have to go. Thanks for calling."

"I'll talk to you tomorrow. Call me."

"Okay." Francis closed his cell phone. "I've got to get out of here. I'll call Joyce from the car." He stood quickly and almost lost his balance. Adrenaline was flowing through his body.

"Hey, be careful," Marco admonished as he rushed to grab Francis's arm.

It's too late for that, Francis thought desperately. Much too late . . .

8

I can't believe this is happening the week before my wedding, Regan thought. She had walked Jack out to the hallway, where he'd opted to take the stairs instead of waiting for the slow-as-molasses elevator. As she stepped back into Alfred and Charisse's salon, Regan could see that her mother was getting that worried look, the look that came across her face when she was deep in thought, mulling over a problem. Or when she was trying to figure out a plot point in one of her books. This time the look seemed to say, "Regan, your wedding is in seven days and we've got a million things to do. Don't get involved in this!"

But my bridal gown is out there somewhere, Regan thought, stolen by a couple of thieves who could have harmed Alfred and Charisse. I need to find out who they are. She smiled to herself, thinking of Brianne's thirst for revenge. I certainly wouldn't want to meet her in a dark alley.

"Alfred, I'd like to slowly go over everything that happened since the break-in."

"We already did that with the police," he answered as he sank further into the curved black leather couch. On the coffee table were the remnants of their lunch.

"I'll make a pot of lavender tea. It's very calming," Charisse said quickly. "With all the anxious brides we get in here, it comes in very handy." She started to clear the table.

"Kit and I will take care of it," Nora offered.

"Of course," Kit agreed, not sounding like she really meant it.

"Thanks, Mom," Regan said. "Charisse, if you don't mind, I do want to talk to both of you together. I know you both spoke to the police, but if we go over everything again, I think it could help."

Charisse pushed back her wavy hair, sat down next to Alfred, and reached for his hand. They've had some night, Regan thought. She couldn't blame Alfred for being agitated.

Regan's notebook was in front of her.

She'd already covered several pages with notes. She cleared her throat and began. "Obviously we want to find out who did this and hopefully get the dresses back."

Alfred moaned. Charisse squeezed his hand.

"You say the two figures were dressed in black with stocking masks that covered their heads?"

Alfred nodded. "When I heard the commotion I opened my eyes. Larry King had on a pair of his bright red suspenders. Then I turned and saw the thieves in their dark drab clothing. What a contrast."

"They didn't say a word?"

"No," Charisse answered. "Alfred and I awoke at the same moment. The two men were in the bedroom, both holding the ropes they used to tie us up. One of them came running around the bed." She paused. "Come to think of it, he moved kind of awkwardly."

"What do you mean?" Regan asked.

Charisse developed a faraway look, then closed her eyes, trying to conjure up images from the previous night. "He was moving fast, but it was as if he was unsure on his feet."

"You're right, darling," Alfred said lovingly. "You see, Regan, movement is so important in our business. When we interview girls to model our dresses, we always want to see how they walk, how they'll present themselves on the runway. We notice more than most people how a person carries themself. One of the thieves did seem to have a little limp."

"Then they tied you up?"

"I should have fought them off," Alfred said with disgust. "But it all happened so quickly. Everything was a blur. After they tied us up, one of them bashed the safe in our closet with I don't know what! The sound was awful!"

"Neither of them said anything?" Regan prodded.

They both shook their heads. "That safe didn't do us much good," Alfred moaned. "It crumbled like a tin can. I used to try hiding our money and jewelry but then I could never remember where I put it."

Like your keys, Regan thought. "You told the police both intruders seemed to be about the same height and weight," she continued.

"Not too tall, not too short," Alfred answered.

How helpful, Regan thought, glancing down at her notes. Sight, sound, taste, and touch, she thought. Charisse and Alfred hadn't gotten a good look at the intruders, hadn't heard them speak, could only have tasted the gags in their mouths, and had already mentioned they were wearing leather gloves. One sense left to explore.

"Did you notice any particular smell?"

Charisse wrinkled her nose. "At least one of them must have just smoked a cigarette."

Regan jotted it down. "You don't have any idea in the least who would have wanted to do this to you?"

"I can't think of a single soul!" Alfred insisted.

"Have you had any displeased clients lately?"

"No, Regan!" This time it was Charisse's turn to get excited. "No matter how difficult any of our clients have been during the process, I promise you that they've all been thrilled with our dresses. We have a scrapbook of wedding pictures with letters thanking us . . ." She started to get up.

"We don't need that right now," Regan

assured her. "Let's concentrate on who might have been displeased. The break-in could very well relate to one of the brides whose dress was stolen. I'll talk to each of them. One bride is due in a little while, you said. Is that right?"

"Yes. She's the worst bride I've ever had. She makes Brianne look like a saint."

Nora and Kit reentered the room carrying two trays. As they poured tea, Regan kept focused on Alfred and Charisse. She knew Alfred got distracted easily and had to keep him focused—especially if another bride-from-hell was about to arrive. "I'll question the bride who is on her way," Regan said, "and I want the names of the other two. We have to let them know what happened right away before they hear about it through the media. That would not be good. When are all their weddings?"

"You, Brianne, and the witch coming in now—I mean the girl coming in now—are all getting married next Saturday," Charisse answered sweetly. "The other two are in three weeks. The five of you are our April Brides."

I knew Jack and I should have gotten married in March, Regan thought. But Nora was worried about snowstorms. Regan's grandmother had been born during a big blizzard in March. Her parents had barely made it to the hospital on time. It became part of the family lore—March is a very unpredictable month weatherwise. Don't plan any big occasions. "Do you have time to replace all the dresses?" Regan asked.

"The thing is . . ." Alfred put his hand to his chest. "What about our May brides?"

"I'm not too worried about them at the moment, Alfred," Regan said a touch impatiently. "They have at least another month."

"Oh, Regan, I know!" Alfred cried. "It's just that it's wedding season and we took on more than we can handle as it is. We wanted to strike while the iron is hot. People are talking about our designs . . . we work sixteen hours a day!"

"We'll get the dresses made," Charisse said firmly. "It will be difficult, but we'll get it done."

"That's good," Regan answered. "I'll talk to the other April Brides and see what I can find out. See if they noticed anything that might be helpful in this investigation. I plan to be on this block tonight at around the same time the thieves broke in."

"Regan . . ." Nora began.

"Don't worry, Mom. Jack will be with me. I want to question people who are out at that time and find out if they saw anything. Maybe someone who walks his dog at that hour every night noticed something. Alfred, I want you to think really hard. When did you last have your keys? If whoever was here last night used them to get in, it would certainly be helpful to know where you might have lost them."

Alfred looked up at the ceiling. "We've been working so much. It's like we never leave here. When did I last see the keys? Hmmmm."

"Did you have your keys in Atlantic City?" Charisse asked him softly.

"Atlantic City?" Regan repeated, her voice rising. "When were you in Atlantic City?"

Alfred waved his hand. "Last Saturday night we needed to get out. So we took a drive down there. I gambled for a few hours. No big deal."

But you never leave home, Regan thought. "Did you win anything?"

"Yes."

"How much?"

"Twenty thousand dollars."

"Twenty thousand dollars! Isn't that how much money you said you had in the safe?"

"Exactly. I put my winnings in there for safekeeping."

"Did you tell the police that?"

"No."

"Why not?"

"I was embarrassed. I thought they might think I have a gambling problem. And believe me, Regan, I report my winnings to the government. I don't want any trouble there. I once worked for a designer who didn't pay his taxes, and they closed him up right before a show! He was ruined!"

"You don't know whether you had your keys with you?"

"Alfred, you did!" Charisse said quickly. "Remember? We were hurrying to get out of here and you ran to get your business cards and the keys were in the drawer with them and you shoved them in your pocket."

"That's right!"

"And you haven't seen them since?" Regan asked.

Alfred shook his head. "No."

"Did you hand out any cards that night?"

Alfred smiled. "Lots of them. You never

know who's going to fall in love and suddenly need one of Alfred and Charisse's
gorgeous gorgeous gowns."

Oh great, Regan thought. You handed out
business cards to strangers in the same
place you lost your keys. Something told
her that she and Jack would be taking a
drive to Atlantic City.

9

In the Upper East Side bank that was having about as bad a day as a bank could, Jack was studying the note the robber had passed to a young female teller.

DON'T PUSH ANY BUTTONS OR SOUND ANY ALARMS. JUST GIVE ME THE MONEY. I'VE GOT A GUN IN MY KNAPSACK AND AM WILLING TO USE IT ON YOUR CUSTOMERS. NO FUNNY MONEY OR YOU'LL BE SORRY.

Jack shook his head. "It looks like it's written by our guy."

"It certainly does," remarked Ed Meredith, one of the investigators from Jack's office. "Same language. Same handwriting. Same kind of paper and ink."

"I'm beginning to think we'll have to post undercover agents at every bank in the city when rain is predicted," Jack said with disgust.

Ed smiled wryly. "April showers bring May flowers."

"Let's hope that's all they bring. You have the security tapes?"

"We're getting them."

In the back office, the striking young African-American teller who was the recipient of the robber's note was sitting in a chair, trying to regain her composure. She was fidgeting, moving her hands from her lap to her hair, which was arranged in stylish cornrows and decorated with colorful beads, and back to her lap again. They were the hands that had touched the note and forked over the money. And now her hands couldn't rest. With wide eyes, she looked up at Jack when he walked through the door.

Jack identified himself and asked her in a soothing tone, "How are you doing?"

"Fine and dandy. Lucky me gets to be the teller the bank robber picks on. Just my luck. Why can't I win the lottery?"

Jack smiled. "Maybe you will."

"Well, I'm not taking any more chances around here. I quit."

"You did?"

"The second that robber walked out the door!"

"I can understand."

"It's not worth it. I'm getting married in a

couple of months. I got a lot of good times ahead of me. I'd rather flip burgers than worry about another lowlife who says he has a gun."

Jack sat down across from her. "I'm getting married, too," he said, anxious to make a connection.

"You are?"

"Yes. Next week. And my fiancée's dress was just stolen from her dressmaker's loft downtown."

The teller's eyes lit up. "That's bad. Not as bad as thinking someone might shoot you. But it's bad. *When* are you getting married?"

"Next Saturday."

"Next Saturday! How come she didn't pick up her dress before now? My mother is guarding mine at home with her dear life. She's afraid something bad is going to happen to it. The day before she married my father, one of her bridesmaids' kids went into my mom's bedroom with a box of crayons." She managed a smile. "I can just imagine the fireworks that day."

"Now that is bad," Jack said, smiling back at her. He was glad to see that she was beginning to relax.

"So how come your fiancée waited so long to pick up her dress?"

"Huh? Oh. Well, she's been living in Los Angeles, so she's just back and . . ."

"Long distance romance? That's no good."

Now Jack's smile was broad. "No it's not. The long distance part is finally over."

"My fiancé, Jamie, lives three blocks away from me. He says that three blocks feels like forever. He should be here soon. He's a nervous wreck."

"I would be, too," Jack said sincerely, thinking of Regan. He was always worried about her, and in her line of work, there was usually good reason. He leaned forward and glanced again at the girl's name tag. "Tara, may I call you that?"

"It's my name," she answered. "I don't know what else you'd call me."

Jack raised his eyebrows. "Tara it is then." He paused. "Could you just go over with me exactly what happened? Tell me everything you remember. Even if a detail seems trivial, it could be important."

Tara nodded and took a sip from the glass of water that a co-worker had brought to her. "I'm sitting here all morning taking care of customers. It was busy. Next thing I know I hear a clap of thunder and it starts to rain. Really hard. We all started joking with each other. We were mad because we close at one and we thought it would be a beautiful afternoon to have off. My fiancé, Jamie, was supposed to pick me up. We were going to Home Depot to look at kitchen cabinets for our new apartment. Next thing I know there's a black-gloved hand pushing a note through my window." She paused. "You read it?"

"Yes."

"No matter how much they train you, you're never prepared for something like this. I slid that money over the counter so fast it would make your head spin. My heart was thumping in my chest so hard, I thought everyone in the bank could hear it. I was so scared I felt like I was having one of those out-of-body experiences—it was as if I was floating up toward that ugly ceiling out there while I watched myself going through the motions down below."

"What did the robber look like?" Jack asked quietly.

"He was white with a dark mustache and beard, and had on oversized tinted glasses.

I couldn't see his eyes, but he had big bushy eyebrows. Not that I looked that hard. It all happened so fast. I was afraid to make eye contact once I read the note. But he was wearing dark clothes and a black raincoat with the hood up."

Jack and Tara both turned toward the door as a man's voice could be heard yelling, "Where is she?"

Tara jumped up as Jamie rushed through the door. Jack smiled as the hulking man scooped his petite fiancée off the ground and held her in his arms.

"I'm getting you out of here, baby," he announced in a booming voice as he swayed her from side to side. "I'm taking you away for a few days so we can both calm down."

"Where are we going?" Tara asked, as the tears started to flow from her eyes. Feeling protected and safe in Jamie's big strong arms, she felt a wonderful relief.

"Las Vegas. We'll have a good time and forget all this."

Some place to calm down, Jack thought.

10

Of Charisse and Alfred's five April Brides, Brianne and Regan were still the only two who definitely knew the bad news about the gowns. Alfred had left messages for Shauna Nickles and Victoria Beardsley, telling them that there was a "little problem." They weren't scheduled to come in for fittings until the following week. Tracy Timber was now a few minutes late for her appointment, which was surprising. Alfred, Charisse, Regan, Nora, and Kit were all waiting for her as though the Grim Reaper were about to appear.

"She's never late," Charisse explained. "She is ultraorganized and efficient."

"Rigid," Alfred offered.

Charisse sweetly ignored him. "I'm afraid the news is going to be a big blow for her."

"She's running her wedding like a marine sergeant," Alfred said. He threw out his hands. "Where is the sense of joy? Show me the love."

Nora and Kit had been sitting silently, taking all this in. Of course neither of them wanted to leave. It was the quietest Regan had seen Kit in a long time. "You know," Nora began. "Planning a wedding is very stressful. There's so much to think about."

"The dress is the most important," Alfred said proudly. "It's the dress that defines the bride. If your dress is bad, then you may as well forget it! People will be talking behind your back for years to come!"

"That's why we have such a problem, Alfred," Regan reminded him. "If this Tracy is so ultraorganized and she's getting married next week . . ."

The downstairs buzzer rang.

As opposed to a collective sigh of relief, there was a collective tensing of muscles in the salon.

Charisse walked over to the intercom but didn't reach it before it buzzed again. This time the buzz was longer. Charisse waited until the noise ended and then pushed the button and spoke into the speaker. "Who's there?" she asked with a lilt, winking at the group.

"Tracy Timber," a clipped voice answered. "I do have an appointment."

"Come right up."

When Tracy appeared at the door with her mother and sister, Regan could tell that this was going to be a painful experience. Tracy was one of those people who had every one of her shoulder-length blond hairs perfectly in place, with a headband to ensure no strays dared escape. She was dressed in preppy clothing and simple gold jewelry. But the rock on her left hand was impressive. She was carrying a briefcase in her right hand, a clipboard in her left.

"The traffic coming in from Connecticut was terrible," Tracy announced. "Once the rain started . . ."

She doesn't know yet, Regan thought. They must not have listened to the radio on the way in.

"No problem . . ." Alfred said, fumbling for words. "Let . . . let me introduce you . . ."

Tracy's mother, Ellen, was an older, more relaxed version of Tracy. Her gold earrings were similar to Tracy's, and she had on well-cut beige slacks and a yellow sweater set. Tracy's younger sister, Adele, had the same features and hair color as her mother and sister but was clearly not cut from the same mold. She looked like she had just rolled out of bed. Wearing wrinkled blue jeans, a denim shirt, and old sneakers, she yawned at least twice before the introductions were complete.

Everyone said hello and shook hands. Tracy's eyes darted back and forth to the long rack where the gowns were usually hanging in wait when clients came for their final fittings.

"Lovely meeting you all," Tracy said without enthusiasm, then glanced at her watch. "Now, let's get down to business, shall we, Alfred. I want to try on my dress one more time and then be on our way. Have you finished up with Regan? You are the bride, aren't you, Regan?"

And the detective, Regan thought, but she just nodded. She felt her throat go dry. Poor Alfred.

"Tracy, why don't you and your mother and sister sit down?" Alfred said, clearly stalling for time.

"I don't want to sit down. I want to try on my dress."

"There's a little problem . . ."

Tracy's cheeks flushed. *"What* is the problem, Alfred?"

"We had a break-in last night, and your dress was stolen. So was Regan's," he added almost joyfully.

Hugging the clipboard to her chest, Tracy looked as though the wind had been knocked out of her. "Could you repeat that?"

Alfred did as he was told.

Regan could see a look of amusement come over Adele's face, but Tracy's mother's expression turned grave. Luckily she didn't seem the type to get overwrought, at least in public. But Tracy's stiff upper lip had vanished.

"My dress is gone? *Gone?* What am I supposed to do? My perfect wedding is in one week." She banged her clipboard. "Everything is set except the dress. Everything."

Charisse ran into the kitchen mumbling about making another pot of lavender tea.

"Honey," Tracy's mother said in a tone that matched her expression. "We'll find you another dress."

"No," Alfred interrupted. "We'll make you a new one. We promise. When you think about it, seven days is plenty of time. Isn't that how long it took God to—"

"That is unacceptable!" Tracy interrupted, her voice quivering with rage. "I have every minute scheduled from now until the time I walk down the aisle. I don't have a second to spare. Do you understand that? Do you?"

Alfred just looked at her.

Tracy unsnapped the cell phone attached to her belt. "I'm going to call my fiancé. He'll tell you a thing or two. He'll sue you." She pressed one key and a moment later barked into the phone. "Jeffrey! The most awful thing has happened! I am so upset! My gown was stolen. I am beside myself! . . . That's right, *stolen.* . . . How can I have a wedding without a gown . . . ? What do you mean we shouldn't go ahead with the wedding? It is not a sign we shouldn't get married, I'll get another gown . . ."

Regan watched as the expression on Tracy's face turned from anger to horror.

"Not the right thing for you now? What are you talking about? I said I'll get another gown . . . You've made up your mind . . . What do you mean it's not me, it's you? I can't believe you're doing this! I can't believe it!" She snapped the phone shut and threw it onto the floor. "Look at what you've done, Alfred! My fiancé dumped me because I don't have a dress!"

Something tells me there are extenuating circumstances, Regan thought.

Tracy ran into the bathroom, her mother in her wake. "Tracy, maybe you caught him at a bad time. Give him a call back!"

Adele shook her head. "The worst part of this is that she was determined to get married before she turned thirty. She was just going to make it by the skin of her teeth."

"When does she turn thirty?" Regan asked.

"In two weeks. They were going to celebrate on the honeymoon." Adele shuffled around the corner to the bathroom, apparently feeling that she should at least attempt to offer some sisterly comfort.

Regan looked over at Alfred. Well at least he doesn't have to worry about replacing Tracy's dress. Unless she manages to find another husband before the day of her Big 3-0.

Kit cleared her throat. "Regan, do you think we should tell her that you're thirty-one and it doesn't bother you that you're getting married over thirty, and I'm thirty-one and I'm not even close to getting married? As a matter of fact, I can tell her that I don't even have a date for your wedding."

Regan smiled. "Kit, somehow I don't think that would go over so well."

"Just a suggestion."

"Well, Alfred, two more April Brides to go. Do you think we'll be hearing from them soon?"

"I hope not. I don't know how much more of this I can take."

11

Thank God for my animals, Joyce thought, as she placed a puppy she'd been grooming in the front window of the pet store. They always want to be with me. Unlike Francis who had called from the road and said that he was going to Atlantic City with Marco. She couldn't wait for that Marco to get lost. He was such a bad influence. Hopefully, Francis could go back to work soon, Marco would leave, and she and Francis could get their life back.

Joyce wanted to settle down. It was about time. She wanted to have kids and animals and buy a house out on Long Island. Just not too close to Francis's mother, who had called and asked if Joyce wanted to come out and spend the night with the folks while Francis was away.

No thank you! she had responded, almost too quickly. She would go home and take it easy. It would be nice to have some peace and quiet in the house. Marco had the television on every second he was awake. In the middle of the night, he'd wake up and turn it on, then the parrot would start to squawk.

Although the parrot enjoyed watching television.

"Hey, Joyce," her co-worker Bunny called to her. "You have another phone call."

"Thanks."

All the workers at Teddy's Pet Store had cell phones, but Teddy insisted the phones remain off in the shop. "All that ringing and beeping and those crazy songs disturb the peace," he declared. "The animals shouldn't have to put up with it!"

Any personal calls would be on the house phone, and they would be brief. "If you're not taking care of a customer, you should be giving love to the animals," he proclaimed.

Joyce hurried to the phone by the register. "Hello," she said as she played with a tiny Velcro ball that was on the counter and intended for cats' amusement.

"Joyce, it's Cindy."

Cindy was Joyce's single neighbor. Nosy

but nice. They saw each other more in the summertime when they threw barbecues together. Cindy was about her age, divorced, and always on the hunt for a new guy. "Hi, Cindy. What's going on?"

"I saw Francis and Marco speed down the block before. Are they heading out of town again?

She's always digging for information, Joyce thought. Cindy should have been an archaeologist. "Another boys' night out," Joyce answered, forcing herself to sound cheery. "It's okay. By the time I'm through here, I'm happy to go home and relax."

"Uh-huh, sure. Listen, Joyce, I'm going into the city with some of the girls tonight. We're going to Little Italy for pasta. The place has music. It'll be fun."

Joyce paused—for a fraction of a second. She loved the energy in Little Italy. Its narrow cobblestone streets, colored lights, and bustling restaurants all made for a great atmosphere. "That sounds great. I'm not that tired."

"You go, girl," Cindy said. "If the boys can go out and play, so can the girls."

"That's for sure."

"What time do you get off work?"

"Five."

"Go home and relax for a couple of hours. Take a nap. I'll pick you up at eight. We'll make it a fun night."

Pasta, a little wine, music, some laughs with the girls. It's what I need, Joyce thought as she hung up the phone.

So what was bothering her?

The front door opened, and a young mother and her son came in. His arm was bandaged.

"What happened to you?" Joyce asked sweetly.

"I fell going up the steps and I had a glass in my hand. I cut my arm, and it bled all over.

Joyce's mind flashed to the bloody paper napkin she'd found in the bathroom wastebasket this morning. Francis and Marco were sleeping when she left for work. She'd forgotten to ask Francis about it when he called.

"I told my mother I'd feel better if she bought me a puppy."

"I'm sure that would make you feel better..." Joyce agreed, leading them to the front window where three little cocker spaniels were scampering around in piles of shredded paper.

I wish I knew what would make *me* feel better, she thought. Maybe a night on the town with the girls will do the trick.

12

Francis and Marco were on the Garden State Parkway in New Jersey heading south to Atlantic City.

"What's the matter?" Marco asked.

"Nothing's the matter. Why should something be the matter?" Francis asked, looking out the side window.

Marco took his hands off the steering wheel to adjust the hand towel he had wrapped around his wrist. The car started to veer to the right.

"Watch it!" Francis yelled.

"You're very uptight."

"Please keep your hands on the wheel."

"I know how to drive. I've never had an accident."

"You also said you've never been arrested."

"Very funny. You've been quiet since you got off the phone with Joyce."

"I feel bad. Last Saturday night I left her home. Now, again this Saturday. It's not right."

"She'll get over it. Listen, I'm in pain. My wrist is killing me."

"Maybe you should go to a doctor in Atlantic City."

"I still don't think it's a good idea."

"You probably need stitches. Just tell the doctor you cut yourself with a knife, that's all. It doesn't mean you committed a crime. Even though you did."

"So did you. What the . . . ? " Marco looked in the rearview mirror. A police car was right behind them flashing its lights.

"Pull over!" came a voice through a bullhorn.

Marco cursed and Francis moaned.

"It's over," Francis said. "We're done. Done!"

"We didn't do anything."

"What about the dresses in the trunk?"

"Oh, yeah."

Marco pulled the aging vehicle to the side of the road and stopped. He quickly pulled his sleeve down so that it completely covered the blue hand towel wrapped around his wrist. Before the officer reached the car, he had his license and registration and insurance papers out, hoping to make the ordeal as quick as possible.

A moment later a burly state trooper was standing slightly back from the car. Marco quickly handed over his documents. The trooper took them and walked back to his vehicle while another police car pulled up behind his.

"Safety in numbers," Francis muttered. "They're out to find drugs. They should know we have a bunch of foufy wedding dresses in the trunk."

"Shut up. We've also got a lot of cash back there, too."

Francis groaned.

They sat and waited for what seemed like forever. The trooper finally got out of his car again. He sauntered back up to Marco's window.

"You in a hurry, boys?"

"No, sir."

"It seemed like you were."

"Really?' Marco feigned surprise. "How fast was I going?"

"Ten miles over the speed limit. Here's your ticket. And here's another ticket for a broken tail light."

"A broken tail light?" Again Marco was aghast.

"You'd better get that fixed real soon. It's dangerous. And your front left tire looks as if it could use some air. Maybe it has a slow leak. Do you want to change it right now?" He stared down at Marco. "Better safe than sorry."

"Change it now?" Marco repeated. "Oh, I don't think so, officer. Perhaps it would be best if we drove to the next rest stop. Maybe I could get the tail light replaced at the same time. And . . . and . . . and . . . I'll put a little air in the tires. And get the car washed, too."

"It could sure use it. Wait a minute." The trooper walked to the back of the car and looked at the tail light. He pulled on a piece of the broken glass.

Francis almost fainted in the front seat. To open the trunk all you had to do was push the button. No key necessary. If the trooper kept fiddling around back there, he'd make four brides very happy.

The trooper walked back to Marco's window. "Your license here says you live in upstate New York. Where are you boys headed?"

Don't say Atlantic City, Francis thought wildly. Don't be that stupid.

"We're going to visit a classmate from our younger days who just had an operation. He's going to be fine, thank God, but we want to cheer him up," Marco answered, doing his best imitation of Eddie Haskell.

"What kind of operation?"

"Knees. Knee. He was a football player and his old injuries were really acting up."

Francis feigned laughter and pointed to his leg. "I was hurt on the job. Been out of work for months. I hate it. Thought I'd go down and commiserate with him."

The trooper's radio squawked, alerting him to a fender bender down the road. He tapped the roof of Marco's car.

"Take it slow, fellas."

"I will, sir. Thank you, sir. Yes, sir."

As the trooper walked back to his car, Francis commented with disgust. "You really laid it on thick, didn't you?"

"What about you? You didn't have to tell him you were injured. Remember, don't give out so much information."

"I'm sorry. I've never been involved in the life of crime before."

"Get used to it."

Marco pulled out onto the highway. A few miles down the road was a rest stop. Marco drove right past it.

"Aren't we going to stop?" Francis asked.

"No."

"Why not?"

"You think I'm going to pull into a busy rest stop? We'll find a gas station that is quiet. We've got those dresses in the back. You want somebody noticing them?"

"Let's just get rid of them. Let's get off at the next exit and find a Dumpster."

"No way. That's money down the drain. They're going to Las Vegas. One hundred thousand brides a year say 'I do' in that town. Surely my pal Marty can find four of them who will pony up a few bucks for those designer gowns. In my humble opinion, old Alfred really does have some talent."

"The note you left said that his designs stink."

"I knew it would get to him." Marco smiled. "I also figured that taping the note inside the refrigerator would be twice as creepy."

As they drove on, Francis desperately wished that he were home with Joyce. Little did he know, she was about to have a wild night on the town.

13

When Tracy reemerged from the bathroom, her eyes had a vacant stare not unlike the ones actors who played psychos in horror movies affected right before they pounced. But her makeup was perfect—she'd clearly powdered her nose and freshened her pink lipstick, Regan noticed.

One wall of the main room of the loft was mirrored, another was all exposed brick. On good days it felt like a happy, open space full of endless possibilities, Regan thought, where excited brides were fitted for the most important dress of their lives. But now, for the second time in twelve hours, it was the setting for personal disaster. The spot where Brianne found her shredded bloodied dress in a heap was exactly where Tracy had been standing when she'd been shot through the heart, so to speak.

Regan was sure that neither one of them

would ever forget every detail of their terrible experiences at Alfred and Charisse's salon. Tracy's pain, of course, was far deeper. After all, what could be worse than having your heart broken a week before your wedding? And better yet, what can turn a basically sane, albeit high-strung person, into a psycho in no time flat?

Getting the royal dump.

Charisse was leaning over the coffee table, pouring tea as though her life depended on it. Nora and Kit were making noise about how wonderful yet another cup of tea would taste. Alfred was slumped on the couch, looking nervous and defeated. When he saw Tracy, he attempted to straighten up.

While her mother and sister stood in the background, Tracy walked over to Alfred and said in a scarily controlled voice, "You have ruined my life. I wanted to pick up my dress two weeks ago. It wasn't ready. And last week it still wasn't ready . . ."

Alfred never mentioned that, Regan thought.

"If it had been ready, it wouldn't have been stolen. And if it hadn't been stolen, I wouldn't have been dumped."

And if you had married that guy, Regan thought, you'd really be miserable. He clearly didn't believe in "for better or for worse."

The room was silent.

"Alfred," Tracy continued. "Do you have anything to say for yourself?"

"Not really."

Tracy shut her eyes as if somehow this would help her process his unexpected response. She opened them again. "Jeffrey, my former fiancé, likes everything to run like clockwork. Just like me. The fact that I didn't make sure my dress was ready when it should have been, and now I don't even have a dress, made him question my competence, I'm sure. My value as a life partner. If I picked someone as irresponsible as you to design my dress, then surely he couldn't expect me to make the proper decisions about . . ." She broke off, her voice cracking.

"Alfred and Charisse are victims of a crime," Regan interjected. "They were tied up all night, and we're lucky they weren't hurt or killed."

Tracy turned her vacant stare in Regan's direction. "You might still have a fiancé, but your dress is gone. How come you're being so understanding?"

"I'm a private investigator. I'm going to try and help Alfred and Charisse straighten out this mess. And hopefully find out who did this."

"Good for you. If you can find any dirt on a guy named Jeffrey Woodall, let me know. If I can't kill him, I want to make his life miserable."

"Dear," Ellen said to her daughter, "don't be so hasty."

"Mother! *One* week before the wedding he calls it off. How could he do such a thing?"

"I never liked him," Adele volunteered enthusiastically. "He's way too uptight."

"Who asked you?" Tracy cried. "Just shut up!"

Adele shrugged. "I was just trying to make you feel better."

"My life is ruined! I'm never going to feel better. I don't care what happens anymore." Tracy rubbed the sides of her forehead. "I'm getting one of my headaches."

"Let's get you home, dear," Ellen suggested. "Tonight we'll go for a nice dinner at the club."

"The club? I can't show my face at the club! That's where my reception was supposed to be!"

"Then we'll order in Chinese."

Charisse was vigorously stirring her tiny cup of tea. "Tracy, this happens more than you think, and it's always for the best. We've been making wedding gowns for years. We started in Alfred's mother's basement out in Indiana." She tried to laugh. "You wouldn't believe how many of them never saw the light of day! Boy, do we have stories! But in the end, it always meant the guy was not the right one! You'll find someone so much better and we'll make you a fantastic new dress—"

"Over my dead body."

"Your next wedding dress is on the house!" Alfred said with gusto.

"I want my money back," Tracy countered in an icy tone. "Then I intend to walk out of here and never come back. This place is nothing but a nightmare."

Charisse went running for the checkbook. "If you don't mind I'll postdate the check. We have to move some money around in the accounts. We were robbed of cash, too, you know. Lots and lots of it. And some of my favorite pieces of vintage jewelry . . ."

"If the check bounces, my lawyer will sue you."

The phone rang. Alfred grabbed it off the table next to the couch. Regan was surprised he didn't let it go to voice mail, but then again he was frantic to avoid this unpleasant conversation. "Hello? Yes, this is Alfred. You like my dresses?" He smiled. "Thank you very much. You're from where? This is a terrible thing . . ." He twirled the cord of the phone, listened, then cupped the phone with his hand. "It's a reporter from the *Galaxy Gossip.* He feels just awful about what happened. He wants to do a human interest story on the five brides who lost their dresses . . ."

Like a woman possessed, Tracy leaped for the phone and disconnected the call. "You imbecile! The last thing I want is my name in the paper!"

Sheepishly, Alfred handed her the receiver. She slammed it down and lowered her face to his. "If my name gets out as being one of your brides, I will ruin you! You understand that? I will ruin you. I don't need for the whole world to find out I was dumped! It's bad enough everyone at the club will figure it out. I will sue you for pain and suffering, invasion of privacy, loss of ability to lead a decent life . . ."

She must have a good lawyer, Regan thought.

The phone started ringing again just as the doorbell buzzed. This time it was Charisse's turn to make an escape. "That must be a delivery," she muttered to herself as she ran to the door, checkbook in hand. "How could they have gotten in downstairs?"

This place is not exactly Fort Knox, Regan wanted to respond. But she kept the thought to herself.

As the phone rang insistently, Charisse pulled open the large metal door. A young female reporter and a cameraman were in the hallway. The bright light above the camera shone into the room as the cameraman aimed his equipment in the direction of the assembled group.

Tracy dove behind the couch. "Trapped like rats!" she wailed.

"We heard about what happened and we'd just love to do a story—" the reporter began.

"This isn't a good time," Charisse insisted as she stepped out into the hallway and started to pull the door closed behind her.

"But we'd just like to help . . ." the reporter was saying as the door shut.

Like a phoenix rising from the ashes, Tracy took a deep breath and slowly pulled herself up from behind the couch. "Now I'm stuck here! I just want to go home."

"Charisse will get rid of them," Alfred promised. "She's good at that kind of thing, but she does it in a sweet way. Then we'll sneak you down the stairwell to your car so no one will see you."

Adele smiled. "Movie-star treatment, Tracy! That's cool."

"I am not a movie star!" Tracy scowled.

"When they get dumped in public, it's really bad," Adele commented. "Everybody in the world starts talking about it. Look at—"

"Mother would you please tell her to stop!"

"Hush, Adele," Ellen said stiffly. "I know you mean well."

"Why would Jeffrey do this to me? Why?" Tracy cried.

"Why is right," Regan echoed.

Tracy looked at Regan, shocked at the show of sympathy.

Regan continued, "Tracy, I'm going to be talking to all the brides whose dresses are gone to see if we can figure out who might have wanted to do this. It could have been a random act, but it could have been done by someone who wanted to hurt one of us. You just never know. You joked about having me investigate your former fiancé but I really would like to check him out."

Tracy started laughing hysterically. "That's wonderful! I'd love to find each and every skeleton he has in his pathologically orderly walk-in closet!"

"Well, I'd just like to see if he could possibly have had anything to do with this. Has he had any trouble with the law before?" Regan asked.

"The only thing he's guilty of is being incredibly boring," Adele retorted.

"Adele!" Tracy snapped. She looked at Regan. "No, he's never been arrested if that's what you mean. He's always so worried about what people think of him. Be my guest in checking him out. I'd love it if you dug up some dirt. I'd kick it in his face!" For the first time since Regan had laid eyes on her, Tracy looked almost happy. "If he did this, then it would be okay if people found out I was dumped. Because I would have been dumped by a nutcase."

"You could become a role model," Adele suggested.

"For what?"

"For being a shining example of 'Be careful what you pray for. You just might get it.' But you'll be the one who dodged the bullet at the last minute."

Tracy wasn't quite sure what to make of this statement. She blinked her eyes and turned to Alfred. "For now, I absolutely don't want people to know my name. Because if he turns out to be innocent, then I'm just the girl who got dumped."

Alfred nodded.

"Or I'll sue you," she added.

Alfred nodded again.

Fifteen minutes later Ellen and Adele pulled around to the front of the building. Regan and Alfred accompanied Tracy down the stairwell. She had on one of Charisse's raincoats, the hood pulled up over her head. Regan was glad it was actually raining. Tracy leaped into the backseat of her mother's

Lexus, the door was shut, and they sped off to the leafy suburbs of Connecticut.

"I wouldn't want to be a passenger in that car," Alfred commented.

"The poor thing," Regan said. "She was crying again."

"She'll get over it. If you find any dirt on her ex, she'll *really* get over it."

"What a responsibility," Regan muttered.

"Revenge is sweet," Alfred said in a tone that implied experience.

"But isn't it a dish best served cold?"

"Regan, it's good any way you can get it."

When they got back upstairs, it was three o'clock. The two other April Brides had not returned Alfred's calls. Charisse had all five brides' files out and was arranging to order fabric for the four dresses Alfred planned to replace.

"Tracy's situation is very sad, but at least that's one less dress we have to worry about," Charisse said cheerfully.

"What if they make up?" Alfred asked.

"She shouldn't take him back," Kit commented.

"No, she shouldn't," Nora agreed with a look of concern. "Alfred and Charisse, do you think you'll be able to replace Regan's dress in one week? If not we've really got to start thinking about . . ."

"Absolutely!" Alfred cried. "Regan will have her dress no matter what. We'll get started on it right away. No thieves or threats are going to keep Alfred and Charisse from their business!"

"Call a locksmith, would you Charisse?" Regan suggested. "I don't want you two in here tonight not knowing if some stranger has a set of your keys."

"Right away, Regan."

"Where do the two remaining brides live?" Regan asked.

"They're both in Manhattan."

"I think I'd better pay them both a visit and deliver the news to them in person. If they're not there, I'll leave a note explaining the situation. Written by you, of course. That way they can't accuse you of not trying in every way possible to contact them. After this experience with Tracy, you'd better be concerned about their privacy. Who knows what their secrets are?"

Charisse sighed. "Anything's possible. They are both a little different . . ."

14

Brianne and her mother had gone to Klein-feld and been greeted cordially.

"Your wedding's next week!" the sales-woman cried in dismay. "Did you get en-gaged five minutes ago?"

Teresa explained the unfortunate situation.

"You're one of the victims of the bridal heist! One of the April Brides!" the sales-woman boomed. "Oh, my God, what a mess. What a mess! Can you imagine if they stole all the dresses we have hanging around here? I can't imagine. Well, you picked our busiest day to stop by without an appoint-ment."

Another saleswoman had wandered over. "Didn't I wait on you two once before?"

Teresa looked guilty. "As a matter of fact you did. But Charisse and Alfred had a de-sign that Brianne just loved. So we went with them," she explained.

Both saleswomen nodded mournfully. "It isn't our policy to work without an appointment, but given your hard luck, we will try and do our best for you," the first one said. "We have sample dresses . . ."

"We appreciate any help you can give us," Teresa said with great relief.

The two saleswomen started pulling dresses off the rack but they couldn't find anything that worked for Brianne. They clucked, frowned, tsk-tsked, and implied that if they had chosen a dress from there in the first place . . . well, then she'd have her dress, wouldn't she?

Brianne was freaking out. She was hot and tired, and the rows and rows of wedding gowns were too much for her. Nothing fit right, and it was too late to order a dress that would really look great. Other brides in the shop were laughing and having fun with their mothers and sisters and friends as they gaily tried on one gown after another, knowing they had time to get whatever dress they wanted. Their happiness made Brianne even more miserable.

Teresa pulled Brianne aside. "Your dead grandmother would light up in the sky if you wore our dress. Let's get out of here and go dig it out of the attic."

"What if it's in bad condition?"

"I wrapped it good. Honestly. I should have had you try it on before you went to those crazy designers."

"Ma, Debbie had her dress made by Alfred and Charisse. It looked beautiful."

"Didn't she split up with him within six months?"

"So?"

"They're bad luck. I'm telling you. Bad luck."

"If I wear your dress and it needs to be altered, then we'll have to take it to them. Who else would do it so fast?"

"It's all right. We'll ignore the bad luck then. But it's good you're going to wear a family dress. Believe me, you can't go wrong. If people don't think it looks gorgeous, you can blame me."

They thanked the saleswomen for their efforts, drove out to Long Island, pulled into the garage, and entered the house through the back door. Brianne's father had just returned from playing a game in his over-50 softball league. He'd already heard the news about the dress but seemed to have gotten over it.

"Aahhh," he groaned. "I pulled a muscle in my leg sliding into home plate."

Teresa rolled her eyes. "You're fifty-five years old. You've got no business sliding around anywhere."

"You better be in good shape to walk me down the aisle next week," Brianne told him.

"Don't worry, baby," he said as he reached in the refrigerator and grabbed a bottle of Gatorade. "No more games until after the wedding. I thought I could play next Saturday morning and still make it to the church on time, but your mother forbade me."

"In no uncertain terms."

He took a chug from the bottle. "Did you get your money back?"

Brianne pulled the check out of her pocket and slapped it in his palm.

"Daddy's little girl."

Brianne gave her father a hug. "I was interviewed on television."

"Let's get a tape and play it at the rehearsal dinner. It'll all work out. You know, honey, the important thing is that you're marrying a good guy. When I think of that creep you went out with last year."

"I know. I know."

"What was his name?"

"Bill."

"That's right. Bill the Pill."

"Good riddance to him," Teresa said. "You see, Brianne, you could still be stuck with someone like that—someone always whining, complaining, and in a bad mood. Instead, you found a nice boy like Pauly. So he's a little rough around the edges. He'll learn."

"He still hasn't called me back. I left him a message hours ago."

"He thought you were going to be busy all day. Maybe he went to see a movie to calm his nerves. All I can say is thank God he finally got a new job. You both work until you have a baby. Then see what's up. Whatever."

"He was only out of work for a few months."

"It still can make a man go bonkers. Especially when he's engaged to be married. Let's go upstairs and check out the dress."

On the second floor of their modest-sized house, Brianne tugged at a rope that hung from the ceiling in the hallway. A trap door swung down, and a set of folded-up wooden stairs followed, losing its fight with gravity. Brianne promptly unfolded them, made sure the bottom section was planted firmly on the hallway floor, and started her ascent.

"Be careful," Teresa ordered.

"I am, I am."

"I'm right behind you."

Brianne reached the top of the flimsy stairs and stepped into the attic, carefully avoiding the insulated sections that were not meant to support anyone who weighed more than three pounds. Step on them and you end up in the extra bedroom. Brianne pulled on a smaller string that was hanging from a lonely lightbulb protruding from the ceiling. The lightbulb made a popping noise as it flashed light for a brief second then died.

"Daaadyyy!" she screamed. "We need another lightbulb."

"Howie!" Teresa screamed, relaying her daughter's message. "We need another lightbulb."

A short time later, guided by another dim bulb, they rummaged through the attic looking for the cherished family dress.

"I don't believe this," Brianne complained after about two minutes. "I thought you said you put it away so carefully."

"I did. But this family has collected a lot of junk over the years. We've got to clean this place out. Oh look, here are some of your school pictures . . ."

"Ma! We can't take time for that now. Where's the dress? I swear if I get my hands on whoever it was who ruined my gown I will kill them. Kill them!"

"Calm down dear. Now let me see. Oh look! It's behind this pole." Teresa pulled aside a carton of junk and reached for the faded white box with a window top that partially revealed the front of the beaded white wedding dress. "Here it is! All packaged nicely from that dry cleaner that went out of business. They did such a good job with wedding dresses. It's such a shame the owner was so nasty and customers stopped going. Who needs to be insulted when you're paying good money?"

Brianne hurried over to take a look at the dress she had never laid eyes on, except in pictures. It was obviously packaged on some sort of form that simulated a woman's chest.

At first glance, Brianne became hopeful that it might work. It looked pretty enough.

Teresa could tell that Brianne's reaction was positive. "Let's take it downstairs, honey, and have you try it on. I promise you it'll be wonderful."

Like a child on Christmas morning, Brianne grabbed the box and hurried down the attic stairs, barely grabbing onto the skimpy railing. Teresa was just a little more careful in her descent down the rickety steps. They hurried into the master bedroom and placed the box on Teresa and Howie's king-sized bed. Brianne held her breath, pulled off the cover of the box, and started to scream bloody murder.

An army of black ants had sprung to life and were frantically running around the top of the dress.

For the second time that day, Brianne fell to her knees in shock and grief over the state of a beleagured wedding gown.

"Howie!" Teresa bellowed. "Get up here! We've got to get this dress out into the back yard! And grab a can of Raid!"

———◆———

15

"I start to feel good when I get near the ocean," Marco declared. "There's something about the salt water. Remember summer after senior year of high school? We made the rounds looking for chicks on every beach from Long Island to South Jersey."

Francis looked glum as they continued down the Garden State Parkway. "We had to keep moving. You promised so many girls you'd call them, we could never go back to the same place twice."

Marco waved his hand at his passenger. "We had fun." He rolled down the window partway and flipped on the radio. "I'm glad the weather is clearing up. I feel like singing."

"We'd better have that tail light fixed," Francis reminded Marco as he checked his cell phone. He was hoping that maybe Joyce would call to say hello. No reason she should. Particularly since he blew her off on another Saturday night.

"Don't worry," Marco said as a deejay's voice came over the tinny speaker.

"You're back with Kenny and Jess. We've got a lot of news here to tell you about, but one of the stranger items of the day is about the wedding gowns that were stolen from a designers' loft in downtown Manhattan—"

"Oh, my God," Francis muttered.

"—four dresses stolen, one slashed and bloodied. All the brides were to be married in the next couple of weeks. 'I'm getting married in the morning...'" he sang, "'but, I've got nothinggg to wear.' Tell me, Jess, what should those brides do?"

"They can always look for a dress on the Internet. You'd be amazed how many gowns are sold there every day. At great discounts."

"Why would someone sell their dress?" Kenny asked.

"Because somebody got coooold feet."

"Gotcha. Eeeww . . . painful stuff."

Jess cooed, "But I can't imagine being one of those brides whose gowns were stolen. When I got married I spent months looking for the perfect dress. When I finally found it I had to go back to the bridal shop for several fittings. It was so much work! To have all that planning and preparation go down the drain is a crime in itself!"

"I wonder where those dresses are now. And what those thieves plan to do with them," Kenny said in his playful radio voice.

"They'll probably try to sell them. But they better not do it in the New York area. This story has been all over the airwaves today."

Marco looked at Francis, smiled, and tapped his head with his forefinger. "You see? I'm always thinking. We'll get rid of them in Las Vegas."

"I've got an idea!" Kenny announced. "Let's start a contest. See who can come up with the most original idea of where the thieves might be hiding those dresses."

Francis turned white.

"That sounds like fun," Jess agreed. "A scavenger hunt for our listeners. Call our phone lines if you have an original idea. And keep a lookout. If you notice anything un- usual—"

"Or happen to spot four designer wed- ding gowns lying around in a Dumpster—" Kenny said as he laughed heartily.

"Then give us a call."

"Let's offer a reward!"

Francis snapped off the radio.

"I told you the Dumpster idea was bad," Marco gloated.

"Marco! We've got to get rid of those dresses. Everyone is going to be looking for them. And I just thought of something. We can't pull into the hotel parking lot. They do random checks of people's trunks." Francis's leg was starting to hurt. "Let's go back home."

"No. That parrot drives me crazy. I need to walk on the beach."

"Then we need to find a big box so we can pack them up and send the dresses off to Vegas."

Marco was silent for a moment. Finally he sighed and agreed. "You're probably right. We don't need to be driving around with the evidence. As it is we've got all the cash and jewelry with us. But that's easier to hide than four wedding gowns."

"Where are we going to find a box?" Francis asked impatiently. "I can't imagine there are too many box stores around here."

"That means we have to buy something that comes in a big box."

"Like what?"

Marco put on the blinker and pulled off at the next exit. "I know you're nervous about leaving Joyce behind tonight—"

"I am," Francis interrupted. "I'm beginning to think I should just marry her. That settled-down life is looking pretty good to me after hanging around with you."

Marco nodded. "Suit yourself. Anyway, buddy, what I was starting to say was that I noticed her dishwasher is leaky. I mentioned it to her, and she said she needed a new one. Now's the time to surprise her with one! When we arrive home tomorrow, you present it to her as a peace offering."

"A dishwasher? That's not the most romantic gift."

"Those gowns won't fit in a ring box! I'm doing my best here!" Marco yelled.

Francis rested his head back against the seat and closed his eyes. He could just picture Joyce's face when he presented her with a new dishwasher minus the box. I'll have to buy a big red bow, he thought.

And I'll make a promise to her that Marco will be gone within the week. He opened his eyes, stole a glance at his partner in crime, then shut them again. I just hope that's a promise I can keep, he thought miserably.

16

Regan pulled Nora's car into the garage of the Reillys' apartment building on Central Park South. For several years, they had kept a pied-à-terre in New York City. At this moment, Nora was particularly grateful that she didn't have to drive all the way to New Jersey before she could collapse.

"What a day this has turned out to be," she sighed.

Turning off the engine, Regan turned to her mother. "I have the feeling that the fun has just begun."

Regan and Kit walked Nora up to the apartment that had a sweeping view of Central Park. The rain had let up, and after a long winter, the park was turning green again.

"Would you like a cup of tea before you head out?" Nora asked.

"I reached my tea quota for the month, Mom."

"A little of Charisse's lavender tea goes a long way," Kit agreed. "You know, Regan, if I ever do meet someone I want to marry, I think eloping might be a good way to go."

"Kit!" Nora laughed. "Your mother would never forgive you."

"Yes, she would. If she thought she had to go through all this, she'd buy me a ladder."

Nora pulled the sliding glass door that opened onto the terrace. "It's nice to get some air in here."

"I tell you what needs a good airing out," Kit began, "Charisse and Alfred's place. They need to bring in one of those experts to get rid of all the negative energy."

"First let them concentrate on getting Regan's dress done," Nora commented.

"If I think there's anything that they're going to focus on, it's getting those dresses made," Regan stated. "Mom, Kit and I have to get going. We'll take cabs to these other two brides' apartments and see if we can catch them in. Jack went back to his office. We're going to meet up with him later. What time will Dad get here?"

"He said by six. We're going to go to Neary's for dinner, then we'll head home.

This next week is going to be so hectic."
Nora paused. Hesitating, she began, "Regan, we have so much to do. I know you want to help Alfred, but this is your wedding. You can't drop everything."

"I know, Mom. We have another week to get ready."

Nora made a face. "Not a whole week dear. We can't figure out who's going to sit where Saturday morning. That alone takes hours."

"Mom, I promise I'll give this case just a couple of days. Then we'll focus completely on the wedding."

Nora smiled at her only child. "You know, Regan, you have waited your whole life for this day. You've met a wonderful guy."

"I know I have," Regan said quietly.

"I want you to be relaxed and rested. There is enough stress to deal with anyway, without all this aggravation."

"Regan can't help herself," Kit interjected. "Her wedding dress was stolen and she's an investigator."

Nora smiled wanly. "I know. It's in her blood. It's like someone telling me not to write. But, Regan, just promise me you'll be careful."

Regan looked at her mother. All of a sudden Nora seemed weary. Regan knew how hard she'd worked on taking care of so many of the details of the wedding while Regan was in Los Angeles. It wasn't fair to make her nervous and worried now. "I promise."

"Okay then." Nora reached out her arms and gave quick hugs to both Regan and Kit. "At this time next week we'll be at the church. Regan, you'll be ready to come down the aisle. Jack will be waiting for you at the altar . . ."

A lump started to form in Regan's throat. "I know, Mom. I know," she said quickly. "I promise I won't screw it up." She gave her mother a kiss. "Let's go, Kit."

"I'm ready. I can't wait to meet these other two brides. You know I was thinking, we should check out Tracy's ex sooner rather than later. Maybe he'd be good for me and he can be my date for your wedding."

"Get out of here!" Nora laughed. "I'll see you two later. But keep me posted!"

"We will."

When they shut the door, Nora went out on the terrace and leaned against the railing. Central Park was so beautiful. A horse and buggy was clipclopping down the road below. Nora smiled. Regan and Jack will be taking one of those from the church on Park Avenue to the reception several blocks away. Jack was going to surprise her. He knew that Regan had loved riding in them when she was a little girl. He'd hired the most charming carriage and made sure the driver would be dressed in tails. It would be waiting outside the church when they came out.

Nora couldn't wait to see the expression on Regan's face. Next week at this time, she mused. I don't think I'll relax until Regan and Jack step out onto the dance floor as husband and wife. She started humming the song they'd chosen, "Till There Was You."

17

Regan and Kit hailed a taxi and gave the address of Victoria Beardsley, who lived on the Upper West Side. They headed across Central Park South, the sight of the towering Time Warner Center in front of them, home of exorbitantly priced condos, upscale shops, and hip restaurants, including the highly praised Per Se, which wasn't a place to go "grab a bite." Reservations could only be made two months in advance for that sumptuous multihour dining experience.

The cab rounded Columbus Circle and made a right on Broadway. It was late Saturday afternoon in early April, and the streets were busy. Shoppers were out in full force. The rain had driven people inside, but the minute the sky cleared, they were back out again. Springtime was in the air.

As they were passing Lincoln Center, Regan received a call on her cell phone from

Jack, who told her about the bank robbery. "Any time it rains, this guy strikes. One of the detectives nicknamed him 'The Drip.' I think it's going to stick."

"I like that," Regan commented. "I'll have to figure out nicknames for the guys we're looking for." She filled him in on Tracy's plight and gave him Jeffrey Woodall's name and address. Jack said he'd run the name and they agreed to meet at his apartment in a couple of hours. They'd take a ride down to Atlantic City to the casino where Alfred had been gambling the week before, and then come back to New York to survey the area outside Charisse and Alfred's loft in the hours after midnight.

"It's going to be a long night," Kit commented when Regan hung up the phone.

"Do you want to go back to my parents' apartment and take it easy?"

"Are you kidding? No way. I might meet somebody in Atlantic City."

Regan smiled. She knew Kit was joking but she also knew that Kit wished she had a special guy she could bring to the wedding. "Don't worry. There will be single guys at the reception. Jack has a cousin around our age and a couple of his friends from college will be there."

"What's wrong with them?"

Regan laughed. "Nothing!"

Traveling up Broadway they passed a multiplex where all the latest movies were playing, bagel shops, restaurants, mobile phone stores, and nail salons, and then Regan spotted Zabar's, the famous gourmet marketplace, on the other side of the street. "I'd love to go in there right now. It always smells great."

"Work calls!" Kit declared.

A couple blocks farther north, the cab turned right. The driver slowed the car and moved haltingly until he found the right address. There were handsome brownstones on the small block, but the old and tired brick building they were now staring at wasn't one of them. Regan paid the fare, and they got out. They approached the front steps and opened the outer door. Regan pushed the buzzer for apartment 4B, the one labeled Beardsley.

They waited, and then she pushed it again.

"Who's there?" a breathless sleepy voice answered.

"Victoria Beardsley?"

"Yes."

"My name is Regan Reilly. I'm here on behalf of Alfred and Charisse, who made your wedding gown . . ."

"Ohhhhh. Yes. Alfred and Charisse." Victoria said, dragging out the words.

Regan looked at Kit quizzically. "May I come up for a moment? I have a letter for you from them."

"Is everything all right?"

"They're all right. There's a problem with their gowns. I'll explain it to you if—"

"I'm in 4B."

The buzzer sounded to release the lock on the inner door.

They walked up the four floors, hearing the everyday sounds of living coming from inside apartments along the way. Rock music, a baby crying, the blare of a television. They passed one apartment where a woman, obviously a professional singer, or at least a fledgling one, was doing her vocal exercises with great gusto.

"Me me me me me me me me me. Me me me me ME ME ME ME ME. Me Me ME ME ME ME ME ME ME ME."

"It's always about you," Kit muttered.

Regan grinned and rolled her eyes. "4B

must be right here to the left." They stopped in front of a door which had several locks and more than a few scratches. "Here goes nothing," Regan whispered as she rang the bell.

Immediately they could hear the snapping sounds of locks being unbolted. The door opened a crack and a set of snapping brown eyes peered out.

"Hi there," Regan said. "I'm Regan Reilly. This is my friend Kit."

"Just a moment." The door shut and the woman released the chain that would have prevented Regan and Kit from storming her apartment. She opened the door again. Barefoot and dressed in a colorful caftan, she waved them in as though she were having a party.

"I'm sorry to disturb you. Did we wake you?" Regan asked.

"I was taking a nap," she said cheerfully. "But I'm up now. I have coffee brewing."

Regan and Kit stepped inside the tiny, dark apartment. A kitchenette on the right opened onto a small room with old wooden floors. Regan had the immediate impression that Victoria was not someone who sweated the small stuff when it came to decorating.

Bookshelves crammed willy-nilly with books, CDs, tapes, and knickknacks covered one wall. Two different-sized framed posters hung on the opposite wall. The seating area consisted of a beige couch dotted with assorted pillows, one overstuffed chair, and a coffee table weighted down by a small television, more books and tapes, and numerous candles. Two stools were pushed up against the kitchenette counter. A door to what Regan guessed was the bedroom was closed. It was clear that not much light could find its way through the one small window on the far wall, as it faced the brick wall of the next building. In real estate terms, the apartment would be termed "private."

"Please come in and sit down," Victoria said as she hurriedly yanked a blanket off the couch.

Regan guessed Victoria to be in her early thirties. She had flowing dark curly hair, wide brown eyes, and flawless skin with a perfect flush to her cheeks. Regan was sure she'd look beautiful in one of Alfred's wedding gowns.

As Regan and Kit sat on the couch, Regan noticed that the book at the top of the stack on the coffee table was about visualization. CREATE WHAT YOU WANT IN LIFE, it said on the cover. The sleeve of one of the tapes on the table urged the viewer to access their inner peace and power. That's good, Regan thought. If she values inner peace, let's hope she takes the news better than Brianne and Tracy.

Regan explained who she was and what had happened.

"That's so sad," Victoria said. She started to giggle and shake her head. "That's really terrible."

Those tapes must work, Regan thought.

"I know you must think I'm a little crazy," Victoria continued as she tried to stop laughing, "but I can just picture how hysterical Alfred must have been." She cupped her hand to her mouth.

Regan couldn't help but laugh herself. "He is a little bent out of shape."

Victoria pointed to her tape on inner peace. "I wanted to lend this to him, but he wasn't interested. He said he enjoys frenzy."

"He thrives on it," Regan agreed. "But I think this is a bit too much frenzy, even for Alfred. He told me you're getting married in three weeks."

"Huh?"

"Your wedding date?"

"Oh, yes. That's right. Three weeks."

"Alfred and Charisse are planning to work night and day to replace our dresses."

"That's great." Victoria shook her head from side to side. "But I don't want Alfred to have a nervous breakdown. I have a girl-friend's dress I can wear. It's beautiful."

"Forget it," Kit cracked. "What will give Alfred a nervous breakdown is if he has to write another refund check."

Victoria grabbed Kit's arm and laughed. "Kit, you're dead on!"

This girl loves inner peace and sharing laughs, Regan thought as she laughed, too. "Where are you getting married, Victoria?"

"Out in the country."

"How nice. Where in the country?"

"Pennsylvania." Victoria jumped up and sauntered toward the kitchenette, humming loudly as she crossed the room. "Coffee?" she asked.

Regan and Kit both declined. She doesn't have to answer my questions, Regan realized. But I sure am curious about her. She's taking this almost too well. "I can't imagine your fiancé will be too happy that you have to go through all this worry about your dress."

"Oh, my fiancé's so wonderful. *Wonderful.* He's just perfect. He won't care." She waved her hand, poured herself a cup of coffee, and floated back to the overstuffed chair. She pulled her feet up under her as she sat back down.

"Where is he now?" Regan asked.

"He lives in Pennsylvania. I met him online. It's so hard to meet men in this city!"

"It's so hard to meet men anywhere," Kit said excitedly. "Which dating service did you use?"

Victoria took a sip of her coffee. "Cupid's Bow."

"I never heard of that one," Kit said. "And I've tried a few. My friend here worries about me when I go on these dates. But I'm careful. Although I haven't met anyone who's good for the long term."

Victoria leaned over and grabbed Kit's hand. "I know how hard it is! But you'll find the right one. I promise. You've got to belieeevvve."

Regan glanced at the cover of the visualization book. *You've Got to Believe* was the subtitle. She got her money's worth out of that, too, Regan thought.

"I belieeevvve," Kit said jokingly. "It's okay.

Before Regan met Jack she didn't have it easy, either. And now you both have found the right person."

"I certainly have," Victoria said. Her beautiful face was glowing.

"The romance with my fiancé was long distance, too," Regan said. "It's not easy. I'm glad it's finally over. Are you moving to Pennsylvania or is your fiancé coming here?"

Victoria made a sweeping motion with her left arm. "We're still going to live separately. You know, we'll visit each other on weekends and holidays."

Regan blinked with surprise.

"Keeps the relationship fresh," Kit volunteered. "You won't have the chance to get on each other's nerves."

Victoria waved her coffee cup and leaned forward. "That's how we feel. We'll see how this arrangement works and then take it from there. I've lived alone for this long, I don't even know how good I'd be at a relationship twenty-four-seven." She rolled her eyes self deprecatingly. "I enjoy my job and I love New York." She lowered her voice to a conspiratorial whisper. "I don't want to leave just yet."

"I love New York, too," Regan said "My fiancé lives in Tribeca. That's where we'll live for now."

"Tribeca is wonderful!" Victoria sighed. "They have such great restaurants and art galleries. It's so hip down there!"

Regan smiled. "Jack has a loft apartment that he was lucky enough to get before the prices went too crazy. We both love it." Regan paused. "Do you work in the city?"

"In Midtown at the Queen's Court Hotel."

"One of the best hotels in Manhattan," Regan commented.

"It is. I check people in on the overnight shift. That's why I was sleeping. I've been doing it for a year now but my body still hasn't gotten used to the schedule. I don't mind though. I'm not a nine-to-five person. I love having my days free and I get a few hours sleep here and there." She paused. "Are you sure I can't get you two anything to drink?"

"No thanks," Kit said. "We've been drinking Charisse's lavender tea all day."

Victoria smiled. "Charisse is such a darling!"

"Charisse is the one who assured me that our gowns would be ready," Regan said. "Victoria, we're trying to figure out if whoever stole the gowns might have had a grudge against Alfred and Charisse or one of the April Brides. Can you think of anyone who knew you were buying your gown from Alfred and Charisse and wanted to screw up your wedding by stealing your dress?"

"No. Not at all," Victoria answered quickly, then smiled. "I did tease my fiancé that he must have broken a lot of hearts along the way."

"What's your fiancé's name?" Kit asked.

Victoria leaned her head to one side. "Frederick."

"Frederick what?" Kit asked innocently.

"Dortmunder. Frederick is so proud of his heritage. He talks about it all the time. His family goes wayyyy back."

Most families go way back somewhere, Regan thought. "What does he do in Pennsylvania?"

"He's a painter. Incredibly talented. At Frederick's house in the country he has a little studio where he spends most of his time. He can't paint in this apartment because there's no light. That's why we spend most of our time together out there. He says that I'm his muse—that he gets inspired when I watch him paint. So I sit there for hours just watching him create these beautiful images."

I'd go nuts, Regan thought, but smiled and said, "Sounds great. Now, Victoria, no matter what you say, if we don't find the dresses very soon, Alfred and Charisse will make you a new one in time for your wedding. I'm just glad that you're not upset. Because let me tell you something—two of the other brides today did not take this as calmly as you have."

"Of course I'm upset. But I've learned that it's best to concentrate on the things in life that really matter." She pointed to her books and tapes. "For the last year I've been studying visualization, learning to listen to the quiet music inside of me. I came to this city from Iowa to try my hand at the whole show-biz thing. I sang and danced in all the plays back home. But in New York the competition is fierce. After several years, it dawned on me that I didn't believe in myself enough! I was introduced to visualization and it changed my life! I wrote my affirmations over and over of what I wanted and at this point in time I wanted to focus on finding love. And I found it! That's what really matters. I'm having fun! The stolen dress doesn't matter in the long run."

"You're absolutely right," Regan said with a nod. "This robbery has gotten a lot of attention from the press. A couple of reporters want to do stories on the five April Brides, as Alfred has dubbed us. One of the other brides is happy to be interviewed. Another, for her own reasons, says absolutely not. Do you have any interest in talking to the press about your reaction to this? They'd love you. You have such a great attitude, and if you want to be in show business, it could give you some good exposure."

"No, Regan," Victoria said without hesitation. "Frederick would disapprove. He believes in the quiet life. He wouldn't want me to get involved in a media circus. I just know he'd find it undignified. He's rather proper."

"So you're not going to pursue show biz anymore?" Regan asked.

"We'll see," Victoria said airily. "But right now I just want to enjoy being in *love*!" she exclaimed, throwing her hands in the air.

"I understand," Regan said as she stood.

"Of course you do! You're in love, too!" Victoria stood. She was a little taller than Regan. "It was so lovely meeting you both," she said as she walked them to the door, once again humming a little tune. "Good luck with your wedding, Regan."

"You, too. You'll be hearing from Alfred about your dress."

"I'm sure it will all work out." Victoria turned to Kit and looked at her with intensity. Her brown eyes were popping. "Remember, you've got to belieeevvve. Draw a treasure map of where you want to go in life and hang it on your wall. Write out your affirmations. To create the life of your dreams, you have to make it happen!"

"I'll check out that dating service when I get home," Kit muttered.

"You do that!"

When Kit and Regan were back out on the street, they both looked at each other. "I liked her," Kit said. "She's a little strange but she has charm."

Regan shrugged as they walked toward the corner.

"What?" Kit asked.

"She's very likable but she doesn't at all seem like someone who's getting married in three weeks. She didn't seem to care about the dress. And there was nothing in that apartment to indicate that she'd sent out invitations or that presents were coming in or anything like that. There are no magazines or books about wedding planning—just visualization and inner peace. If you pay that much money for one of Alfred's dresses, you must be having some sort of special ceremony."

"Maybe it's all out at Frederick's studio," Kit quipped. "Next to his paintbrushes."

"Could be," Regan said, then frowned. "If he's such an incredibly talented artist, then how come the only thing she has on her wall are a couple of framed prints? Wouldn't she have at least one of his paintings on display?"

"You'd think."

"I've got to tell you something, Kit. They don't sound like the greatest pair. She doesn't want to leave the city. He doesn't want to leave the country. She's gregarious and likes to have fun. He's worried about getting his name in the paper. Let me tell you, if he wants to sell his paintings, it would help if people knew about them. It could help her, too. But she obviously doesn't want to upset him."

"Frederick must be some hunk."

"I don't know what he is."

Kit shrugged. "Have you ever heard that opposites attract?"

"Sure I have. But something doesn't seem right." Regan hailed a cab. They got in, and she gave the address of the last April Bride. "We're going across Central Park to Fifth Avenue," she told the driver. "Fifth Avenue and Seventy-fifth Street."

"You got it lady," he said and took off like a shot. "You live there? That's a nice address."

"No, I don't."

"That's okay. As long as you're happy. You know what I mean? To me the important thing is to be happy. I'm okay. My wife's okay. We're happy."

Regan leaned back and smiled at Kit as the driver continued his monologue about the meaning of life. She was sure it wouldn't end until they arrived at the home of the fifth April Bride.

Whoever she turned out to be.

18

Jack returned to his corner office at One Police Plaza. It wasn't unusual for him to be found at work on a Saturday. But today there were especially compelling reasons to be there.

As of next Saturday, he'd be gone for over two weeks.

The Drip had struck again and was still free to roam the streets.

Jack sighed. There were bank robberies every day in New York City. With a little luck and planning, robbers often could get away with it. They couldn't get that much more than a few thousand dollars each time. But for the same person to succeed several times in the last three months—as Jack and his colleagues suspected—was the cause of a lot of frustration in Jack's office.

The detectives had interviewed everyone in the banks at the time of the robberies, as well as people outside who might have seen something that would be helpful to the investigation. But because each robbery had taken place when rain, sleet, or snow was coming down, everyone's focus had been on themselves. Even more than usual. It wasn't a big time for observing your fellow man when you were trying to stay dry and avoid getting poked by umbrellas.

Jack and his colleagues had looked at the tape of the last robbery several times. The profiler, Len Fisher, had said to Jack, "It looks like The Drip. Same shaped face. He's got a different beard and mustache this time but he's about the same size. He's wearing another ugly raincoat and thick black rubber shoes." They'd compared the tape to the one from the robbery two weeks before. "You see. He moves the same way. He's good at his disguises, though. Even though this one is slightly different, he's still recognizable from the last rainy day robbery."

"Looks like he took a few lessons from Willie Sutton."

Len nodded. "Willie took his work very seriously," he'd said wryly.

Jack had been fascinated by Willie Sutton, the famed bank robber born in Brooklyn in 1901 whose career lasted from the late 1920s to 1952 when he was caught for the last time. He'd served a number of prison terms. Nicknamed The Actor because of his ability to take on so many different looks, he was the master of disguise. Hollowed-out corks widened his nostrils, loose clothing hid his shape. He sometimes donned uniforms of workers, such as deliverymen, so he wouldn't seem suspicious. In 1969, he was freed from prison. Before his death in 1980, he appeared in commercials for a bank credit card and showed up as a celebrity at bank openings.

God Bless America, Jack thought.

Legend had it that when Willie was asked why he robbed banks, he answered, "Because that's where the money is." But in later years he said that a reporter had made up that quote. "I robbed banks because I enjoyed it. I loved it. I was more alive when I was inside a bank robbing it, than at any other time in my life . . . I enjoyed it so much that one or two weeks later I'd be out looking for the next job."

Jack sighed as he sat at his desk. The Drip's first robbery was at the beginning of January. He might be looking for his next job but he couldn't strike again until the weather was on his side. And sunny skies were predicted for the next several days. There was nothing The Drip could do about that except maybe try a rain dance. Or move to Seattle.

Tapping his fingers on the top of the desk, Jack looked off, deep in thought. Does this guy do it for the thrill? Or just the money? Or both?

One of the detectives had found a credit card slip on the floor of the bank. Over a thousand dollars had been charged at Dan's Discount Den. The name on the receipt was Chris Diamond. It was being checked. With any luck it had been dropped by the robber. Of course, Jack knew that if it had been dropped by the robber, there was a good chance the card wasn't his.

One of the most prevalent crimes these days was credit card theft, and even worse, identity theft, Jack mused. Even if The Drip had a stolen credit card, he probably wasn't smart enough to be involved with identity theft. If he were, he wouldn't be wasting his time going out in broad daylight and robbing banks of a couple grand. Instead he'd be making far more money using other

people's identity to take out loans or pur-
chase high-price items like luxury cars.

We have the security tapes, the notes,
and possibly a credit card receipt to help us
find this guy, Jack thought. If only there had
been some DNA on any of the notes he'd
left. The scientific advances in recent years
in matching DNA samples had been revolu-
tionary. But so far The Drip hadn't blessed
them with any of his. He was smart enough
to wear gloves.

"Hey, Boss."

Jack looked up. Sgt. Keith Waters, Jack's
top assistant, was standing in the doorway.
A handsome black man in his late thirties,
Keith possessed a restless energy. He loved
his work and could be found in the office at
all hours. "That credit card receipt?" Keith
said.

"Yes." Jack felt his pulse quicken.

"The credit card company got in touch
with the owner of the card, Chris Diamond.
He's been out of the country for a couple of
weeks working on a project in London."

"So he wasn't shopping at Dan's Discount Den in Queens the other day?"

"He assured them in no uncertain terms
that he'd never heard of the place. And no,

he didn't give anyone permission to use his card."

"Where does he live?"

"Connecticut."

"Did you find out what the thousand dollars was spent on?"

"We're working on it. But The Drip's taste in clothes could easily be satisfied by shopping at Dan's. It's not exactly designer stuff." Keith pointed to the outer office where several of the detectives had their desks, "Joe said his wife doesn't buy many clothes there, but she loves the place. They sell everything, so it's one-stop shopping. But get this. Last Halloween she bought costumes there for the kids. They have a big department that's stocked year round with all sorts of wigs, fake beards, and mustaches. She said they look real." Keith laughed. "As a matter of fact, so real that the sight of her six-year-old wearing the beard gave her the creeps. The kids love that department."

"Let's hope The Drip loves it, too. Maybe he did his one-stop shopping there. Everything he needs to report for work at the bank. Raincoat, beard, ugly black shoes . . ."

Keith smiled. "He could have gotten everything on his list."

"Any chance at all we can get prints off the slip?"

"We're working on that, too."

"Keep me posted. I'm going to be leaving in a little while to go meet Regan."

Keith shook his head and whistled. "Those stolen dresses are the talk of the town."

"I know."

"And Regan's in the middle of it."

Jack smiled. "That doesn't surprise you, does it?"

"Not at all, Boss. That Regan is something else. We're all looking forward to next Saturday. Your wedding is going to be some bash. Three hundred people, huh?"

Jack nodded. "Somewhere around that number." An uneasy feeling came over him. He wished that he didn't have to wait another week. He wished that Regan's dress hadn't been stolen. She was putting up a good front, but it had to be difficult for her. Jack stood. "It will be a good time, Keith. I wish it were tomorrow." He picked up a piece of paper off his desk. "I'd like you to do a background check on somebody. He might only be guilty of being a louse, but his name is Jeffrey Woodall . . ."

19

When the taxi pulled up to 75th and Fifth, the driver wound up his dissertation on the meaning of life. Regan quickly paid him as the doorman of Shauna's ritzy building hurried over to open the cab door.

"Thanks, lady," the driver said. "And remember, don't feel bad you don't live here."

"I don't," Regan assured him as she climbed out after Kit.

"Can I help you?" the doorman asked.

"We're here to see Shauna Nickles."

"And you are?"

"Regan Reilly. I'm here on behalf of the designers of her wedding dress."

The doorman smiled.

Regan wasn't sure whether she saw a look of sly amusement flash across his face. But it quickly faded as he resumed his professional air, ushering them to the front door.

"The concierge will call upstairs for you," he said, pointing inside.

Regan and Kit crossed the polished marble lobby and stopped at a gleaming wood desk. As Regan identified herself to the concierge, his expression remained impassive. When she was finished speaking, he picked up the house phone and pressed a button. A moment later, he said, "Mr. Ney, I have some young women here to see Shauna about her wedding dress."

A nod of his head indicated they were allowed admittance. In the elevator, a white-gloved attendant took them to the tenth floor.

"Down the hall to your left," he told them gravely.

"Thank you."

As they walked down the floral-carpeted hallway, Kit whispered, "Are you sure you're not depressed you don't live here?"

"Positive," Regan replied as she rang the bell. "This place doesn't look like a lot of laughs." The door opened, and an elderly man in a well-cut suit and conservative tie was standing before them. Regan guessed that he was in his mideighties.

"Hello—" Regan began.

"Come in," he ordered in a somewhat cranky tone. He gestured toward the ornately decorated living room that looked out over the treetops of Central Park. "I'm Arnold Ney."

Regan and Kit obeyed his command and stepped inside.

The apartment was a far cry from the one they had just visited. A large Persian rug was the centerpiece of a living room filled with antiques. A gold framed portrait of a regal-looking woman with silver hair, dressed in a ball gown, hung over the delicate silk couch. Regan was somehow sure that that couch was not intended for naps. It certainly couldn't be used to stretch out on and watch the ball game because there was no television in sight, nothing, actually, to suggest that the tenants lived in a modern world. A grand piano had its place by the window and was covered with family pictures.

"So," Regan began, addressing the man who was now shooing them farther into the room. "We just need to speak to Shauna for a few minutes."

"I know." Arnold stopped and cocked his head in the direction of the hallway. "Shauna!"

he called. "Shauna!" He turned back to them. "She'll be here in a minute."

"Thank you," Regan said as she and Kit sat on the formal silk couch. Arnold took his place in a wing chair by the fireplace. "This apartment is so lovely. Did Shauna grow up here?"

Arnold furrowed his brow and looked over at Regan like she was nuts. "Grow up here? She just moved in a few months ago to plan the wedding."

"Oh," Regan murmured. Kit looked at her with an expression that said, "I'm glad it wasn't me who asked that."

"I'm coming!" Shauna called breezily as she entered the room. Regan guessed her to be about forty. She was petite, with curly, light brown hair and an elfin expression on her plain yet pleasant face. Her outfit was far more casual than her surroundings— khaki pants, Birkenstock sandals, and a peasant top. Regan was willing to lay odds that she ate granola for breakfast.

Avoiding too many pleasantries, Arnold introduced them.

Shauna had a twinkle in her eye as she sat in a chair near the couch and said to

Regan, "I understand you have bad news for me."

"Bad news? What bad news?" Arnold asked.

"My dress has been stolen!" Shauna answered, slightly raising her voice. She then turned toward Regan and Kit. "I just spoke to Alfred."

"Your dress has been stolen?" Arnold repeated.

"Stolen! Isn't it the worst? But don't worry! Alfred promised he'd make me a new one in time for the wedding."

"The wedding is in *three* weeks," Arnold said, holding up that many fingers.

"He said he'd get it done."

Regan had experienced a lot of strange situations in the past several hours but nothing quite like this. Was this man the groom? She didn't dare ask. "Alfred and Charisse are so sorry," she began. "They hate to inconvenience you—"

"I love them. And I *love* their gowns," Shauna enthused. "I'm not into designer clothes, but Alfred's vintage look is so perfect on me. Arnie saw pictures. He thinks the dress looks romantic. Right, Arnie?"

"I like their dresses," he answered, waving his hand dismissively.

What is their relationship? Regan wondered. She couldn't come out and just ask. She'd try another tack. "I ordered my wedding dress from Alfred. My fiancé asked me what it was like, but I wouldn't tell him . . ." Regan let her voice trail off.

This time it was Shauna's turn to look at Regan like she was nuts. "You don't think?"

"What?" Regan asked, playing dumb.

Shauna started laughing hysterically. "Arnie, did you hear that?"

"What?"

"I think she thinks we're a couple."

"Oh, that's a good one. Wait till Pamela hears!" He finally laughed, making one of the oddest sounds Regan had ever heard. "Kkkkkkk," he laughed. "Kkkkkkk."

"I didn't think that . . ." Regan protested.

"Heyyyyy, what's happening?"

Regan turned her head. A thirtyish young man with shoulder-length dark hair, a pierced ear, and, like Alfred, sporting several day's worth of stubble on his face, came strutting into the room. He was clad in jeans that were ripped in the places where they were supposed to be ripped these days, and a white T-shirt that showed off his great form. To say that his hip look seemed out of place in the surroundings was an understatement.

Shauna turned and looked at him lovingly. "This is my fiancé, Tyler."

"Heyyyyy," Tyler said again, waving at the group.

What do you know? Regan thought. Here I thought Shauna was marrying someone at least forty years older. It's more like ten years younger! "Hello," she said to Tyler. "We're just talking to Shauna about her missing wedding dress."

"What a bummer."

"It's okay," Regan said. "Shauna will have a dress for your wedding. Alfred and Charisse just wanted to make sure you all knew what happened and assure you that everything would be fine."

Shauna reached for Tyler's hand while she stared at Regan. "Alfred told me the whole story." With her free hand she pointed at the portrait over the couch. "Pamela is the one who will really be disappointed if I don't have the dress for the wedding. She loves good clothes. We put a lot of time and energy into picking out that dress." Shauna grinned.

"She thinks it makes me look like a princess."

"Awesome," Tyler opined, "awesome."

"You're getting married in three weeks, right?" Regan asked.

"Yes."

"Tell her not to worry. They'll have it done," Regan said with a confidence she didn't necessarily feel. Offhandedly, she asked, "Where are you getting married?"

"At Pamela and Arnie's club on East 65th Street. It will be a small ceremony with about fifty guests. It's going to be so elegant and wonderful."

"Those two are like children to us," Arnie grunted. "When Pamela and I met them out in Santa Fe, they were so friendly. We felt like we knew them for years."

Shauna smiled. "Tyler and I sell the best turquoise jewelry in the town square in Santa Fe. Arnie bought a beautiful necklace for Pamela and then invited us to join them for dinner." Shauna paused. "Thank God we were there. Pamela started to choke on a piece of steak. Tyler saved her life."

Tyler nodded and gave the thumbs up.

Arnie looked down, clearly uncomfortable that tears were welling in his eyes.

"So we bonded," Shauna declared. "The next night we went out to dinner again. This time to a vegetarian restaurant. Pamela wanted to know why we weren't married. We told her we were saving up but would probably end up going to a justice of the peace. Pamela had a fit! She said that we have to come to New York to get married in style. So here we are! Like a family."

"How nice," Regan murmured.

"They're good kids," Arnie grunted.

"I just feel so lucky about everything. So lucky. I love Tyler so much and then to meet a terrific couple like Arnie and Pamela . . ." Now it was her eyes that welled up with tears. "My parents passed away when I was a child. Maybe that's why I never was interested in having a real wedding and settling down. To have met a couple who treat me like the daughter they never had . . ."

"And me like a second son," Tyler interjected. "Right, Pops!"

"Stop!" Arnie ordered. "Or you'll make me start bawling again."

"I'm so happy for you," Regan said.

Shauna nodded, her impish face caught between tears and a smile. "You must be very close to Alfred and Charisse," she said as she batted her makeup-free eyes.

"I've gotten to know them a little over the last few months as they worked on my dress. But I'm also a private investigator so I can't help getting involved in this case. I'll ask you the question I'm asking all the brides who were affected by the break-in. Do you know of anyone who might have done this to hurt you and Tyler? Or Arnie and Pamela? Is there anyone who might not have wanted you to have that dress?"

Tyler looked befuddled. "No. Hardly anyone knows us around here."

"Can't imagine," Arnie said dismissively.

"That would be so hurtful," Shauna declared.

Regan took that for a no. "Okay. One more question. This case has attracted a lot of attention. Reporters are dying to write about the brides whose dresses are gone. It's such an emotional subject. Shauna, would you be willing to talk to the press about your story?"

"Absolutely not!" Arnie barked. "I have enough people after me for money. I don't need the world to know that we're paying for the wedding. It would turn something nice that's just between the four of us into something crass. And I'd have more people hounding me with their hard luck stories!"

"I understand," Regan said. Did Shauna look disappointed? She wasn't sure.

"Arnold Ney worked hard for every dollar he made! I don't need any more solicitations."

"Calm down, Arnie," Shauna said soothingly. She hurried over and gave him a kiss on the cheek.

Regan and Kit made their escape as fast as they could.

"Whew!" Kit said when they were out on the street. "Out of the five April Brides, you and Brianne are the most normal."

"Whatever normal is," Regan said. "Let's get a cab. I need to see Jack."

"If you guys want to be alone tonight, and maybe even elope, it won't hurt my feelings one bit."

Regan smiled. "Don't tempt me."

———◆———

20

Several miles off the Garden State Parkway, and not that far from Atlantic City, Marco and Francis wandered into a store that was nationally famous for its great bargains on appliances. A salesman approached them with his most winning smile.

"My name is Roy. What can I do for you this afternoon?" he asked.

"We're looking for a dishwasher," Marco said matter-of-factly.

Roy clapped his hands together. "A dishwasher? No problem. For some reason I thought you guys would be in the market for power drills or electric chainsaws."

"We're not," Marco answered in a now unfriendly tone.

"The dishwasher is a present for my girlfriend," Francis hastened to add.

"Fantastic!" Roy enthused. "I have a super-duper model she's just going to love. It gets the dishes clean as a whistle and it's so quiet you barely know it's on." He pointed to a large machine.

"Got one a little smaller?"

A half hour later Marco and Francis pulled the car up to the back of the store where they could load Joyce's present into the back seat. Smiling Roy was waiting. He was an enthusiastic salesman who saw to it that his customer received the best possible service from the time they walked through the door until they pulled away with their purchases.

"Hey guys!" he boomed, tapping Marco's trunk. "Pop this baby open and we'll load you up."

"Our trunk is full," Marco said gruffly. "We're going to put it in the backseat. First we want to take it out of the box."

"Now?"

"Now. But we want to keep the box in case we have to return the dishwasher."

"That's all right!" Roy said, always eager to please. "If you bring it back, you won't need the box—"

"*I want the box!*" Marco snarled.

"It's all yours!" Roy blurted nervously.

They pulled the front seat all the way forward, wedged the dishwasher into the back-seat, and crammed the cardboard box in next to it. Marco and Francis drove off, the sight of smiling, waving Roy receding from the rearview mirror.

They couldn't hear the comments he was making under his breath.

"He was suspicious of us," Francis moaned.

"No he wasn't. All he cares about is his commission."

"What now?"

"Time to find a secluded spot."

Francis sighed. "Around here?"

"Hopefully."

They drove around and around and around, not wanting to veer too far from their final destination of Atlantic City. Marco cut down side streets, but they couldn't find anywhere that would give them the privacy they needed. Eventually, he turned onto a two-lane road that became increasingly wooded and suddenly took a sharp curve. Once around the bend, Marco whistled with satisfaction at the sign ahead.

WELCOME TO THE HEAVENLY REST CEMETERY
GATE CLOSES AT DUSK

The imposing, black-iron gate was wide open.

"Hurry!" Francis ordered. "I don't know what time dusk is but I think it's around now."

Marco stepped on the gas. They sailed through the entryway, past a religious statue whose outstretched arms welcomed them, and glided down a sloping road. Rows of tombstones could be seen in all directions. At a fork in the road, they went left and up a hill. Large mausoleums were facing each other on either side of the narrow path. Marco pulled over and stopped the car. Without a word, they both got out.

All was silent except for the rustling of the breeze and the occasional chirp of a bird.

"Do you think it's safe?" Francis asked anxiously.

"It's closing time," Marco said. "Everybody's gone except maybe the guy who'll lock up."

They pulled the empty dishwasher box out of the backseat, placed it on the ground behind the car, and opened the trunk. The four wedding gowns were in a jumble. One by one they pulled them out and stuffed them down into the rough cardboard container.

"I hope they'll all fit," Francis fretted.

"We'll make them fit," Marco said resolutely as he gave a final squash to the dresses that Alfred and Charisse had labored over so lovingly. "Give me the tape."

Francis leaned in the trunk and grabbed a roll of masking tape they'd used with the ropes to bind Alfred and Charisse's hands.

Marco closed the sides, sealed the box, and they tossed it into the trunk. Quickly, they got back in the car and drove off.

A moment later a visitor to the cemetery teetered out from behind one of the mausoleums. Something on the ground caught her eye. The elderly woman leaned down and picked up a beautiful, antique-white lace button that had fallen off one of the dresses. "Oh, darling," she whispered as she walked back to her husband's tombstone. "Whenever I visit, you always give me a sign that you know I'm here, don't you?" Smiling, she examined the button that reminded her of the buttons on her wedding dress. The dress she'd worn exactly sixty years ago today. "It's got a tiny logo with the initials *A* and *C* on the back," she said aloud. "Too bad they're not our initials, sweetheart, but I'll treasure it all the same."

A moment later her driver pulled up. He turned off the radio before she got in the car. He'd been listening to Jess and Kenny.

21

The Saturday before a guy gets married is expected to be stressful, but it shouldn't be this stressful, Pauly Sanders thought as he returned to his spacious two-bedroom apartment on the Upper East Side. His roommate had moved out the month before to make way for Brianne. The minute he was gone, a van pulled up with a slew of Brianne's belongings and several cans of paint.

"This place needs work," she insisted.

To Pauly, it looked just fine. He'd been lucky to buy it before the market got too crazy. And he'd been lucky to keep it when he was unemployed. A funny feeling hit him in the stomach. Being unemployed and engaged hadn't been the world's greatest combination. He'd be starting his new job when they returned from their honeymoon. He couldn't wait to get back to work and start collecting a paycheck again.

In the foyer of his apartment he pulled off his dark wet raincoat and dropped it along with his knapsack on the floor. He kicked off his heavy black shoes and left them there.

"One of the last times I'll be able to get away with that," he mumbled as he trudged into the bedroom. He changed into dry clothes, sat on the bed, and pulled on a pair of white gym socks. Trying to catch his breath, he looked around.

Brianne and the decorator she worked for had been traipsing in and out of the apartment every other day, planning their "touch-ups." It was enough to make a man crazy. Pauly's bachelor pad was being gussied up with flowery window treatments and fancy pillows, pillows that were not meant for resting one's weary head on.

But he loved Brianne. She was a piece of goods. She didn't take any of his garbage. She was the first girl he truly fell in love with, and he didn't want to lose her.

The phone rang. He grabbed the cordless next to the bed. It was his beloved.

"Hey, baby," he said.

"Don't 'baby' me! Where have you been?" Brianne practically shrieked.

"What's wrong?"

"What's wrong? I've had the crisis of my life and I haven't been able to reach you. Didn't you check your messages?"

"No. I was doing a lot of thinking. And I was busy. To tell you the truth, I thought you were going to be tied up with your mother. This is a reflective day for me. My last Saturday as a bachelor."

"Don't give me reflective!" Brianne screamed. "Didn't you see me on NY1?"

Pauly's phone beeped, which meant another caller wanted his ear. "Hold on a second, baby." He pressed the call-waiting button. "Hello."

"Pauly! Did you see Brianne on NY1?" It was Pauly's best man, Tony.

"As a matter of fact I didn't. And I'm catching a lot of flak for it now. I don't even know why she was on. Let me call you back." Pauly clicked the button. "Brianne, that was Tony. He saw you on NY1."

"How did he think I looked?"

"He didn't say. I didn't give him a chance. Honey, what happened?"

Pauly laid back on the bed as Brianne explained everything that had happened, down to the last detail. "And the dress was not only covered with ants, it had been eaten by moths. My mother wants to call and scream at the dry cleaner, but he went out of business twenty years ago."

"Maybe you could wear my sister's dress."

Brianne howled in protest.

"Maybe not."

"She just got married a month ago! I'm not going to be seen in her dress. The champagne stains aren't even dry. Besides, she had no right getting married before us. We were engaged first."

"All right. All right. I was just trying to help."

"I'm sorry, Pauly. I don't want you to think I'm difficult."

Pauly rolled his eyes. He started to sing softly. "I love you just the way you are."

"Our wedding song," Brianne said quietly.

"Yeah."

"I love you just the way you are, too," Brianne said without a trace of sentiment.

"That's what we decided," Pauly croaked. "No putting each other on pedestals. No unrealistic expectations. For better or for worse. No matter what, we're there for each other."

"What did you do?" Brianne asked, suddenly suspicious.

Pauly sat up quickly and looked out at his dark wet raincoat sprawled on the floor of the foyer, his knapsack and shoes next to it. "Nothing."

"Are you sure?"

"Positive."

"Did you pick up the ushers' cuff links from the jeweler?"

"Oh, I forgot."

"Did you pick up your new suit from the tailor?"

"No."

"What have you been doing all day?"

"I've been really nervous."

"So, I guess you didn't return the television to Dan's Discount Den?"

"I thought we were going to k-keep it," he stammered.

"No, we weren't. I want a little television for the kitchen counter to keep me company when I cook you nice dinners. You've lost too much weight these past few months. That TV we bought is too big."

"Maybe we can ride over there tomorrow, and you can bring it in."

"Me?"

"I'm embarrassed to return things. I've always been that way. My mother used to return clothes after she wore them, and I couldn't stand it."

"You never told me that."

"I was too embarrassed. But it's true. It affected me."

"Pauly?"

"Yes."

"We haven't used the TV. We barely took it out of the box. It's still wrapped in plastic. There's no issue here. Just your issue about your mother. She doesn't seem like the type who would return clothes after wearing them."

"All right, Brianne. All right. What are you going to do about your dress?" he asked, clearly wanting to change the subject.

"My father called and threatened Alfred. Said he'd better have a new dress made for me by Wednesday."

"Wednesday!"

Brianne managed to laugh. "Thursday at the latest. This has been some day, Pauly. Tonight when I go out with the girls, I plan to just let it rip."

Pauly glanced at his reflection in the full-length mirror that was hanging next to the closet. His five-foot-eight-inch frame looked haggard. His dark hair was matted down.

"That's it, baby. Just have fun tonight. We may as well try to enjoy life while we can. I'll try to have a good time tonight, too."

"Are you sure nothing happened?"

"Yes. Why?"

"You just sound weird. You're talking about your bachelor party with your best friends—you shouldn't have to try too hard to have fun. Just don't have *too* good a time. Oh—I don't suppose you went to the bank today."

"Why would I go to the bank today?" he asked, his voice tense.

"To get our travelers' checks. Remember?"

"I thought I'd do that Monday."

"Well I guess you have all next week. We've been going through a lot of money lately. That's why I want to be sure to have travelers' checks for our honeymoon. Unlike cash, if the checks are stolen, they can be replaced."

Pauly swallowed hard. "Getting married is expensive."

"Try being the bride. Then you'd know expensive."

"No thanks."

"One day I hope you'll be the father of the bride," Brianne said softly. "When this is all over, we're going to be so happy, right, Pauly? We're going to have a wonderful life together."

Nervous apprehension swept through Pauly's body. "Of course we are," he said, forcing himself to sound confident. "Of course we are."

22

Joyce had had an unusually rough day at the pet store. Most of her customers were nice normal people who, like her, were animal lovers. But not today. Joyce figured that there must be a full moon lurking. In the couple of hours before closing time, the eccentrics had come out of the woodwork.

Teddy, the store's owner, had seen a catalogue that advertised life preservers for dogs. As a lark, he ordered a dozen. They'd come in and to everyone's surprise had sold out almost immediately. Some of the store's longtime customers had their noses out of joint that they weren't notified in advance about this latest canine accessory.

"Of course I would have bought two," one woman announced haughtily. "Joyce, I'm surprised at you. You should have set them aside for me. Lucky and Jigsaw both love to go swimming out in the Hamptons."

Joyce knew that the closest those dogs got to the Hamptons was the fire hydrant at the end of their block. "I'll call the manufacturer and see if we can get more in," she promised sweetly.

Another customer was getting married and had ordered a doggy necklace to match the one her fiancé had given her. It hadn't come in yet. The wedding was six months away, but the bride was in a tizzy.

"This is making me incredibly nervous," the bride complained as she petted her little black poodle. The poodle looked bored as it stared at Joyce.

"We have plenty of time," Joyce assured the bride.

"Fifi wants her necklace now, don't you, Fifi," the woman said, kissing the poodle on the top of his fluffy head. "Fifi wants to look pretty at my wedding."

Fifi yawned as the customer in line behind them rolled her eyes. "Hey, lady, did you hear about the stolen wedding dresses in Manhattan? Two guys broke into a fancy designers' loft in the middle of the night and made off with several wedding dresses and all the money and jewelry in the safe. Now *that's* something to be upset about. How would you like to be getting married next week and have no dress?"

Fifi's mommy did not seem particularly concerned. "You can find wedding gowns everywhere. Not these necklaces. Joyce, please call me the moment it arrives."

"I will."

"Come along, Fifi. Mommy wants to buy you a special treat."

Fifi didn't protest. Actually, the dog had no choice. She was still in her mother's arms. Together they exited the store.

"I'm telling you," the next customer began as she took the doggie toys out of her shopping basket and placed them on the counter, "if that designer had a dog like my King, those dresses would have gone nowhere, that's for sure. King would have taken a piece out of those two guys' hides. My King would never let anyone hurt me."

"They say it's two guys?" Joyce asked off handedly as she rung up the purchases.

"Yeah, two guys. How much do I owe you?"

"Thirty-nine ninety-seven."

"It's worth every penny. King will be so happy."

When Joyce finally arrived home, she was

grateful that the house was empty except for the parrot who would always be there for her. When she bought Romeo, she was told that the life span of your average parrot is seventy years. That gave them a lot of time together. It also gave Romeo a lot of time to pick up new phrases.

"Lazy bums! Lazy bums! Arrrhhhhh."

"No, Romeo, it's just me," Joyce said, walking over to the cage. "The lazy bums have gone out for the night."

"You're so chicken! You're so chicken!"

"What?" Joyce asked her bird. She'd never heard him use this expression before.

"You're so chicken!"

"What are you talking about?" Joyce laughed.

"You're so chicken!"

"Did Marco teach you that?"

"Hello!"

"Hello, Romeo." Joyce reached out and patted his feathers. She loved her bright green parrot with his yellow crown, and appreciated his companionship, but wished she could have a dog as well. The problem was, Francis was allergic to dogs and cats. In a million years, no dating service would have paired them up, but as Joyce explained to her mother, "What looks good on paper doesn't always work in real life. And vice versa."

"Vice versa, my foot," argued her mother, an animal lover if there ever was one. "It's never going to work. And a dog, unlike most people, will never let you down."

Joyce gave Romeo his favorite treat, yogurt covered raisins, then walked into the bathroom. Again she noticed the bloody paper napkins in the garbage. Francis had a bad nosebleed a couple months ago. All of a sudden she felt panicked. What if there was something really wrong with him? She hurried into the kitchen and started to dial his cell phone. But before the connection went through she hung up.

Why should I call him? she thought as she stood there with the phone in her hand. He's obviously well enough to take off for Atlantic City for the evening. The phone rang, startling her out of her reverie. It was Cindy.

"Are you ready to go out and paint the town red tonight?" Cindy asked.

"I will be," Joyce answered.

"Good. I'll pick you up at eight. After dinner we're going to a new place called Club Zee. It's in the Meatpacking District and it's really cool. I just heard from one of my friends who lives near there on West Fourteenth Street. She'll be at Club Zee tonight with a big group of friends, and they really plan to let loose."

"Great," Joyce said, trying to sound enthusiastic. Her energy was waning and she was tempted not to go. But she knew Cindy would be upset if she backed out now.

"It will be great! My friend's group is taking out a girl who's getting married next week—the poor girl's wedding dress was shredded at a break-in in Manhattan. Four other dresses were stolen . . ."

"I just heard about that!" Joyce interrupted.

Cindy laughed. "My friend said if this girl Brianne ever gets her hands on the guys who did it, God pity them. She's one tough broad. Her father just put up a ten-thousand-dollar reward for anyone who supplies information leading to an arrest."

"Sounds like we're gonna have an interesting evening."

"We'll make it interesting. I'll pick you up at eight."

"You're so chicken!" Romeo squawked as Joyce hung up the phone.

Joyce smiled as she headed into the bathroom. A nice hot bath will relax me, she thought. But when she looked down again at the sight of the bloody napkin, her sense of unease intensified. She shook her head and realized again that she was fed up with having Marco around. I'm going to have to lay down the law, she thought. If Francis doesn't get rid of him, then I'll throw them both out. Who knows? Maybe I'll meet someone new tonight.

Somehow Joyce sensed that the winds of change were blowing around her life. She took off her clothes, stepped into the tub, and eased her body down into the soothing warm water.

"You're so chicken!" Romeo squawked from down the hall. "You're so chicken!"

Joyce stood up and pushed the bathroom door closed with a loud bang. It almost felt symbolic. I'm not taking it anymore, she told herself. As she sat back down, she felt liberated. Tonight, I start a new way of life. It's my way or the highway. Francis is going to be surprised. But life is full of surprises.

She couldn't have guessed how many were in store for her.

23

When Regan and Kit stepped out of the cab at Jack's apartment building in Tribeca, Kit looked up and sighed. "Your Home Sweet Home, Regan."

Regan smiled. "I love it. I can't believe this place used to be a warehouse."

Jack's paternal grandfather had been an extremely successful businessman who, when he died, left a generous inheritance to each of his grandchildren. Jack had wisely put some of that money in real estate, buying an apartment that he hoped someday to share with his soul mate. Until Regan came along, Jack had been afraid he'd never find her. Now, as the song went, he never wanted to let her go.

His maternal grandfather had been a police lieutenant. After graduating from Boston College, Jack decided that he, too, wanted to pursue a career in law enforcement. He'd risen quickly through the ranks of the NYPD, from patrolman to captain, and now was head of the Major Case Squad. His goal was to become the police commissioner of New York City. Few doubted that he would make it.

Jack was waiting for them upstairs in the roomy apartment. "How's my bride?" he asked as he opened the door, leaned over, and gave Regan a quick kiss.

"Much better now," Regan answered with a smile as she looked up at him, always amazed at how handsome he was and how happy he made her feel. "We've had quite the afternoon."

"And our bridesmaid?" Jack asked Kit, planting a kiss on her cheek.

"I feel better, too, just knowing we're on our way to Atlantic City. Maybe I'll hit the jackpot at one of those slot machines. Then I can retire."

"Maybe we'll hit the jackpot and find out some useful information about our dress thieves," Regan said hopefully as she walked into the large, airy living room. Several of the boxes she had sent from California were lined up against the wall.

"I talked to the head of security at Gambler's Palace," Jack informed them.

"Stan Visoff is a former FBI agent I met a couple of times. He's getting out the security tapes from last Saturday night for us."

"Great," Regan said as she silently admired her surroundings. Jack had decorated the apartment with oriental rugs, antiques, traditional furniture, and interesting artwork that he bought in the neighborhood galleries. Like Alfred and Charisse's loft, the apartment had an exposed brick wall that gave a feeling of country charm. Regan felt completely at home. Blending her life with Jack's felt so easy and so right.

"Wait till you hear about the other April Brides," Kit began enthusiastically.

"I'd love to as soon as we get in the car," Jack said quickly. "We'd better get going if we want to get back tonight at a reasonable enough hour to check out the activity in Alfred and Charisse's neighborhood."

Ten minutes later they were heading for the Holland Tunnel.

"So tell me," Jack said, "how did the other brides take the news?"

"Surprisingly well," Regan answered, "especially considering the reactions of the first two."

Kit leaned forward from the backseat.

"Besides your lovely fiancée, these April Brides of Alfred's take the cake. The two we visited this afternoon were so blasé about their missing gowns, I couldn't believe it. One of them is into visualization and inner peace. She's into inner peace so much that she and her future husband don't plan to live together when they get married. They'll just pay each other visits."

Jack chuckled and grabbed Regan's hand. "That won't be us."

Regan smiled. "No way."

"The other bride," Kit continued, "well, talk about hitting the jackpot . . ." She told Jack about their visit to the Fifth Avenue apartment.

"Arnie Ney?" Jack asked. "That name sounds familiar."

"He's rich," Kit volunteered. "And doesn't want his name in the paper. He doesn't want anyone else bugging him for money."

Regan turned to Jack. "And how was the rest of your day? Any leads on the bank robbery?"

Jack shook his head and filled them in. "The bank teller is also getting married soon. Her fiancé came and picked her up.

He was a wreck. He's whisking her off to Las Vegas for a couple days of R and R."

"Kind of makes the whole experience worth it," Kit sighed.

"She was pretty upset. I just wish we could get this guy soon."

"If by this time next week we have the bank robber and two dress thieves behind bars, we can fly off without giving a thought to our work," Regan said.

Jack turned to her. "When we take off for Ireland, we have to make a pact to leave this all behind."

They were planning to spend several days in Ireland, staying at two different castles in the countryside, and visiting some of their ancestors' birthplaces. As an engagement present, a friend of Regan's had given them a year's subscription to Roots@Relatives.com, an Internet service that helped trace your ancestry. The card read, "To Regan and Jack— I hope you don't discover you're kissing cousins." They decided to find out. Then it was on to London and Paris.

As Regan thought about their plans for Ireland, she mused aloud. "The bride who is into visualization said that her fiancé's family went 'wayyyy' back. I'd love to be able to check them out on Roots@Relatives. When people imply how impressive their family lineage is, it makes me curious what they call impressive."

"Please!" Kit gasped. "Anyone can put on a tiara and claim to be from royalty. I met a guy at a party who said he was a prince. I'd never heard of the country. I Googled it. They hadn't heard of it, either."

Jack and Regan laughed. "I'm just so curious about Victoria and Frederick's relationship," Regan said. "The few things she said about him give me the impression he's pompous. Maybe I should call her and offer to look up his family in Roots@Relatives. They provide census records and birth certificates. It's really interesting. They already sent me a picture of the boat my great-grandfather came over from Ireland on. If Frederick's family really is so grand, I bet he'd love to get copies of those old records."

"He'd probably be afraid that you'd uncover a family scandal. Have you ever met anyone who doesn't have at least one embarrassing relative?" Kit asked, then sat back in her seat. "As long as she's not upset about the dress, leave well enough alone."

Regan shrugged. "We'll see. I'd better give Alfred a call and let him know that all the victims have been notified." She pulled her cell phone out of her purse and pressed in his number.

"Alfred, it's Regan," she said when he answered.

"I was just about to call you!" he said excitedly.

"Is anything else wrong?"

"There's always something wrong. But something right has happened, too."

"Do tell," Regan said. "I love good news."

"That hot new cable network, Tiger News, wants to have us on their Sunday morning show, *Patrick and Jeannie*!"

"Us?" Regan asked.

"Me and Charisse and the April Brides! They've been doing specials on planning spring weddings. One of the producers is familiar with my dresses and absolutely adores them! She thinks this would be a great human-interest story."

"Well, you know Tracy won't do it. And you can forget Victoria and Shauna. Neither of them wants publicity."

Alfred groaned. "Brianne couldn't find another dress. So her father called and threatened me. He said I'd better have a new dress for her or else."

"There's a human-interest story for you," Regan remarked.

"I'm afraid to call her. Would you call her for me?"

"And say what?"

"That we're going to be on Patrick and Jeannie's show tomorrow morning and she should join us."

"I don't know, Alfred."

"Please, Regan! That show is so popular! They're going to show pictures of my beautiful dresses. It would mean so much for my business. It might even help us get the dresses back. *Please,* Regan! This is national television!!!!"

"What's her number?"

"Thank you, Regan. Thank you. I love you so much."

"Love you, too."

Jack turned and looked quizzically at Regan. She shrugged as Alfred gave her Brianne's number. "What time do we have to be there?"

"Eight o'clock."

"I'm not going to get much sleep tonight," Regan commented.

"Charisse and I aren't going to get any sleep for the next three weeks!"

When Regan hung up, she looked at Jack, then at Kit. "I'm going on TV tomorrow morning."

"Huh?" they both answered at once.

Regan explained as she dialed Brianne's cell phone number.

"Hello," Brianne answered in the same gruff tone Regan had experienced that morning.

"Brianne, this is Regan Reilly. How are you doing?"

"I've had better days. But I'm at my apartment with my girlfriends. It's one of my last nights here. We're revving up to go out tonight."

"That's good. I know it's been rough for you," Regan said, trying to sound sympathetic, then asked her about the *Patrick and Jeannie* show.

"What?!" Brianne exclaimed. "Are you kidding me?" She called out to her friends. "Listen to this, guys! They want me on that new *Patrick and Jeannie* show tomorrow morning!"

Regan could hear a chorus of cheers and

shouts of encouragement. "Brianne! You're going to be a star!"

"The only bad thing," Brianne continued, "is that I have to be there at 8 A.M."

A chorus of boos erupted. "We'll just have to stay out all night!" one of Brianne's girl-friends cried. It was followed by another chorus of cheers.

They're having no problem getting psy-ched up for their night out, Regan thought. "So you'll do it?" Regan said loudly into her phone, hoping Brianne would hear her.

"Yes! Can I bring my fiancé?"

"Of course. The studios always have a greenroom that's stocked with coffee and donuts. He can wait there while we're on the air."

"What about the other brides whose dresses are gone?"

"They all have their reasons for not want-ing to do publicity."

"Must mean they're guilty of something."

"No," Regan protested. "It might be hard to believe these days, but some people aren't interested in being on television or having their name in the paper."

"It's very hard to believe. Regan, this is

my bachelorette party tonight. I might not look my best in the morning."

"I'm going to have a long night, too. But don't worry. They have makeup artists on these shows who can perform miracles."

Brianne laughed as she warmed up to Regan. "We're going downtown tonight to a new place called Club Zee. It's in the Meat-packing District on Fourteenth Street. Drop by if you'd like."

"Thanks, Brianne. I kind of doubt we'll make it. But I'll call you if there are any new developments before tomorrow morning."

"Okay."

"Remember, Brianne, next week at this time we'll both be dancing at our weddings. We will! . . . Okay, bye." Regan snapped her phone shut.

"Is she going to be your new best friend?" Kit asked from the back seat.

"Highly unlikely, Kit. But let me tell you something. Her group sounds as if they're going to have a grand old time tonight. She invited us to stop by the club where they'll be later on."

"Maybe we should take her up on it," Kit suggested.

Regan raised her eyebrows. "It might be a

good idea to check in on Brianne. If she doesn't make it to the show tomorrow morning, Alfred will fall apart."

Jack shook his head as he steered the car onto the Jersey Turnpike. He turned to Regan and smiled. "Are all our Saturday nights going to be this exciting?" he asked.

"Till death do you part," Kit answered from the backseat.

Somehow her words didn't have the humor she intended.

24

After their side trip to the cemetery, Francis and Marco had searched in vain for a post office that was still open. Rain, hail, sleet, and snow might never prevent the United States Postal Service from making their appointed rounds, but closing time on Saturday would halt them in their tracks.

The only thing Francis and Marco did accomplish was getting their taillight fixed. And it was by accident. At one of the many gas stations where they stopped to see if anyone knew of an open FedEx or post office, the attendant admonished them about their broken taillight.

"No post offices open now. But what you should do is let me fix that taillight for you. You're going to get yourself a ticket," he said with an expression that seemed to warn he'd call the cops himself if Marco didn't let him make the buck fixing it.

"I know it's broken," Marco grumbled.

"It's Saturday night. Cops around here are always on the lookout for trouble. I wouldn't drive around for too long with that thing."

"Fix it then," Marco snapped.

After the light was replaced, the attendant stuffed the money in his pocket. Impatiently, Marco pulled out of the gas station.

"I'm hungry and my leg is bothering me," Francis whined.

"How do you think my wrist feels? It's sore as hell. I'm lucky I didn't hit an artery. I need to see a doctor."

"Why don't we stop at that diner ahead and grab a couple of burgers?" Francis suggested. "We'll both feel better."

Marco nodded. He steered the car into the parking lot of Madge's 24 Hour diner. Wordlessly they went inside, grabbed a booth, and then placed their orders with a waitress who clearly was not experiencing career satisfaction.

But when the food arrived it was hot and the beer was cold. The cheeseburgers and french fries hit the spot, wherever that spot is.

Marco wiped his mouth with a flimsy paper napkin. "I didn't realize how hungry I was. We haven't eaten much today."

"We didn't sleep much last night, either," Francis complained. "I'm tired. I wish we were home."

Marco looked around the empty, dreary diner and then whispered, "Cheer up! We have twenty thousand dollars cash and we're on our way to Atlantic City! Once you walk into the casino and hear all those bells and whistles and the clatter of coins spilling out of the slot machines, you'll perk up. Believe me! Let's turn our twenty thousand into forty!"

Francis could have kicked himself as he heard himself asking, "You think we could double our money tonight?"

"Yes! I'm going into the men's room to rinse off my wrist. It might be getting germs. I'll be right back."

As Francis sat alone, the depressing surroundings got to him. The diner where Ma works is much nicer than this, he thought. Then he remembered what she had said on the phone earlier today—that at work they were all talking about the stolen wedding dresses. A wave of guilt and dread washed over him. After downing the cheeseburger and beer, he'd felt good, but that sense of well-being quickly vanished. They had to get rid of those dresses. And it looked like it would be Monday before they could get them out of their possession.

When Marco emerged from the rest room, he grabbed the check off their table. They paid the bill, grabbed toothpicks and stale mints from the bowl by the cash register, and headed out to the car. One of the lights from the parking light shone right into the backseat, illuminating Joyce's dishwasher like a coveted prize on a game show.

Before too long they were on the Atlantic City Causeway heading east. It was already nine o'clock. Marco flipped on the radio.

"If you see anything," the reporter was saying, "please call Crime Stoppers. Those wedding dresses have to be somewhere. Police are on the lookout."

Marco flipped off the radio.

Neither of them said a word. But the air was thick with tension.

The neon lights atop the towering casinos in Atlantic City finally came into view, beckoning them with the promise of Lady Luck. "Gambler's Palace. Our lucky charm," Marco said in an effort to change the mood in the car. But when they headed for the entrance to the Gambler's Palace multilevel parking lot, Marco slammed on the brakes. Before cars could gain entry, drivers were being asked to open their trunks. "What the . . . ? " Marco muttered.

"Oh, my God!" Francis cried. "We've got to get out of here."

Marco did a quick U-turn. "When you said they might be inspecting the trunks, I thought you were being paranoid."

"I never thought it would really happen. Maybe we should just go home. With this dishwasher in the backseat we look like idiots. I'm really tired—"

"No!" Marco insisted. "We have to get these dresses to Las Vegas. The only way is to drive them there."

"You go," Francis said. "I'll take a bus home."

"You're coming with me."

"I can't."

"Why not?"

"What do I tell Joyce?"

"Figure something out. We'll be back in a couple of days. I might even let you fly back. I'll go on to California."

"You will?" Francis said hopefully.

"Don't sound so happy."

"I'm not happy. Believe me, I'm not happy."

"I know I've worn out my welcome with Joyce. It might even be understandable. We'll drive to Vegas, I'll get my arm stitched up, we'll have Marty sell the dresses, then we'll divide up the proceeds. Don't forget we also have our twenty thousand dollars cash to play with. Minus what it cost us for lunch."

Francis sank back in his seat. Marco was right. Driving across the country seemed like the right thing to do. As Marco put in a call to his friend in Las Vegas, Francis tried to cheer himself with the thought that he'd be free of Marco very soon, with at least ten thousand dollars in his pocket. He promised himself that he wouldn't gamble the money away. He'd hurry home from Vegas and take Joyce out for a nice dinner. He'd even be willing to try new allergy pills so she could buy the dog she wanted.

The furthest thing from Marco's and Francis's minds was the possibility that a passenger in the car that had been right behind them in line for the parking lot had taken notice of their hasty departure.

It was Jack Reilly's car.

25

Jeffrey Woodall felt a sense of relief and excitement that he had never known in all his born days. He'd gotten rid of Tracy, and the best part was he'd been handed the opportunity on a silver platter. He didn't have to sit her down and say, "We need to talk." When she told him her dress was stolen, he blurted out his true feelings, feelings that had been building up for weeks.

Now he was opening a bottle of champagne at his apartment on Central Park West in Manhattan and he was positively giddy. He'd spent the afternoon making the necessary phone calls, letting his half of the guest list know that they could make other plans for Saturday, April 9th, assuring those who already sent presents that they would be returned.

Jeffrey's mother was mortified. Jeffrey's father didn't say much. He never did. It was from his father that Jeffrey had inherited his limited ability to communicate.

"What am I going to tell my friends?" his mother asked.

"Tell them that it just didn't work out."

"Our tickets are nonrefundable. Maybe we'll come to New York and take in a show."

"May as well," Jeffrey said, although he wished they wouldn't. He had other ways he wanted to spend his time. Blond, wealthy, attractive, and thirty-two years old, Jeffrey was a catch. That is, if you didn't mind someone who was uptight, obsessed with order and cleanliness, and crippled by insecurity.

He came from a respected family in Chicago and had moved to New York after business school. He'd been working at the same insurance company for seven years, set on an unwavering rigid course, always afraid to step outside the box. But now that was all about to change. His head had been turned by someone new, someone who would soften his edges. Someone who would dare him to be himself, liberate him, set him free. He and Tracy weren't a good match, he convinced himself, because they were too much alike. Too worried about what other people think. Too worried about living in the right place, belonging to the right clubs, getting their future children into the best schools. His new love was the yin to his yang. She was the opposite of what he had always thought he wanted.

Jeffrey felt like he might finally have found the key to life's happiness. He was ready to change—it was worth the risk. And the funny thing was this woman who left him intoxicated didn't go to a top school or have an incredible job. He marveled at that. He never thought he'd be able to love someone who wasn't of a certain ilk.

He couldn't wait to get to know her better. It had all happened so fast, but the day he met her he knew his life would never be the same.

His buzzer sounded. Jeffrey answered and listened to the doorman announce his visitor. "Send her up," he said with a smile. He hurriedly poured two glasses of champagne from one of the bottles left over from one of the many engagement parties he and Tracy had thrown. He had a spreadsheet calculating all the costs leading up to the marriage. What a waste. Luckily he had taken out travel insurance for their honeymoon trip to the Caribbean. He'd get some of that money back.

Unless of course he dared take that trip with someone else . . .

The doorbell rang.

Jeffrey glanced at his reflection in the mirror by the door, smoothed back his hair, and opened the door. He smiled at the sight of her. She was so incredibly beautiful.

"Darling," she said as she rushed into his arms.

He held her tight. "Can this really be happening?" he whispered. She smelled so good.

"I can't believe it myself."

"I've never felt this way before."

"Me, neither," she sighed. "Are you really free to love me and me alone?"

"Oh, yes. And you, did you get rid of him?"

She sighed.

He led her inside and shut the door. Cupping her face in his hands, he asked her softly, "Victoria, please tell me that you called off your wedding to Frederick."

She smiled up at him. "Don't worry, darling. Frederick is of no concern to us whatsoever . . ."

26

"That car was certainly in a hurry to get out of here," Regan observed from the front seat of Jack's car as she tried to decipher its license plate number. They had just pulled into the line outside the parking lot of Gambler's Palace. Regan grabbed her ever-present notepad out of her purse and jotted down the few numbers she was able to make out. "I don't think they wanted anyone to inspect their trunk."

"Maybe they didn't want to wait," Kit suggested.

"Maybe," Regan agreed. "This could be useless information. Which over the years I've collected plenty of. But you never know. It was a gray sedan, right, Jack?"

"Yes. Two people were in the car. A guy was driving. I couldn't tell whether his passenger was a man or a woman." Jack looked in his rearview mirror. "The red sports car behind us is also turning around. A young couple. Who knows? Maybe they had a couple drinks and are afraid of being stopped."

Kit turned around, craning her neck to get the license plate of the second departing car. She recited it to Regan, who dutifully jotted it down.

"I could sit here all night and collect license plate numbers," Regan joked. "But when something like that happens right in my face, I have to take notice."

When they got to the front of the line, the guard made a quick inspection of Jack's trunk, then waved them through. They parked and took an elevator up to the casino level where they were immediately blitzed by the sights and sounds emanating from the numerous rows of slot machines. Flashing lights and jaunty musical notes filled the air and seemed to celebrate with lucky winners as they scooped up the clinking coins.

"We'll head right to Stan's office," Jack said as they made their way across the cavernous room.

Stan had been expecting them. A solid, stocky guy in his late fifties, he greeted Jack with a hearty handshake. Even though they didn't know each other well, there was the immediate camaraderie shared by those in law enforcement, the bond of wanting to get the bad guy. "Good to see you, Jack."

Jack introduced Regan and Kit. "It looks like you're having a busy night. We had our trunk inspected on the way in."

"There's a benefit in the Grand Ballroom tonight. Several politicians from the state are attending. On nights like these, we like to play it safe."

Jack nodded.

"I have the tapes from the table where you say your friend was last Saturday night."

"That's great," Regan said. "Thanks so much."

"I think I'll go play the one-armed bandits," Kit said eagerly. "See if I can make enough money to buy you a wedding present."

"We're rooting for you," Jack replied with a smile.

"Keep your cell phone out," Regan advised. "I'll call you when we're finished. It looks like it's easy to get lost around here."

Stan took Regan into an empty office where they could view the tapes. He inserted the first one into the DVD player. "I'll be back later."

"Here goes nothing," Regan murmured as the image of Alfred seated at a gambling table filled the screen.

27

Shauna, Tyler, Pamela, and Arnold had enjoyed a cocktail at the apartment and then they'd cabbed to Il Tinello on West 56th Street, just off Fifth Avenue. Il Tinello was an upscale, elegant Italian restaurant. The dining room was comfortable, the food delicious, and the white-jacketed waiters were quietly attentive. It had an old-world feeling and Mario, the owner, always took good care of the Neys. They'd been dining there almost weekly for over fifteen years.

"I cannot believe this whole business about your dress," Pamela said in her well-bred tone. She was dressed in a silk pantsuit and wearing some of her favorite pieces of exquisite jewelry—a sapphire necklace with matching earrings and a diamond bracelet. "Planning this wedding is quite an experience."

Shauna smiled at her. "I don't care what I

wear. This has been so amazing, getting to know you and Arnold. That's what is so important. And that Tyler and I will finally be married."

Arnold sipped his wine. "What were you two waiting for? Why didn't you get married a long time ago?"

Pamela looked at her husband sternly. "Arnold, Shauna told us already. She doesn't have family." Pamela turned back to Shauna. "Are you sure that there aren't any cousins you want to invite? Anyone at all?"

Tears glistened in Shauna's eyes. "Honestly, I have no one. No one but Tyler. And now you."

"What about you, Tyler?" Pamela asked gently. "I've been going over the guest list. I just wish that there were some people who you could share this day with."

"Whoa," Tyler answered as he took a bite out of his dinner roll, then looked off into the distance as he chewed.

Normally Pamela would have winced at the sight of someone biting into a roll instead of breaking off a delicate piece, but for Tyler she felt nothing but affection. His breach of manners was almost endearing. He knew the Heimlich maneuver and had saved her life. He could lick his knife for all she cared.

Finally Tyler swallowed, took a sip of his water, then put his hand over Shauna's. "Before Shauna and I met, we both felt like we were alone on this planet. Then we found each other. It was as if we were the only two people in the universe, man. You two are teaching us what it means to have family." He paused and stared into Shauna's eyes. "Should we tell them?"

"Tell us what?" Arnold demanded.

Shauna giggled. "Tyler, you can't tease them like that. Now we have to tell them." She turned to Arnold and Pamela. "We didn't know whether we should wait until after we were officially married to tell you because we were afraid you'd disapprove. But you know we have been living together."

Arnold and Pamela both shrugged as if to say "What can you do?"

"The thing is . . ." Shauna continued.

"We're pregnant!" Tyler interrupted, then banged the table excitedly with his fist. "We're pregnant, and if it's a boy he'll be Arnold; a girl, Pamela. And we hope to have a couple more. We'll keep trying until we get an Arnold and a Pamela." He banged the table again and looked around. The people at the next table looked over with disdain as the silverware jingled.

Pamela's mouth dropped. "Ohhh," she said. "Ohhhh, my word."

"We are so happy," Shauna continued. "We thought we couldn't have children. But I'm convinced it's the love that you've shown us that has made this happen for us. We want you to be our child's surrogate grandparents."

Even Arnold smiled.

Pamela's mouth quivered as she said, "I've longed to be a grandmother. And I know Arnold would love to be someone's Papa. Our son is married, but I think that he and our daughter-in-law have gotten used to a life without children."

Shauna brought her hands together as if in prayer. Soulfully, she said, "I know that I'm at an age where it isn't so easy to have a child. That's why I'm so grateful."

"We had our Alex later in life," Pamela noted. "I didn't want to ask if you had plans for a family. I thought it might be a sensitive subject."

"Ask us anything," Tyler exulted. "We're family. This baby will be all of ours."

"There's nothing that would please us more than to spoil a child. Isn't that right, Arnold?"

Arnold nodded.

"That means that over the holidays this year we'll have a new baby in our midst," Pamela said joyfully. "Oh it'll be so wonderful."

Tyler raised his glass. "Here's to little Arnie or Pammy! They'll be here by Thanksgiving!"

They all laughed and clinked glasses.

After coffee and a dessert of raspberries covered with whipped cream, the two couples sauntered up Fifth Avenue. The April air was cool and fresh, and they decided to walk the nearly twenty blocks home. "That was some rain we had today," Pamela said, shaking her head. "Tyler, I saw your black raincoat hanging in the back hallway. It was soaked. So were those big black shoes of yours. You always seem to get stuck in the rain! Couldn't you get a cab today?"

"I was out running errands and couldn't get a cab when the storm hit. It doesn't matter. I like walking in the rain."

"Well, at least you were wearing a raincoat! That storm came upon us so suddenly

I think it caught most people unprepared. When I left this morning I had no idea it was going to rain."

"It comes from living out in the open," Tyler explained. "You get in tune with nature. You just know what's coming."

"I suppose. I just hope you don't catch a cold."

"I'll be fine," Tyler assured her.

"We don't want a bridegroom with a case of the sniffles," Pamela laughed. "Or a Daddy. When we get upstairs, I'll give you Vitamin C."

"You're the best, Pamela," Tyler murmured. "I wish my mother had been as caring."

Pamela smiled. "I always loved being a mother."

"I know I will, too," Shauna said serenely. "I just hope everything turns out okay. I'm not that far along."

"Everything will be fine!" Pamela insisted.

In the apartment, Pamela and Arnold said their good nights and retired to their room. After they got ready for bed and turned out the light, Pamela reached for Arnold's hand. "Honey, I've been thinking. Maybe we should change our will and provide for Shauna and Tyler. They are starting a family, and it's so tough these days. And they do plan to name their children after us."

In the dark, Arnold made a face. "I suppose we could do that. But I'd like to see them enjoy money while we're both alive. Maybe we should get them a decent place to live and set up a trust fund for the baby. But what about Alex?"

"There's plenty of money to go around. Our son has enough money of his own, and it doesn't look like he'll ever have to worry about supporting children."

Arnold grunted. "I suppose you're right. I'll call the lawyer on Monday."

Pamela closed her eyes. "I can't believe we're finally going to have a baby named after one of us."

"Took long enough," Arnold said. "We may as well make the most of it before we die."

The two of them fell fast asleep.

28

The Timber family had never known such hysteria. They usually reacted to any of life's upheavals in a quiet reserved manner. Not this time.

Tracy was sprawled on the couch in the family room of her parents' gracious Connecticut home, gulping her second cosmopolitan. Her face was streaked with tears. Montgomery, Tracy's dear old dad, had built a fire in the large stone hearth even though it wasn't really cold. It gave him something to do, and he thought it would offer comfort.

"Dear, I think you'd better slow up your drinking," Tracy's mother, Ellen, advised. "You haven't touched any of your chicken with cashews. I ordered that specially for you."

"My life is ruined," Tracy slurred.

"No, it's not," Montgomery insisted. "You're

a Timber. You can do a lot better than Jeffrey Woodall and you know it!"

"I just hope that detective, Regan Reilly, discovers something about Jeffrey that ruins his life!" Tracy spewed. "I hope they find out he cheated on his taxes and they send him to jail!" She took another large sip of the pink elixir.

Tracy's mother shook her head. "I just don't understand what happened. He must have gotten cold feet."

"Don't ever take him back!" Montgomery barked. "You are a Timber! Always remember you are a Timber! You are proud! Our family fought in the American Revolution. Never forget that!"

Tracy raised her right hand. "I'm a Timber. And it looks like I'm never going to be anything else."

Tracy's sister, Adele, was curled up in an overstuffed chair, examining her hair for split ends. "You're going to be so happy about this in a few months, believe me! You dodged a bullet. I can't believe he actually kept a record of how much he spent taking you out to dinner before you got engaged. What a creep."

"I want revenge!"

Ellen nodded. "That Regan Reilly is a lovely girl. I'm sure if there's anything to find out about Jeffrey, she will. But, dear, what does it matter?"

"It matters a lot. I want him to suffer like I'm suffering right now. I want him to feel pain!"

Ellen sat down next to her daughter. "Grandma called earlier when you were soaking in the tub."

Tracy frowned. "All she's been saying since I got engaged was that she was so happy she was alive to see me get married."

"That's true," Ellen agreed. "But at ninety-two she's still going strong. She told me something that I never knew. She said she wanted you to know that before she married Grandpa, she got dumped, too."

Adele's split ends no longer held as much interest. "Grandma got dumped?" she repeated, her voice rising.

"I never knew it. But she said there was a boy who proposed to her, and they told everyone they were engaged to be married, and then he ran off with a new girl who moved to town. Grandma was happy to report that they experienced nothing but misery their whole lives. She, of course, married Grandpa and lived happily ever after."

"Good for Grandma!" Adele enthused.

"Grandma also said that she couldn't imagine life without your grandfather. And she reminded me that I wouldn't have been born if she had married her first fiancé, which means you wouldn't have been born either."

"So someday I'll have a kid who wouldn't have been born if I weren't in misery right now."

"Exactly. Which goes to show—"

"Goes to show what? The man I was in love with doesn't want me!" Tracy started to sob yet again.

The doorbell rang.

Montgomery, happy to get out of the room, ran for the front door. When he opened it, Tracy's three best friends were standing there.

Catherine Heaney, Tracy's closest friend since college, spoke first. "Mr. Timber, I know that Tracy said she didn't want to see anyone. But we're her girlfriends, and this is the girlfriend ambulance. We're here to take her out and we're not taking no for an answer."

"Please!" Montgomery said ecstatically. "That sounds like a great idea!"

When they entered the den, and Tracy saw the three girls who would have been her bridesmaids, she burst into another round of tears. They rushed over, and the four sorority sisters huddled together.

"I never liked him."

"Not good enough for you."

"Boring."

In the background, Adele was shaking her head in earnest agreement. "Stuffy," she added. "Uptight."

"Quiet, Adele," Ellen reprimanded her daughter.

"We're taking you out," Catherine told Tracy.

"I can't go out," Tracy sniffled.

"You have to. You can't just sit here and be miserable."

"But I'm humiliated! I don't want to run into anyone I know!" Tracy wailed.

"We figured that," Catherine said. "So we're taking you to a biker bar a couple miles out of town. It's a dump, but they have a dartboard!" Catherine pulled an unflattering picture of Jeffrey out of her purse that she'd blown up to eight by ten. "We're going to pin his mug over the bull's eye."

Tracy looked at the picture. It took her a moment to react, but she started to laugh like she hadn't for a very long time. "This is just the beginning," she vowed as she got to her feet, somewhat unsteadily. "I'm going to live to make him regret what he did if it takes me the rest of my life," she said with a hiccup, half laughing, half crying.

Ellen sighed. "Tracy dear. Just go out and have a good time. Think of how well getting dumped turned out for Grandma."

29

Regan and Jack viewed the tapes for nearly two hours. Several players came and went, but Alfred stayed put at the craps table. And why not? He kept winning, making no attempt to hide his glee.

"If I'd have known Alfred was going to entertain us for this long, I'd have brought along a bucket of popcorn," Regan commented. "He does ham it up." They watched as Alfred clapped his hands and pumped his fist in victory.

"And he's been served a few drinks," Jack remarked. "I could have used some popcorn this afternoon. We watched the security tapes of the bank robbery over and over."

"Did it help at all?" Regan asked.

"Not yet. I keep thinking that there must be something on all the tapes of those first robberies that date back to January that we're missing."

They watched the screen as Alfred finally got up to leave the gambling table. He reached into his jacket pocket and pulled out what looked like a jumble of cash and papers. He wobbled slightly, steadied himself, and handed out his business cards to several of the players, all men.

"There are the business cards he mentioned," Regan said. "I can just imagine what he's saying."

"None of the players look like they can use a wedding dress."

Alfred waved to the group as if he were their departing leader, bowed, and walked off.

"I already knew Alfred liked to make a grand entrance when he walked into a room," Regan said. "Now I see he's into grand exits as well."

Jack sighed and turned to Regan. "What do you want to do now?"

"I guess we'll just . . . wait a minute, Jack . . . look . . ."

Another one of the players got up from the table and leaned down, apparently picking something up off the ground, very close to where Alfred had been standing. When the young man straightened up, he walked off quickly without a backward glance.

"The keys," Regan said. "Could he have just picked up Alfred's keys?"

Another guy got up from the table and hurried to catch up with the player who had left after Alfred.

"That second man looks like he's favoring one leg," Regan said, cautiously optimistic. "Alfred and Charisse said that one of the thieves walked with a limp."

Jack pressed a button, and they watched that last moment again, slowing the action several times. Then they went even farther back. "Those two guys were already at the table when Alfred sat down," Jack observed. "They were sitting next to each other. Let's get Stan back in here and see if he can get close-ups on those two. It would also be nice if the dealer from that night is on duty."

Twenty minutes later they were showing the images to a man of about forty with gelled brown hair, a deep tan, and perfectly manicured hands. The dealer leaned forward in his chair as he stared at the screen. "Who could forget that guy in the velvet jacket? You say his name is Alfred?"

"Yes," Regan answered.

"He was lucky. He sat down and started to win right away. As he kept winning, he started to get carried away. Your average gambler at least tries to keep a poker face the whole time they're playing. Not Alfie. He was gloating. I could tell it was irritating those other two guys. They'd been winning before he came to the table."

"They'd been winning?" Regan repeated.

The dealer nodded. "They lost everything to him."

There's motivation for you, Regan thought.

"That's why they got up when Alfred left. He'd just relieved them of their last chips. I remember being surprised that Alfred even handed them his business card. I heard them trade barbs about each other's clothes."

"Really?" Regan said.

"Your man Alfred was in a green velvet jacket. The other two were wearing old jeans and sweatshirts." He shrugged. "What can I tell you? They don't have the same taste."

"That they don't," Regan agreed. "Anything else you can tell us about them?"

"They were young. In their mid- to late

twenties. They knew the rules of the game. Especially the dark-haired one."

"Would you recognize them if you saw them again?"

"Probably. If I see them, I'll let the boss here know."

Stan nodded. "We'll keep on top of this."

Regan handed the dealer her card. "If you remember anything else about those two, anything at all, please let me know."

He nodded and got up to leave.

Stan shut the door behind him. "Jack, I'll get the images of those two reproduced to show to our staff so they can be on the lookout. They're not passport photos, but I think our employees can get a good idea of what these two look like. I'll have stills made for you as well. I'll also make you a copy of the tape. It'll take us a few minutes."

Regan looked thoughtful.

"What is it, Regan?" Jack asked.

Regan shook her head. "These two could very well be the ones we're looking for. It's just what to do next."

"We'll keep on it," Stan assured her. "I'll have the staff at the front desk look at the images. See if anyone remembers checking them in. There's a good chance they'll be back. If they do grace us with their presence again, we'll find out who they are."

"Thanks," Regan said. "We're heading back to the neighborhood where the robbery took place last night. With a few of these photos, maybe we can jar someone's memory who was out at three o'clock in the morning. Jack, why don't we take a stroll around the floor while Stan gets the pictures ready?"

"Sure," Jack said as he stood. "Maybe our friends will surprise us and be out there attempting to reverse their losses."

"That'd be a stroke of luck," Regan commented.

Out in the casino, Regan and Jack did a tour of the whole room. There was no sign of the men who resembled the two they were looking for. They found Kit, who was down to her last few coins at a slot machine.

"I can't believe it!" she yelped. "I was way ahead about fifteen minutes ago. If I had walked away I could have bought you two your china gravy boat as well as a place setting."

"These little machines really get you to dream big," Regan said with a laugh. "That's why you usually end up losing all your money."

"What about you?" Kit asked. "Did you find out anything helpful?"

"I certainly hope so," Regan said as the three of them headed back to Stan's office.

Jack smiled but was lost in thought. His mind kept returning to the bank's security tapes. His gut told him that there was more to the case than met the eye, as they say.

He also felt that if they didn't catch the robber soon, he'd elude them forever.

30

At the cavernous Club Zee, Brianne and her friends were having a great night—the music was loud and the drinks were flowing. They'd had dinner at Carmine's on West 44th Street, a family-style Italian restaurant that attracted large parties of rambunctious diners. The portions were enormous, the atmosphere energetic. Brianne had opened her gag gifts, and they'd made jokes about wedding gowns. Before she and her buddies moved on to Club Zee, Brianne was introduced by the bartender as one of the April Brides whose gown was stolen. Brianne stood on a bar stool and took her bows. She was a celebrity for the evening and was loving every minute of it.

Now they had procured a special spot on the Zee balcony overlooking the crowded dance floor. A banquette and several leather chairs surrounded a low glass table. The whole scene was very hip.

You had to scream to be heard.

The crowd Joyce was traveling with gained admittance to the club and joined the group on the balcony. Two squeezed into the banquette and two stole chairs from other tables.

Cindy's friend Beth made the introductions.

"And the guest of honor is my friend Brianne whose bloody wedding gown is making headlines!" she shouted, barely audible above the deejay.

Brianne beamed as though she didn't have a care in the world. She was with her best friends. Life was good. She had Pauly and she was going on national television in the morning.

Joyce, on the other hand, wasn't feeling so great. She'd had a couple of shots of tequila, then wine with dinner. Her head was spinning, and she felt depressed.

Club Zee had a policy of playing a popular song from different eras every half hour. Julio Iglesias's song "To All the Girls I've Loved Before" came over the speakers at exactly eleven o'clock. The whole crowd started to sing. Cindy ran down to the dance floor. When the song was over and the thumping music started up again, Beth proposed a toast.

"To all the men Brianne loved before."

"There have been some real winners!" Brianne said, rolling her eyes. "I'm so blessed to have found Pauly! To think that I used to let Bill the Pill leave me alone on all those Saturday nights. How did I put up with that for so long?"

Joyce got up from the table, hurried to the bathroom, and threw up. Her life was miserable. She should never have let Francis talk her into letting Marco stay for so long. Joyce came out of the stall and rinsed her mouth with water from the sink. I need air, she thought. I'll go outside for a little walk.

When Cindy returned to the table from the dance floor, she looked around. "Where's Joyce?" she asked.

"I think she went to the bathroom," Brianne answered.

Fifteen minutes later Cindy went to look for her.

But she was nowhere to be found.

31

Francis and Marco had been heading west on Interstate 80 for a couple of hours. The road was dark and depressing. Las Vegas seemed very far away. "This isn't worth it," Francis declared, breaking a long silence. "It's going to take too much time."

"Francis, relax! This is business. We're not on vacation, we're going to make money. When you have the extra dough in your pocket, you're going to thank me. Suck it up and call Joyce. You'll feel better once you get that over with. Tell her you'll be back in a couple of days."

Silently Francis picked up his cell phone, opened it, and grimaced. "My battery is going to die soon. And I don't have my charger." He dialed Joyce's number. Her voice mail came on. "Hi, this is Joyce. Leave me a message."

"Honey, it's Francis. Give me a call. I hope you're having a good time."

When he hung up, Marco mimicked him. "Honey, it's Francis . . ."

"She's a good person," Francis said. "We've both been taking advantage of her sweet nature."

"I told you, I'll be out of there very soon. Then you two can resume your exciting life together."

"I like my life with Joyce," Francis said defensively. He longed to be home. He wished he were sitting with Joyce watching television, hearing about her day at the pet store. In her quiet way, she was funny. The parrot who couldn't stand him would be in the background squawking. Francis missed that, too. All the comforts of home. If I get out of this mess, he silently promised God, I'll be so good you won't believe it.

He tried Joyce's cell phone three more times in the next half hour. She still wasn't answering. He knew his battery was on its last legs so he left her a message to please call him on Marco's phone and resumed staring out at the seemingly unending road in front of them. The unending white line. With each passing mile, his anxiety mounted. He fidgeted in his seat and caught sight of the dishwasher. Turning to Marco, he blurted, "I'll buy Joyce another dish-washer. I think we should get rid of this one. It's making me nervous. It'll just attract attention wherever we stop along the way."

"Now you're talking sense, buddy," Marco said. "I'll get off at the next exit, and we'll leave it on the side of the road some-where. Maybe someone with a sink full of dirty dishes will get lucky."

Francis breathed a sigh of relief. But he'd breathe an even bigger sigh of relief when Joyce called him back.

What was taking her so long?

Sunday, April 3rd
12:10 A.M.

———◆———

32

"So what you have," Kit concluded, once again ensconced in the backseat of Jack's car, "is an image of two guys who might have gotten a hold of Alfred's keys. Or might not have."

"Big cases have been broken with less information," Regan said. "And if these two are the ones who have my wedding dress, it's worth hunting them down. Although I'll admit it's not much to go on."

"Hell hath no fury like a woman whose wedding gown has been stolen or destroyed," Jack said with a smile.

"That goes for three of us," Regan said. "But those other two brides didn't display an ounce of fury."

"One of them doesn't want publicity," Kit added, "and the other isn't allowed to get any if she wants Arnie to foot the bill for her wedding."

Regan frowned.

Jack reached over and touched her forehead. "Isn't your mother always telling you not to frown?"

"I'm thinking, I'm thinking. I just can't get over how that Victoria didn't seem at all like someone who was getting married in a few weeks."

Jack rubbed her forehead. "At the moment you don't seem like someone getting married to a prince among men in one week."

Regan smiled. "Like I told my mother, I'll give this case a couple of days and then go back to our wedding plans. But this case does involve criminals who have thrown a wrench into those very wedding plans." She paused. "To my prince."

"Regan, I want to get my hands on these guys as much as you do," Jack said softly. "So tell us what else you were thinking before I got you off track."

Regan hardly needed encouragement. "The two brides we visited this afternoon were both unusual," she said. "I'll ask Alfred more about their backgrounds. After all, aren't we supposed to investigate people who are closely connected to a crime like this? Even the supposed victims?"

"You can't rule anybody out," Jack answered. "Those women have obviously been in and out of the loft. They might have known there was a safe back in the bedroom. Either one of them could have gotten their hands on Alfred's keys if they were just lying out in the salon. Who knows?" Jack asked with a roll of his eyes, "Maybe one of them didn't want to have to pay for her dress."

"My father would have loved it if I'd figured out a way to get that dress for free."

"You're doing a good job of it right now," Jack said. "Alfred should supply you with gowns for life."

"I doubt that will happen."

Jack adjusted the earpiece of his Bluetooth cell phone. "I think I'll check in with the office."

One of the young detectives answered. "Hey, boss. We've got a couple things to tell you. Not too much came up on Jeffrey Woodall on a preliminary check. So Keith stopped by his apartment building on the way home and made a few inquiries. Seems he's got a new lady friend up there tonight."

Jack relayed the information to Regan and Kit.

"What a shock," Kit proclaimed from what felt to her like the peanut gallery.

"And we found out what had been purchased at Dan's Discount Den with the stolen credit card. Turns out a small television was on the bill as well as men's raincoats, shoes, and clothing. And yes, some lifelike beards and mustaches from the costume department."

"I'm surprised The Drip didn't splurge on a big screen TV," Jack grumbled. "Keep me posted." When he pushed the disconnect button on his phone, Jack turned to Regan. "It seems The Drip bought his disguises at Dan's Discount Den with a stolen credit card, and Jeffrey Woodall has a new lady in his life."

"They're both Drips," Kit declared. "Guys have it made. A jerk like Jeffrey Woodall can just pick up the phone the day he dumps his fiancée and arrange a date for that night."

"Poor Tracy," Regan lamented. "I'd love to get a look at this other girl. And find out how long Mr. Woodall has known her."

"Tracy will freak when she finds out," Kit said. "Love. Ain't it grand?"

Regan and Jack glanced at each other quickly, a look that seemed to say, "Thank

God we're out of the singles scene. Thank God we have each other."

It took two and a half more hours to get back to the city. When they arrived at Alfred and Charisse's building, they were able to park right in front. Charisse said they'd be sewing dresses around the clock and insisted Regan call when they were back from Atlantic City.

"Regan!" Alfred cried sleepily, picking up the phone on the third ring. "We just fell into bed. We're so exhausted and we want to look rested and refreshed on television tomorrow."

At least somebody will be rested and refreshed, Regan thought. "Okay, Alfred, I'll see you at the studio. We're downstairs and are going to see if there's anyone who saw anything last night."

"Wonderful. Best of luck. I'd invite you up but we must must must get some shuteye."

Regan looked at her phone and tried to remember her mother's advice about frowning. But this time she couldn't help it.

For the next hour the three of them canvassed the neighborhood. They interviewed a couple of people who were walking their dogs. Nobody had seen anything unusual the night before. They stopped in a bar down the street. Nobody had anything to report. Regan knew that the tenants in Alfred and Charisse's building had already been interviewed by the police, but when she saw the couple who had let them into the building that morning amble up the block, she asked them a few questions.

"Our loft is above Alfred and Charisse's," the young woman said. "We didn't hear anything. I wish we had. Naturally it makes us nervous to be in a building where something like this happened."

The young man, whose demeanor had turned deadly serious, sighed. "When we bought our loft we were concerned about being in a building where one of the tenants conducted a business. People are coming in and out all the time. It raises security issues."

"You were nice enough to let us in this morning," Regan said.

"I shouldn't have done that," he stated.

"No, you probably shouldn't have," Regan agreed, trying to keep the sarcasm out of her voice. She gave them her card. "Please give me a call if you come up with anything at all that might be helpful to the investigation."

"We will."

As they walked away, Regan turned to Jack and Kit. "Three o'clock in the morning on a dark street like this is a good time to strike. It looks like our guys made a clean getaway. They disappeared without a trace."

Jack put his arm around her. "Maybe we should call it a night."

As Regan leaned against his shoulder, her cell phone started to ring.

"Uh-oh," Kit said as Regan reached in her purse. "Phone calls at this hour don't bear good tidings."

"Hello," Regan said quickly.

"Regan, it's Brianne. I know it's late . . ."

"Hi, Brianne. Sorry we couldn't make it to the club tonight."

"Regan, one of the girls we were partying with is missing."

"Missing?"

"She's been gone for several hours. She went to the ladies' room and never came back. I just met her tonight, but her friend Cindy is really worried, and I thought you might be able to help us. Would you speak to Cindy?"

"Of course," Regan said quickly, then waited as Brianne handed over the phone.

"Hello, Regan?" Cindy said anxiously.

"Yes, it's me."

"I'm sorry to bother you, but my friend is gone. It's not like her to disappear like this. She's a quiet type. I convinced her to come out with us tonight because her boyfriend is out of town. I can't reach her on her cell phone or at home." Her voice broke. "I'm really worried."

"There could be some logical explanation," Regan said, trying to sound positive. "Was she arguing with her boyfriend?"

"I don't think she was thrilled that he went out of town on Saturday night."

"Maybe she met someone else."

"She would have let me know if she were leaving. We've been driving around for hours looking for her. We drove along the water," Cindy said, her voice quivering. "We stopped a patrol car, and they said it's too soon to consider her a missing person. But they said they'd keep an eye out for her."

"Where are you?" Regan asked.

"We've been all over, but right now we're on Washington Street."

"I'm on the street in front of Alfred and

Charisse's loft. Why don't you come by here? It shouldn't take you long to drive across town, especially at this hour. Then we'll figure out what to do next."

"Thanks so much, Regan. I really appreciate your help."

Ten minutes later a car full of young women pulled up. The earlier excitement of the evening was gone. They were all sobered by Joyce's absence. Brianne introduced Regan who in turn introduced Jack.

"She's an adult, and it's Saturday night," Jack reminded them. "She could have decided to go someplace else and lost track of time. Did she have much to drink?"

"We were doing tequila shots," Cindy reported, "and then had wine with dinner. Joyce hardly ever drinks but she seemed okay."

Oh boy, Regan thought. Tequila is potent. "Where does she live?"

"In Queens. Out by LaGuardia Airport. Across the street from me."

"Do you have her boyfriend's number? Or her parents'?" Regan asked.

Cindy shook her head. "No. I'm sure they're written down somewhere at her house. I feel terrible. It's my fault. I told her she had to come out tonight. I don't know what to do."

Regan and Jack looked at each other. "We should take a ride out to Queens," Jack said.

Regan nodded.

"Ladies," Jack said, leaning down to the car window. "Let's go out to Joyce's place. Cindy, why don't you ride with us? I'll call in her description and make sure all the patrol cars in the area are on the lookout. With any luck she'll be home sleeping when we get there."

"Thank you so much," Cindy said quickly as she opened the car door and jumped out. "We've *got* to find her."

33

Joyce felt woozy, and her head was pounding. She tried to open her eyes, but they felt incredibly heavy. She realized she was covered by a blanket. A couple of dogs were asleep at her feet. Where am I? she wondered. Am I dreaming? Joyce groaned and put her hand to her forehead. It was covered with a damp washcloth. She turned and gasped. A woman who had to be pushing eighty, with wild gray hair, a weathered, wrinkled face, and teeth that cried out for a dental hygienist, was leaning over her.

"Missy, how do you feel?" the woman asked in a raspy voice.

Terrified, Joyce thought drowsily. She tried to talk, but it was an effort to say much. "My head hurts," she uttered. "What happened to me?"

The old lady smiled. "I was just getting home from taking four of my doggies for a walk when you came down the block. Don't you remember you said how much you love dogs? You bent over to pet them, and my Porgy was so excited he jumped up on you. You got caught up in all their leashes and fell down the steps outside. I felt so bad! You hit your head, and I think you hurt your foot, but I helped you inside my little apartment. I like to take care of people. I want to take care of you."

"Thank you," Joyce said. "But I'd better get home."

"No! You have to rest. The tea you sipped before is special. It will make you feel better."

"What kind of tea?" Joyce asked. And why am I so out of it? she wondered as she felt her eyes closing. She quickly fell back into a deep sleep.

Joyce's host shrugged and walked back to the stove, where she resumed stirring a pot of soup. Her four dogs were asleep in the small, cluttered, dimly lit room. "We have to be quiet, fellas," she whispered to them. "Our company is sleeping and will be for a little while. I hope you guys don't mind I gave her some of your medicine." The old woman paused. "It's so nice to entertain again. I hope she likes my cooking."

34

As Jack sped up the FDR Drive, Cindy clenched her fists and stared out the window at the dark waters of the East River. She'd read stories about people who were out for the night, drank too much, and ended up slipping or being pushed into the river's punishing currents. Not Joyce, she thought, please, not Joyce. "It's just not like her to leave without saying good-bye," Cindy blurted out. "She's quiet and considerate."

Regan turned around to face Kit and Cindy, who were both in the backseat. "There could be an explanation for this, Cindy," she said calmly. "People who we are convinced would never act a certain way often surprise us. And she had been drinking. Let's hope Joyce ended up at another club and is now asleep at home."

"But she's still not answering her phone . . ." Cindy said, her voice trailing off.

Jack had radioed the central dispatcher, who sent out a bulletin that patrol cars in Manhattan, particularly downtown, should be on the alert for a petite twenty-seven-year-old woman with light brown hair and green eyes, last seen wearing blue jeans and a black jacket. Of course that description could fit any number of young women out on Saturday night in New York City. Because she wasn't considered a missing person yet, it was an unofficial alert. Someone from Jack's office was calling the area hospitals to see if she had been taken to an emergency room.

They crossed the Triboro Bridge into Queens and a few minutes later were driving down a block of small, two-family houses. As far as the eye could see, every parking spot was taken. "It's the third house on the left," Cindy said.

Jack stopped in front of Joyce's house. There were no lights on. The carful of bachelorettes pulled up behind them.

"Cindy, I think you should go knock on the door," Jack advised. "Joyce is a grown woman and has a right to her privacy. If she's there, she doesn't need to have a crowd of people standing on her doorstep in the middle of the night."

Wordlessly, Cindy got out of the car and hurried up the steps. She rang the bell and waited. She knocked on the door several times. Then she held her hand on the bell so it rang continuously—making enough noise to wake the dead.

But there was no response.

Cindy hurried back down the steps, shaking her head. "She used to leave a key hidden by the back door. Let's go see if it's still there."

"I don't have the authority to go into her house," Jack said. "As a member of the NYPD, I'd be violating her rights."

"I wouldn't be violating her rights," Cindy said, her voice breaking. "Joyce once called and asked me to feed her parrot when she stayed at her mother's longer than expected. She knows where I keep my extra key, and I know where her key is hidden. We're friends." She paused. "But I don't want to go in there alone. Regan, would you please come with me?"

Regan knew that it would be fine for her to go inside the apartment. She was a private citizen. "Of course I'll go with you," she said as she reached for the door.

Jack grabbed her hand and squeezed it. "Be careful."

"I will." Regan got out and followed Cindy across the tiny yard and around to the back door. The light of a small television glowed through the kitchen window.

"The television's on! Maybe she's asleep," Regan said hopefully.

"She always keeps the television on for her parrot when no one is home."

Everyone wants company, Regan thought, wondering what channel the parrot liked to watch.

"I hope the key is still here," Cindy said as she bent over and picked up a loose slate from the small stone patio outside Joyce's door. "It is!" she said excitedly. She pulled the single key out of the dirt, straightened up, and waved her fist.

Regan's mind went back to the security tape she had viewed in Atlantic City—the guy bending over and picking something up off the ground. But he didn't wave his hand in victory. He hurried off, trying to avoid notice.

Cindy inserted the key in the lock and pushed the door open.

"Hello!" the parrot cried. "Hello!"

"Hello, Romeo," Cindy said as she flicked on the light. "The poor thing was probably going crazy with me ringing the phone all night and then the bell."

Especially when he's trying to watch the tube, Regan thought. A black-and-white movie that looked like it was made in the 1940s was playing on the screen. "Let's take a quick look around and make sure Joyce is not here sleeping."

"Okay."

They went into the small but cozy living room and turned on a light, then walked down the hall. As they both expected, the bedroom was empty. Regan turned on the light in the bathroom. Everything felt so still and quiet. She didn't step inside, didn't want to intrude on Joyce's space. At least not yet. And I hope I don't have to, she thought, as she flicked off the light.

The bloody napkins in the garbage can went undetected.

Back in the kitchen, Cindy and Regan looked at the list of names and numbers pinned to a small bulletin board next to the phone.

"Francis is her boyfriend," Cindy said. "He lives here with her."

"And he went out of town with a friend?"

Cindy nodded.

"Do you know where they went?"

"No. I don't think Joyce wanted to talk about it. She was vague. Said something about a boys' night out."

Regan sighed, staring at Francis's cell phone number. "The problem is," she said, "if Joyce is out with someone else right now, I'm sure she wouldn't want her boyfriend to find out. Especially like this."

Cindy shook her head emphatically. "I don't believe she's out with anyone, Regan. And if she is, then Francis better learn that he can't leave Joyce alone on a weekend and expect her to sit around waiting for him. Who knows what he's up to? If you don't feel right about calling him, I will."

"Until she's considered a missing person, you should be the one to make the call," Regan advised. "You're her friend. You have the right to look out for her. I will help you in any way I can. Then if she's not back by tomorrow—"

"Don't even say it," Cindy interrupted. "I understand you want to protect Joyce. But believe me, she is in danger right now. Something went wrong, I know it." She picked up the phone and dialed.

Francis's voice mail picked up. "Hey, this is Francis. Leave a message."

"Francis," Cindy said. "This is Cindy. Please call me. It's about Joyce. Have you heard from her? We went out tonight, and I don't know where she is." She gave her cell number and hung up. "I wonder why he isn't answering at three o'clock in the morning."

"Lazy bums!" the parrot cried. "Lazy bums."

Regan looked quizzically at the bird cage. "What ever happened to 'Polly want a cracker?' "

"That parrot is something else. The only person that parrot likes is Joyce," Cindy said. "Everyone else gets on his nerves."

"I read somewhere that parrots mate for life," Regan mused. "As pets they get attached to one person and that's it."

"I wish one of the guys I dated felt that way," Cindy grumbled as she stared at the list of names. "Joyce's mother is on a cruise in Europe. She lives out on the north fork of Long Island." Cindy managed a smile. "She was here a couple weeks ago but had to leave her two dogs in the car because Francis is allergic to them. It makes her nuts. She told Francis his allergies are all in his head."

"Nice," Regan said. "My mother and I are both allergic to dogs. It's no joke. It doesn't mean we don't like them. Where is Joyce's father?"

"Good question. He split years ago."

"Does Joyce have any brothers or sisters?"

"No. She's an only child."

Like me, Regan thought.

"Joyce says that's why she is so attached to animals. They were her companions growing up, especially dogs."

"But now she can't have them because of Francis."

Joyce rolled her eyes. "That's right."

"She must be in love," Regan said.

"Who knows? I have the feeling that things aren't so wonderful lately. The friend Francis is out with has been staying with them for a couple months. Now they're out without her on a Saturday night."

Regan sighed. "I don't think there's much more we can do right now, Cindy. Except wait."

"I know you have to get back. I'm going to stay here. I'll just stretch out on the couch. I doubt I'll sleep but I want to be here if she gets home."

"Do you want to ask one of your friends to join you?"

Cindy shook her head. "No. None of the others know Joyce. I'll be fine by myself."

Regan put her hand on Cindy's arm. "The police are looking for her. Try to get some rest. I'm staying at my parents' in the city tonight." She pulled her business card out of her pocket. "Call me the minute you hear something. We're going on a morning show in a few hours about our stolen wedding dresses."

"Brianne was so excited about that." Cindy paused. "If Joyce isn't back yet, would you be able to mention it on the show?"

Regan shook her head. "I don't think so, Cindy. If she didn't come home tonight because she's met a new guy, it could be very embarrassing for her to have been discussed on national television. Now, if by tomorrow afternoon she hasn't returned . . ." Regan shrugged.

"I understand. I'm just so worried."

"I know."

"Joyce!" Romeo cried. "Joyce!"

Cindy walked over to the cage. "He misses her." She stuck her fingers through the bars to pet the parrot. Romeo quickly bent over and tried to bite her. Cindy yanked her hand back, inadvertently opening the cage door. The parrot grabbed his chance for freedom and flew the coop.

"Hello!" he cried as he sailed past Regan, heading for the living room. "Pretty girl!"

I like that bird, Regan thought as she followed Cindy into the living room. Romeo was having a grand time, flapping his wings and circling the room.

"Come on, Romeo!" Cindy cried. "Come on."

He swooped down onto the floor behind the couch where Marco's belongings had been piling up for the last couple of months. Cindy kneeled on the couch, bent over, and grabbed the energetic bird. Something shiny was hanging from his beak. Still bent over, she pulled the metal object out and tossed it back onto one of Marco's bags. Straightening up, she turned to Regan who was looking around the room. "I'll get him back in his cage."

"Okay. I'll head outside."

Cindy couldn't have possibly guessed that the object she tossed aside so casually was actually something quite significant.

Alfred's keys.

35

As Jack, Regan, and Kit drove back into Manhattan, the light of the new day was starting to make its appearance. Streaks of red and blue filled the sky.

"I'd love to grab a steak at Elaine's, but by now even they've rolled up the carpet," Regan said, referring to Elaine Kaufman's legendary restaurant on the Upper East Side that had been open until four in the morning for the last forty years. "I suppose it will be good to get a couple of hours sleep before going on national television."

"What are you going to wear?" Kit asked.

"I don't know. I'll have to see what I have in the closet at my parents' apartment," Regan answered. "It's hard to believe that when we started this day we thought we'd be asleep in bed in New Jersey right now."

"You called your mother to tell her about the show, didn't you?" asked Jack.

"Yes. She'd love for us to drive out there tomorrow for brunch. Obviously she doesn't know about the missing Joyce yet."

Jack sighed. "We'll have to see what develops."

"If you don't mind, I think I'll watch the show from the comfort of bed," Kit said.

"I don't blame you," Regan answered. They were now driving along Central Park South toward the Reillys' apartment building. "It seems to me that there's no quieter time in Manhattan than Sunday morning at dawn."

"The crowds have gone home," Jack said.

"Except for Joyce," Regan said quietly.

Jack pulled into the driveway. The second the car stopped Kit jumped out of the back. "See you later, Jack," she said wearily.

"Good night, Kit." Jack put his arms around Regan and held her close. "I love you, my crazy April Bride," he said.

"I love you, too." They kissed, and after a moment Regan turned to go. Then she turned back and kissed Jack again. "Are we really getting married next Saturday?"

Jack smiled. "That's the plan."

"And miles to go before we wed."

"That's what it feels like." Jack looked at her tenderly and smoothed her hair. "I can't wait for our honeymoon. I can't wait until we're on that plane and on our way. Just the two of us . . . finally."

"Just the two of us," Regan said softly. "But first we're going to have a great time at our wedding with our family and friends. No matter what I end up wearing."

Jack laughed. "Get some sleep, baby. I'll pick you up at seven forty-five."

Upstairs Kit was already out cold in Regan's room. Regan crashed on her parents' bed. She set the alarm for seven o'clock, closed her eyes, and immediately lost consciousness.

36

"Francis, wake up!" Marco yelled. "You've got to drive. I can't keep my eyes open." He pulled into a service area. Marco tugged on Francis's shoulder. "Wake up!"

Francis blinked his eyes open. He had been hoping this was all a bad dream. It wasn't. Marco was a mere foot away, and by this time neither one of them was a pretty sight. "Where are we?"

"Pennsylvania."

"We haven't even hit the Midwest yet."

"We're making progress."

"I need caffeine."

"Go get it. I have to go to the bathroom."

In the coffee shop, Francis bought a large cup of joe and a couple of jelly donuts. He brought his purchases back to the car. Marco was already asleep in the backseat, drool dripping out of the side of his mouth. Even when he's sleeping, he looks like he's up to no good, Francis thought.

A moment later, Francis pulled out onto the highway. Marco's cell phone was in the well next to the driver's seat. I'll call Joyce again in a few hours, he thought. Hopefully, she's sleeping and when she wakes up she won't be mad at me.

But deep down he knew that his goose was cooked.

37

Regan's alarm went off when it was supposed to. Seven o'clock. Forcing herself to get right out of bed, she headed straight for the shower. The hot water on her shoulders felt so good. She washed her hair and hurried out across the hallway to her bedroom on the other side of the apartment. She tiptoed in. Kit was fast asleep. What a weekend she's had, Regan thought. I hope she hits it off with one of Jack's friends at the wedding.

Kit had even joked about inviting Tracy's ex. Jeffrey Woodall turned out to be an even bigger jerk than Regan could have imagined. Who was the girl he'd taken up with?

Regan pulled a pair of dark pants, a raspberry-colored cashmere sweater, and black jacket out of the closet. She fished around and found a pair of high-heeled boots.

At seven forty-five, she was combing her

hair when the buzzer sounded from down-stairs.

Regan answered. "I'll be right down."

Jack and Regan drove through the won-derfully quiet streets to the studio of Tiger News on the far west side of Manhattan by the Hudson River. Tiger was a new cable network and they were getting great ratings. Their popular Sunday morning show was a mix of news, entertainment, sports, and chat.

Alfred and Charisse were already in the greenroom drinking coffee and looking fresh as daisies when Regan and Jack arrived.

"Regan, darling!" Alfred exclaimed, giving her a big kiss.

He's thrilled with all this, Regan thought. I guess any publicity is good publicity. "Are you ready for your close-up?" she asked.

Alfred laughed. "We are indeed. We got here early. They've already done Charisse's makeup and powdered my nose. Oh my. I just have one little thing to tell you."

Regan paused. "What?"

"I gather you haven't seen the *New York Post* this morning?"

"Not yet."

Alfred picked a copy of the paper off the

chair and held it up. WEDDING DRESS BLUES the headline screamed.

Regan took the newspaper from his hands. A picture of Alfred and Charisse staring forlornly at Brianne's shredded dress took up half the front page with instructions for the reader to turn to Page 3 for the full details. Regan did so. Another headline screamed ROBBERY AT ALFRED AND CHARISSE'S COUTURE SALON TURNS FIVE APRIL BRIDES INTO MODERN DAY CINDERELLAS.

"Cinderellas?" Jack said in a stunned tone.

"She had nothing to wear to the ball," Regan muttered.

The article began:

You thought Cinderella had problems? Minutes before the Prince's big ball she was sartorially challenged. Luckily, her fairy godmother showed up with a gorgeous gown that fit perfectly. How would you like to be a bride about to be married in the next few weeks only to discover that the dress of your dreams has been stolen or shredded? Downtown designers Alfred and Charisse were the victims of a brazen robbery at

3:00 A.M. Saturday but insist that they will act as fairy godmothers and make new dresses in time for the following brides' big day . . .

"They list all the names!" Regan gasped.

"It's unfortunate," Alfred said, as he sipped his coffee.

"How did they get the names? You knew that Tracy, Victoria, and Shauna didn't want their names mentioned. Especially Tracy."

"I don't know. Honest. I don't know. I didn't tell them."

"Then who did?"

"I didn't tell," Charisse said breathlessly. "The reporters called back a couple times last night while we were working on your dress, Regan."

"It's coming along beautifully," Alfred interjected.

Regan ignored his weak attempt to smooth things over. "Was there anyone else with you last night?"

"Our assistant who works with us once in a while. He came up for a couple of hours. He answered the phone for us while we were working. So many people were calling. There was so much excitement."

"There's your leak," Jack said matter-of-factly.

Regan shook her head and looked down at the paper. "I hope Tracy doesn't sue you."

The names of the brides were there for the world to see: Regan Reilly, Brianne Barth, Tracy Timber, Victoria Beardsley, and Shauna Nickles.

The article continued:

Regan Reilly was on the scene yesterday. Reilly, who happens to be a private investigator, is set to marry the head of the NYPD Major Case Squad, Jack Reilly, next Saturday afternoon at Saint Ignatius Loyola Church in Manhattan. She is the daughter of mystery novelist Nora Regan Reilly . . .

"How did they find all this out?" Regan asked.

Jack raised one eyebrow. "The same way you do, my sweet."

The elevator door next to the greenroom opened. Brianne hurried off, followed by a guy who looked like he would rather be anywhere else.

Brianne introduced him. He was Pauly, her fiancé.

Pauly said hello and immediately headed for the food. He helped himself to a donut and a glass of juice, inhaling both, then helped himself to seconds.

"Regan, have you heard anything more about Joyce?" Brianne asked.

Regan shook her head. "Did you see the paper this morning?"

"No. It's so early. I'm surprised I made it in time."

Regan showed them the article.

"Look at that, Pauly," Brianne said with a smile. "I'm famous."

"Uh-huh," he mumbled as he read the story over Brianne's shoulder.

What's with him? Regan wondered. He seems so nervous.

"You're the head of the Major Case Squad?" he asked, pointing at Jack.

"Yes."

"Oh."

A producer's assistant appeared in the doorway. "We're ready for Regan and Brianne in makeup. Right across the hall."

"Make them look bridelike," Alfred advised. "Nothing too harsh or dramatic."

The assistant pretended she didn't hear him.

A makeup artist and hair stylist worked side by side in the small room. Regan was always amazed at how fast those people could bring out the best in whoever ended up plopped in their chairs. Over the years she'd been to plenty of these studios with her mother. The hair stylist, armed with a blow dryer, round brush, and can of spray went to work on Regan's crowning glory while the makeup artist skillfully and quickly touched up Brianne. Then they switched places. Within minutes they were being shepherded into the freezing cold studio.

In one corner of the vast room, a seating arrangement for six had been set up. A life-size photo of one of Alfred and Charisses's dresses was in the background.

Alfred clapped his hands when he saw his creation. "Marvelous!" he cried.

The attractive young hosts, Patrick and Jeannie, were set to do the interview together. Jeannie was tan and blond, Patrick was black-haired and blue-eyed, with chiseled features. They were dressed in their "weekend clothes"—designer blue jeans, boots, and sweaters. The show was trying to capture the segment of the Sunday morning television audience that would enjoy starting their day with the two fun and easygoing anchors. As viewers at home sipped their coffee and read the newspaper, Patrick and Jeannie would be doing the same, shooting the breeze with each other and their guests.

Today's guests were seated and miked.

Patrick and Jeannie hurried over from the anchor desk with big smiles. They sat down and adjusted their mikes. Patrick winked at the group.

When the cameras rolled, Jeannie introduced the segment.

"It's wedding season," she began. "A time when brides are running around trying to get everything done. Well, how would you like to be a bride who, on top of all the other things that can go wrong, learns that her wedding dress has been stolen just a week, *one week,* before her wedding? It happened to two of our guests."

The camera focused on Regan and Brianne as Jeannie gave their names.

I feel like an idiot, Regan thought.

"We also have the incredibly talented designers, Alfred and Charisse, with us. In the last couple of years they've had write-ups in numerous fashion magazines because the wedding dresses they design are so gorgeous. Take a look," Jeannie said, pointing to the life-size photo. "But, unfortunately for them, they made the wedding dresses that were stolen. Still, when I get married, I want you to make my dress!" Jeannie giggled.

"We will," Alfred promised with a big smile while Charisse waved demurely at the camera.

Jeannie told the viewers the tale of the robbery, then turned with a look of wide-eyed sympathy to Alfred and Charisse. "How are you two doing today?"

"We're exhausted," Alfred said. "We were up all night sewing. No matter what, we will have the dresses ready for Regan and Brianne. They've both been so wonderful and patient."

Patient? Regan thought. Brianne's father threatened you, and I got two hours sleep last night because I'm out trying to solve this case. I don't call that patient.

Patrick leaned in. "We know that Brianne walked into your salon to find her wedding dress in a heap on the floor all slashed with drops of blood on it. Tell us what that was like, Brianne."

"Oh, please," Brianne said, rolling her eyes. "It was unbelievable."

"I understand that you went home and dug out your mother's wedding gown but it was full of bugs?"

Brianne smiled and laughed like it was the funniest thing in the world. "My mother was so upset," she began.

After Brianne finished sharing her anecdotes, Patrick looked at Regan. "And here we have bride-to-be Regan Reilly, who is also a private investigator."

"Eeeww," Jeannie said. "How fun!"

"You're working on this case, right, Regan?" Patrick asked.

"As you can imagine, I have more than a passing interest in it," Regan joked. "The NYPD is also investigating."

"Your fiancé is a member of the NYPD. I see here that he is the head of the Major Case Squad, Jack Reilly."

"Yes," Regan answered with a genuine smile.

Patrick looked earnest. "So you're kind of a crime-fighting duo. The two Reillys!"

Jack's going to kill me, Regan thought. "We both enjoy our work."

"Tell us about this investigation."

"Basically, we're looking for two men who came into Alfred and Charisse's loft, tied them up, broke into the safe, stole a large amount of cash and jewelry, and made off with the dresses."

Jeannie's face looked quizzical. "How did they get in?"

"There was no sign of forced entry," Regan answered.

"I'm always losing my keys," Alfred confessed dramatically.

Regan became convinced Alfred would do anything to get camera time.

"Gotta be careful about that, folks," Patrick warned. "See what can happen when you lose your keys."

"Change your locks!" Jeannie urged the viewers. Then she turned to Alfred and Charisse. "Weren't you scared when the intruders tied you up?"

"Poor Charisse was terrified," Alfred answered.

Patrick looked down at his notes. "Three other brides were affected by this crime. Tracy Timber . . ."

Regan cringed.

"Victoria Beardsley, and Shauna Nickles. Where are they this morning? I'm sure they have interesting stories."

You have no idea, Regan thought. At this very moment Tracy is probably having another meltdown in Connecticut.

"Alfred, do you know how they are coping with this?" Jeannie asked.

Alfred started to stammer. Charisse cut him off. "Of the five April Brides, Regan and Brianne are the two we're concentrating on right now. They are both getting married next Saturday. We have a little more time to replace the other dresses."

"Good luck," Patrick said. He turned full face to the camera. "We want to help catch these guys. And you viewers out there, watching from coast to coast, often make the difference. If you see anything or have any information, please call our hotline. Help our April Brides, Regan Reilly, Brianne Barth, Tracy Timber, Victoria Beardsley, and Shauna Nickles, get their dresses back."

Jeannie nodded. "Take another look at this spectacular vintage-style dress behind us. This is Alfred and Charisse's creation. All four of the stolen gowns look similar to this one. Those dresses have to be somewhere! Our hotline number is . . ."

Patrick held up the copy of the *New York Post* for the camera. WEDDING DRESS BLUES. He sighed dramatically, then shook his head and smiled. "I can tell you right now my wife wouldn't have been happy if this had happened a week before our wedding. Folks, we'll be right back."

The segment was over.

Patrick pulled off his mike. "Thank you all for coming in this morning. I'm sure there will be quite a reaction to this story."

I have no doubt about that, Regan thought.

"Thanks so much," Jeannie echoed as the twosome hurried back to their anchor chairs.

Jack and Pauly were inside the studio. They'd been invited to watch the segment live instead of waiting in the greenroom and seeing it on the monitor.

Regan walked up to Jack and smiled. "Sorry, Batman."

Jack put his arm around her and whispered in her ear. "We make a great duo. And not just as crime fighters."

The phone lines of Tiger News were already lighting up.

Jack and Regan, Pauly and Brianne, and Alfred and Charisse all got into the elevator together and descended to the lobby.

They were exiting the building together when an assistant came running after them. "Miss Reilly, my boss thought that you might be interested in one of our callers . . .

38

In the large and tasteful guest room of the Neys' apartment, Tyler and Shauna were just waking up. Tyler picked up the remote control, as he did on most mornings, and flicked on the television. As usual, he constantly changed the channel, giving each program about a nanosecond to grab his attention. If it didn't, he kept going.

He almost missed the segment on the April Brides. Almost, but not quite. He had already started to push the remote when Regan Reilly's face appeared onscreen.

"Shauna," he said, tapping her back. "Look at this!"

"What?" Shauna asked drowsily.

"Look!"

They both watched the segment. When the news anchor read Shauna's name they slowly looked at each other. Shauna threw back the covers and got out of bed. She looked at the clock. "Pamela should be getting ready for church right now. I'm going to go in and see if I can help her."

"That's a great idea," Tyler said quietly.

39

Pamela and Arnold could always be found in the front row of St. Bartholomew's Episcopal Church on Park Avenue at the nine o'clock service on Sunday mornings. But today they had gotten there a little late and were seated toward the back.

So already things felt a little off.

After all the excitement last night, they got off to a slower start this morning. Pamela had prepared Arnold his oatmeal and coffee, grateful that Shauna and Tyler were late sleepers. It was wonderful having them stay at the apartment, but sometimes she felt the need for more elbow room.

Now they were going to have a child. And it will be named after one of us, Pamela thought as Father Tully preached to the congregation about God's grace. It would be wonderful to hold a baby in her arms. So why was she feeling so unsettled? It should be a happy day.

Pamela smoothed back her hair with her left hand and realized that her earring was missing. Quickly she felt her other ear. That earring was in place. It was one of her favorite pairs, the large diamonds in a gold setting that Arnold had given her on their wedding anniversary last year. Did I drop it, she wondered in a panic. She looked around her seat. I shouldn't be worried about jewelry when I'm in church, but that pair is so special.

I hope I find it when I get home.

Pamela sat back in her seat. She thought about the dinner last night. They had toasted the baby. Shauna had had several glasses of wine. Maybe it was because they were celebrating, Pamela thought, but she shouldn't be drinking if she's pregnant.

If she's pregnant.

Pamela's hand went back up to her left ear. This morning when I was getting ready, Shauna came into the bedroom. I had the safe open. Arnie was calling for me to hurry. Shauna was going on and on about the baby. I didn't want to be rude so I tried to listen, but it was so distracting. I left the bedroom before Shauna, mostly to get away from her constant chatter.

But I don't remember closing the safe.

Pamela's heart started to beat faster. She felt light-headed. All my jewels are in there, she thought. They're worth several hundred thousand dollars. Was Shauna distracting her on purpose? All of a sudden the story of Shauna's pregnancy didn't ring true. Pamela tried to calm herself. But she couldn't. She was starting to feel physically ill. She tapped on her husband's arm. God will forgive me, she thought. "Arnold, I don't feel well. I have to get home."

Shauna and Tyler were throwing their things together as fast as they could.

"A bird in the hand," Tyler crowed as he held up the bag they'd swiped from Pamela's closet and filled with her jewelry. "I thought we'd have a bigger payday from Pammy and Arnold but we'll have to make do with these gems."

"I should have used a different name," Shauna said. "But when we met them I had no idea it would come to this."

They zipped up their suitcases.

* * *

Regan and Jack followed the assistant up to the newsroom at Tiger News Network. They were ushered into a private office. The news producer, a woman in her forties, was waiting for them. Her glasses were resting on top of her head, a large cup of coffee was next to the stack of papers on her desk. She got up quickly and introduced herself.

"My name is Dana Mansley. We're getting a lot of calls about the piece on the missing dresses," she said. "Most of them probably won't amount to anything. But this guy sounded like someone you'd want to talk to." She picked up her phone, pressed a button, and handed it to Regan.

"Hello, this is Regan Reilly."

"Hello there, Regan. This is Horace Banks. How are you?"

"Good. How are you?"

"Most things are good, but I'm still legally married to a Shauna Nickles who disappeared a couple years ago. I want to get a divorce because I have a little lady I'd like to marry. By the way, she thinks that dress they showed today was really pretty."

"I'll tell the designers," Regan assured him.

"Anyway, it takes a while before you can declare someone legally dead, you know what I mean?"

"Yes, I do."

"If this is my wife, Shauna Nickles, I'd like to get in touch with her. I heard she'd taken up with a younger guy. She shouldn't be getting married anyway if she's still married to me."

"No, she shouldn't. Let's see if we have the right Shauna Nickles. Can you describe her to me?"

"She's forty-eight years old but doesn't look it. She's cute, or at least I used to think she was cute. She's petite, with light brown hair, and big green eyes. I always called her a sparrow with a good figure."

Interesting description, Regan thought. But it sounds like Shauna. "Do you have a description of the guy?"

"All I heard was that he was young, dark, and handsome," Horace laughed. "The opposite of me. I'm just glad that he's not rich! The two of them supposedly wander around like a couple of gypsies."

As Regan processed this information, she could hear a woman in the background assuring Horace that he was as handsome as could be.

"Where are you calling from?" Regan asked.

"We live in northern Texas."

Not that far from Santa Fe, Regan thought. "The Shauna I met said she didn't have family."

Horace groaned. "She used that line on people when she wanted to gain their sympathy. For the stupidest things. Let me tell you something, she's bad news. A real trickster. Truth be told, I wasn't sure if I should call because she doesn't seem like the type to bother with a fancy gown for her wedding. But I had to. If it's her, I want my divorce."

Regan's pulse quickened, but she kept her cool. "Horace, let me take your number. I'll find out what I can and get back to you."

When Regan hung up, Dana looked up at her questioningly. "I'll check into this," Regan said diplomatically. The last thing she wanted to do was slander Shauna to a news producer. "Please keep me posted about any other calls."

Dana nodded. "Keep us in the loop, too. We'd like to follow this story."

"Sure thing," Regan promised.

But when Regan and Jack were on their way out, she turned to him. "Jack, let's pay a visit to Fifth Avenue. Fast. If Shauna is this guy's wife and she's heard her name's out there in the newspaper and on television, there's no telling what she and her fiancé might pull on the Neys. It's obvious they're very wealthy and would be a perfect target for a couple of crooks."

When they got in Jack's car, he turned on his siren. They sped across town to Madison Avenue, made a left, and headed uptown.

Shauna pressed the button for the elevator. "This place was nice while it lasted," she said to Tyler in a low tone.

The door opened and Walter, the elevator operator, looked at them with surprise. "Leaving us?" he asked.

"We're taking a couple days away. Arnold and Pamela could probably use a break," Shauna said with a laugh. Sweetly she asked, "Could you let them know downstairs we'd like a cab?"

"Of course," Walter replied solemnly as

he pressed the taxi signal. "I saw your name in the paper today, Ms. Nickles."

"You did?"

"Yes. I'm sorry about what happened to your wedding dress."

"Me, too," Shauna said. "It's just terrible what those thieves did."

"It certainly is," Tyler agreed.

The door opened at the ground floor, and Shauna and Tyler hurried off.

Arnold and Pamela grabbed a cab in front of the church and gave the driver their address.

"What's the matter?" Arnold asked.

"You know how sometimes you just get a feeling that something is terribly wrong? That you've been so stupid?" Pamela asked, fanning herself with her white glove. Perspiration had broken out on her forehead.

Arnold looked into her eyes. "Do you mean about Shauna and Tyler?"

"Yes," Pamela gasped.

"I hope they haven't taken us for a couple of old fools."

Pamela started to cry.

* * *

Regan and Jack turned the corner onto Fifth Avenue as Shauna and Tyler were about to get into a cab.

"There they are!" Regan cried. "They're leaving."

"What are you going to do?" Jack asked.

"I'll just talk to them for a minute." Regan jumped out. "Shauna!" she called and hurried over as the doorman finished loading their suitcases into the trunk of the taxi. Shauna had a velour floral bag thrown over her shoulder that looked like it was filled to capacity. It also didn't look like her style.

Shauna turned. The expression on her face was not nearly as happy as it had been the day before.

"I'd like to talk to you," Regan said as she approached her.

"I can't right now. We have a plane to catch." Shauna said impatiently.

Tyler was on the other side of the cab, with the door open.

"It'll just take a minute," Regan said.

"We don't have a minute!" Tyler said, trying to sound in control. "We're very late already."

Another taxi pulled up. Pamela started to

get out. She was screaming, "That's my bag!" Regan's head turned for a split second. In that moment, Tyler and Shauna took off. They ran across Fifth Avenue toward Central Park.

Regan ran after them. Jack jumped out of his car and crossed Fifth Avenue in a flash. They both hoisted themselves over the low stone wall that bordered the park and resumed their chase.

Jack ran ahead in hot pursuit of Tyler while Regan raced after Shauna.

She's a fast runner, Regan thought. I wish I didn't have these boots on. But Shauna had the heavy bag. There must be some goodies in there, Regan mused, pushing her body as hard as she could.

People out for a Sunday morning in the park were astonished to see the wild chase of Shauna and Tyler happening right before their eyes. Many scurried away in fear, others took out their cameras.

With a burst of speed, Regan ran across the road full of bicyclists and joggers, caught up with Shauna, threw her arms around her from behind, and they both stumbled to the ground. Regan firmly placed her knee on Shauna's back. Panting, she grabbed the bag that had fallen to the ground and unzipped it.

It was filled with magnificent sparkling jewelry.

"Were you going to sell this on the street in Santa Fe?" Regan asked sarcastically.

Shauna didn't answer.

"Regan!" Jack called. He was approaching fast with two police officers. "We've got the groom. Now we have a pair of bracelets for the bride."

"Allow me," Regan said, as she took the handcuffs from Jack and snapped them on Shauna's tiny wrists.

40

When Joyce started to regain consciousness, it didn't take long for her to realize she
was not at home sweet home. It wasn't a
bad dream—she was in the same dingy,
creepy room she'd found herself in the night
before. And she felt as if she'd been asleep
for a very long time.

The old lady was sitting in a chair, her
head nodding, her hands folded. She was
wearing a pair of old black pants covered
with animal hair, sneakers, and a brown
ratty cardigan. Dogs were stretched out
everywhere.

Joyce had a tremendous headache and
she was thirsty. She tried to sit up, but the
pain across her forehead got worse. I feel so
weak, she thought, as she lay back down.
One of the dogs lying at her feet woofed
halfheartedly then put his head back down.

The old lady's eyes flew open. She

hoisted herself out of the chair and moved toward Joyce.

Joyce felt herself shrink back.

"Good morning," the woman rasped. "I'm so glad you're awake! But you had a good night's rest. That's so important. Now we can talk. My name is Hattie."

"I'm Joyce."

"I'm going to take good care of you. You got some lump there on your forehead. It's what they call an egg!" Hattie started to cackle, waving her hands with glee. "My dogs, Porgy, Ginger, Pang, and Thor, have been worried about you. You were out cold last night. They all wanted to lick your face when you fell down the steps. Now how about breakfast?"

"My head hurts. I'd better get home."

Hattie's face turned dark. "Absolutely not! You have to let me nurse you back to health! My best friend just died. I should have helped her get better. I should have! Now I have to help you."

"But I'm okay."

"No, you're not!" Hattie insisted. "You just said your head hurt."

Joyce decided to try and placate her. "I'm

kind of thirsty," she said. "Could I please have a glass of water?"

"The water's kind of rusty. It needs to be boiled. Problem with these old pipes. Why don't I make you a nice cup of tea?"

"Okay."

Joyce tried to sit up again, but the effort was too much. "Is my purse around here?"

"Huh?"

"My purse."

"I didn't see no purse."

"It has my cell phone in it."

"I haven't heard anything ringing."

"Could I use your phone?"

"I don't have a phone. When you got nobody to call, you don't need a phone."

"You say that I fell right outside. Would you mind looking to see if my purse is on the ground? It's black and has a shoulder strap."

Hattie shrugged. She went over to the front door, which faced the steps that ran up the side of the building to street level, and opened it. A couple of leaves had blown down and landed outside the door, but that was it. Hattie quickly ascended a couple of the steps, turned her head, and peered out. Everything was calm and quiet. Just as quickly she went back inside. She shut the door and locked it. "Nope. No purse. Somebody probably stole it."

This is crazy, Joyce thought. I've got to get out of here. I believe her story. She didn't kidnap me. I drank too much and got myself into this mess. She's nothing but a good Samaritan who's a little nuts. At least I hope that's all she is. But I've got to go home.

Hattie turned on the kettle. A few minutes later she brought Joyce a steaming cup of hot herbal tea. "This will make you feel better," she said. Her weathered face wore an intense expression. She grabbed a pillow and shoved it down behind Joyce's head.

Joyce sat up and slowly took a sip of the hot brew. If I weren't so thirsty, she thought, I'd never drink this. Some of these herbal teas taste awful. As she sipped, she wondered if anyone was looking for her. Francis was who knows where, her mother was on a cruise, but at least Cindy must be worried. I've got to let her know I'm okay. All of a sudden a dog started barking ferociously. But it wasn't one of the four dogs in the room.

"Shut up!" Hattie yelled. "My friend's dog

is in the bedroom. I don't know what to do with him. He's big and a little mean. He doesn't get along with the other dogs."

"Is he throwing himself against the door?" Joyce asked as a loud thumping noise shook the apartment.

"Yup," Hattie said. "He hasn't been feeling good. I think he's sad that his master died. I'm sad, too. But I don't know what to do! And he won't eat his food."

When Joyce's eyes started to droop again, she realized she'd made a mistake. I shouldn't be so tired, she thought. This nutcase must have laced the tea with drugs. Luckily, I didn't drink too much of it. She put the cup down and fell back asleep.

41

Tom Belfiore lived on the west side of lower Manhattan in Battery Park City. On weekend mornings he loved to take his Irish setter out for a bout of fresh air and exercise. Sometimes he and Greeny went all the way up to Central Park and joined other New Yorkers, with or without dogs, who enjoyed running around the reservoir. Sometimes Tom stayed in the downtown area where he lived, choosing to run along the Esplanade in Battery Park where he could enjoy the sight of boats floating by and the Statue of Liberty in the distance. Along the eastern bank of the Hudson River there were grassy open fields, picnic tables, and watery coves. For man and dog alike, it was a great place to experience nature.

A new dog run at Kowsky Plaza even had water fountains for dogs to splash in and mounds for them to jump over. That was Greeny's favorite.

This Sunday morning Tom opted to stay downtown. A young and attractive ad salesman for a sports magazine, he enjoyed the outdoors as much as his dog. But taking Greeny for a walk or run in Manhattan was always an experience. The adventurous mutt loved to sniff out and explore every nook and cranny in his path.

Today was no exception.

After spending time at the dog run, they wandered north, ambling through Tribeca, SoHo, and Greenwich Village, almost all the way to the Meatpacking District. They turned down one of the little side streets off Washington, and were heading back over toward the river. Greeny had his nose down, slowly examining every inch of pavement. He led Tom over toward the curb, then suddenly dove between two parked cars. Such rapid movement usually meant he had spotted a much smaller creature and felt confident enough to give chase.

"Come on, Greeny," Tom urged. "Let's go."

But Greeny's head was down. Something had caught his attention. He was straining the leash as he attempted to make his way under one of the cars.

Tom leaned over and tried to see what Greeny's fuss was all about. Then he saw it. A woman's purse. Tom nudged his dog to get out of the way, bent down, and picked up the bag. "Good boy," Tom said, petting Greeny's head. "Somebody must have lost their purse, but you found it, didn't you? Good boy!" Greeny wagged his tail joyfully.

Tom unzipped the small black bag and smiled at the sight of a Hershey's chocolate bar. Next to it was a small cell phone. He reached his hand in, pulled out a driver's license, and looked at the picture. A woman named Joyce who lived in Queens. She's cute, Tom thought. The only other items in the purse were a credit card in her name and keys. No cash. A hard-core thief would have used the credit card and taken the cell phone. Someone probably took the money and ran.

"We're making a special stop, Greeny," Tom said, "then we'll go down by the river." The nearest police station was several blocks away. When Tom and Greeny walked in together, Tom smiled at the sergeant behind the desk. "I'm being a good citizen and returning a purse that my bloodhound here discovered on the street. I think he picked up on the scent of the chocolate bar inside."

The sergeant smiled good-naturedly. "Does it have any other hidden treasures?" he asked as Tom handed it over.

"No, but if she's offering a reward, I'd be happy to accept it."

The sergeant dumped the contents on his desk. He picked up Joyce's driver's license, looked at the name, and grimaced.

"What's the matter?" Tom asked.

"This girl was out last night with her friends at a club. It seems she disappeared into thin air."

"Oh, my God," Tom said quietly.

"Where did you find this?"

"On Jane Street. One block from the river."

"This doesn't bode well," the sergeant said quietly. He took all of Tom's information for the police report.

When Tom went back outside, he couldn't stop thinking about Joyce from Queens.

———◆———

42

Victoria loved being in Jeffrey's apartment. It was so elegant. They were able to spend just three precious hours together before she had to report to work at midnight. As they snuggled on the couch, sipping champagne and taking in the view of Central Park, they reminisced about their chance meeting.

"It was such a stroke of luck that we ended up on that elevator together," Jeffrey cooed. "If Tracy hadn't left her wedding shoes in the car, I would never have had to run up to Alfred's salon to drop them off. To think you were leaving at that very moment. And then the elevator got stuck with us in it!"

"Just long enough for you to kiss me!" Victoria giggled. "The attraction between us was too much to fight."

"You were standing so close to me. When

you grabbed my hand and said you were scared, I felt electricity," Jeffrey sighed. "I knew at that moment I could never go back to Tracy."

"Poor Tracy," Victoria said as she put her head on Jeffrey's shoulder. "In time she'll understand."

"I doubt it."

"It doesn't really matter, does it?" Victoria asked, looking up at him.

"Not at all. But believe me, Tracy will never understand. What about Frederick? How did he take the news when you broke up with him?"

"He felt terrible. So did I. But I told him to visualize the wonderful life ahead of him."

"What did he say to that?"

"He hung up on me."

"I can't say I blame him," Jeffrey laughed. "Ohhhhhhh," he said, giving Victoria a big hug. "I can't wait to get to know you better. I can't wait until this mess blows over and we can go out in public together. I want to show you off!"

Victoria swooned. "All's fair in love and war, Jeffrey! I keep pinching myself. I can't believe I found you. I knew that if I just kept on believing, then real true love would come into my life."

"Didn't you think you'd found true love with Frederick? At least in the beginning?"

"No," Victoria answered honestly. "I've never felt like this before." She looked at her watch. "I'd better go. I'll miss you, darling."

Jeffrey walked to the door, and they kissed again. "I'll be dreaming about you tonight, my sweet," he whispered.

"And I'll be daydreaming about you."

At the hotel where Victoria worked in midtown, it was quiet during the witching hours. Not too many people checked in or out in the middle of the night. Workers on the late night shift ended up having a lot of time on their hands.

Victoria spent the night smiling, thinking about her future with Jeffrey. She was good for him, and he was good for her. Poor Tracy, Victoria thought. She must be devastated.

At around 6 A.M., one of the hotel employees dropped off the morning papers at the front desk. When Victoria saw the headline of the *New York Post,* her mouth dropped. But when she opened the page and saw her name in bold print, her adrenaline really started pumping. It was a feeling she couldn't say she disliked.

"I didn't know you were getting married!"

Victoria spun around.

Her co-worker Daisy, who'd been on a break, was standing inches from her. "I just saw the newspaper!" she cried. "Why didn't you tell me?"

Victoria smiled. "My fiancé is very private. We just wanted to have a quiet wedding . . ."

"I didn't even know you had a boyfriend! We're here together all these nights, and I do nothing but complain about my love life and you don't tell me anything! Who is the lucky man?"

"His name is Frederick and he lives in Pennsylvania."

"I'm going to throw you a shower!"

"No."

"Why not? It will be a fun excuse to get everyone who works here together. No big deal. But it said you were an April Bride. When are you getting married?"

"As you know, I'm working every weekend. We were going to take a couple days in the middle of the week and get married ourselves. Just a few friends and his family will be with us."

Daisy looked down at the newspaper and pointed at the picture of one of Alfred's dresses. "You got yourself an expensive dress for a small, middle-of-the-week wedding!"

"Frederick is a painter. He plans to do a life-sized portrait of me in my wedding dress. I knew it had to be special."

"How romantic! Are you going on a honeymoon?"

"We'll go to the Poconos for a couple of days," Victoria said quickly. "He's busy and I'm busy, so we'll take a longer vacation in the summer when the weather is nice."

"I know what you mean. Give me a beach chair and I'm happy. So what's Frederick like?"

The expression on Victoria's face turned positively saintly. "He's wonderful. And he's incredibly talented. His work is magnificent."

"Yeah. What does he look like?" Daisy asked, always getting to the point.

"Handsome. Handsome. Oh, just so handsome."

Daisy giggled with abandon. "I love it! What

does your mother say about your dress being stolen? She must be freaked." Daisy's eyes opened wide. She stared straight at Victoria.

"Actually," Victoria said, "my mother doesn't know I'm getting married. She doesn't approve of Frederick."

"Really? Why not?" Daisy was clearly enjoying every detail, the juicier the better.

"My mother was hoping I'd marry someone who offered more stability. Frederick is a dreamy artist. So she doesn't even know that we were planning to get married."

"She doesn't? Girl, she's going to find out now!"

"Maybe not. She and my father are living abroad. I was going to tell her after we were married so she wouldn't try and talk me out of it. I just hope Jef—"

Daisy waited, her wide-eyed stare never wavering.

"I just hope Frederick doesn't get upset that my name is in the paper. He shuns crowds and attention. When I'm with him out at his home, it's just us and the rolling hills. I have to say I love it."

"When are you going to quit your job?" Daisy asked.

"I'm not going to."

"You're not?" Daisy asked, astonished. "Why not?"

"I will eventually. But Frederick likes to be alone so he can paint. I like to be alone as well. For now I'll go out and visit on my days off. It's exactly what we both want."

"How modern!" Daisy said excitedly. "It'll probably work better. Less chance of getting on each other's nerves."

"Absence makes the heart grow fonder," Victoria said as a middle-aged man stepped off the elevator and approached the front desk, wheeling his black suitcase. Victoria turned to Daisy. "I'll take this." She smiled bewitchingly at the customer. "Leaving us so soon, Mr. Flach?"

Daisy watched as the customer's face lit up.

"You have a good memory," Flach said, clearly flattered.

"I never forget a handsome man," Victoria cooed.

What a flirt she is, Daisy thought as she headed to the back office. And she's always dressed so sexily in those expensive outfits. Frederick better watch out, she thought. Leaving Victoria alone for too long in the city could mean trouble. Daisy laughed. Biiiggg trouble.

I want to find a man, Daisy mused. I'm going to have to start taking lessons from Victoria. Maybe I'll ask her about that visualization stuff she's so big on. I've seen her reading those books. She said it helps you figure out what you really want. Then you have to go for it, no matter what it takes to get there.

Daisy shook her head and laughed. It sure looks like Victoria succeeded.

———◆———

43

While Shauna and Tyler were hauled off in the back of a police car, Regan and Jack went up to Pamela and Arnold's apartment for a quick chat.

"Thank you, thank you," Pamela cried.

"I'm sorry if I was rude to you yesterday, Regan," Arnold said contritely. "Turns out it's a good thing Shauna got publicity. Otherwise those two miserable ingrates would be off with all of Pamela's jewelry." Arnold's face turned beet red. "I just can't believe we trusted those two in the first place."

"Calm down, dear," Pamela said. She turned to Regan and Jack. "This is embarrassing, but Tyler did save my life."

"They took advantage of your gratitude," Regan said.

"She even told us she was pregnant," Pamela said. "They said they'd name the baby after one of us. I'm sure they were lying."

"We'll soon find out," Jack replied with a raised eyebrow.

Regan looked thoughtful. "They've been here since January? They weren't working that whole time?"

Pamela shrugged. "Tyler did odd jobs for us. We gave him cash but not that much. He chauffeured us in our car when we had to go out in the evening. Shauna did some cooking. They made themselves so helpful. Shauna kept saying she had to get busy and make more jewelry to sell after the wedding. But it never seemed to happen."

Regan rolled her eyes.

"I know, Regan. It's ridiculous."

"Well, whatever," Regan said. "The police will be going through their suitcases to see if there's anything else that belongs to you. Be sure to check around to make sure there's nothing else missing that they might have taken in these last three months and already sold."

"We'll go over this place with a fine-tooth comb," Arnold declared.

"For all we know they could have been in on the robbery at the bridal salon," Jack said. "Where were they on Friday night?"

"They went out to a concert. We watched

a movie in bed, then went to sleep early. We never hear them when they come in. I have no idea what time they got home," Pamela replied wearily.

"I'm sure you two could use a rest," Regan said. "We'll be in touch."

By the time Regan and Jack got back downstairs, reporters were already camped outside the building. Regan had contacted the Tiger News Network. They had, after all, been the reason that Shauna and Tyler were thwarted.

"Regan Reilly," one of the reporters began, "one of the April Brides turns out to be a jewel thief. What do you have to say about that?"

"I'm glad she's been caught."

"What about her stolen dress?"

"What about it? Alfred and Charisse have one less dress they have to worry about replacing."

The reporters laughed.

"You were on the air with Brianne Barth this morning. Have you talked to Tracy Timber or Victoria Beardsley today?"

"I haven't had any reason to."

"Do you think you will?"

"I can't say."

When Regan and Jack got back in the car, her cell phone rang. It was Alfred. He was delighted with all the excitement about Shauna.

"What did you think of her?" Regan asked.

"She was a phony," Alfred cried.

"We know that now, Alfred," Regan said with a slight shake of her head.

Jack's cell phone rang. He answered it, listened, and put his hand on Regan's arm. "Joyce's purse was found this morning downtown. Her cell phone and license were in it. No cash."

Regan's face looked grave. "Alfred, I've got to go. I'll talk to you later."

44

Cindy had spent a mostly sleepless night on the couch in Joyce's apartment. She tried to watch television, but her mind couldn't focus on anything but the fact that Joyce was missing. Where could she be? She tried Joyce's cell phone a number of times, not expecting an answer, and not getting one.

What am I going to tell her mother? Cindy worried. She hasn't been well. She went on the cruise for a little rest and relaxation. Sure she was laid-back, but she'd been having health problems and she always worried about Joyce. When Joyce had had the surgery on her foot last year and they'd given her too much medication, her mother had been frantic. Joyce was out of it for a couple of days. She couldn't handle more than an aspirin. And last night Joyce probably had too much to drink. Who knows what could have happened to her?

At around eight thirty Cindy fell asleep. She awoke when Joyce's phone rang. Racing into the kitchen, she grabbed the receiver. "Hello," she said quickly.

"Who's this?" a male voice asked.

"Who's this?" Cindy answered tartly.

"This is Francis. I'm looking for Joyce."

"Francis, this is Cindy."

"Oh, hi, Cindy," Francis answered, sounding guilty. "Is Joyce there?"

"No."

"Where is she?"

Cindy clenched the phone. "I don't know, Francis." The call waiting beeped. "Hold on a second. Maybe this is Joyce." Cindy pressed the flash button. "Hello."

"Cindy, it's Regan. You haven't heard from Joyce have you?"

"No, I haven't. Her boyfriend is on the other line."

"Where is he?"

"I don't know. He just called."

"Cindy, I'm sorry to tell you that Joyce's purse was found downtown."

"Oh, no!" Tears stung Cindy's eyes. "What could have happened to her?"

"I don't know. The police are looking for her. We want to post her picture all over downtown where she was last seen. Are there any good photos of her at the house we could use?"

"Yes. Lots," Cindy sniffled. "I'll get a couple of them out."

"Jack and I are on our way right now." Regan then told Cindy about the adventure with Shauna and Tyler.

"I missed the show this morning," Cindy said. "I finally fell asleep for a little while."

"Thanks to that show we thwarted two jewel thieves. I'm going to see if the producer would be willing to run Joyce's picture. Now that her purse has been found."

"I understand," Cindy said quietly. "What should I tell her boyfriend?"

"Tell him the truth. I'd like to talk to him. Tell him that I'll call him back when we get to Joyce's."

"Okay, Regan." Cindy clicked back. "Francis?"

"Yes, Cindy. What's going on?"

"I hate to tell you this, but Joyce is missing. She went to the bathroom last night at a club we were at and never came back." Cindy's voice broke. "They just found her purse downtown."

"What? Oh, my God!" Francis wailed.

"That was a private investigator on the phone. Her name is Regan Reilly and she was here last night. She's investigating the stolen wedding dresses that everyone is talking about. Now she's involved in this. Her boyfriend is the head of the Major Case Squad. They're coming here in a few minutes to get a picture of Joyce. Regan wants to talk to you."

Francis whimpered.

"Where are you?" Cindy asked.

There was no answer.

The line went dead.

45

"What happened?" Marco asked after Francis closed the cell phone and flung it across the seat.

"Joyce is missing!" Francis said. He was practically hyperventilating.

"Missing?"

"Since last night. They found her purse on the street in Manhattan this morning. The cops have been at the house. They're coming back. One of the investigators is that Regan Reilly we saw on NY1. She's also looking for the wedding dresses!" he yelped, pointing with his thumb to the trunk. "And I just hung up on Cindy. I got so scared. I'd better call back."

Marco grabbed the phone. "No! Are you crazy? Stay out of it for now."

"But I just hung up on Joyce's friend. It makes me look suspicious!"

"Of what? You were so upset you didn't

know what you were doing. It's understandable."

"But what about Joyce? She disappeared last night when she was out with her friends."

"I've done that plenty of times. Nobody went looking for me!"

"I've got to go back."

"You can't! Going back would put us in the middle of an investigation. And we're guilty! Listen, the cops are looking for Joyce. Let's keep going to Vegas. That's all we can do right now."

"I should at least call."

"*No!* Then you have to tell them where you are. Or go back. Neither of which is an option. You're her bereft boyfriend and hung up because you're going out of your mind."

"That's for sure," Francis said miserably as he stared out at the road.

———◆———

46

Shauna and Tyler were being questioned separately. They were both insistent they had nothing to do with the break-in at Alfred and Charisse's salon.

"You had a lot of cash in your suitcase," one of the detectives said to Tyler. "You want to tell me where you got it?"

"We don't have a bank account here in New York. We've been traveling. That's why we were carrying such a large amount of money."

"Twelve thousand dollars?"

"Yes."

"That's a lot of cash to have sitting around. And three months is a long time to hang around the city without a job. What have you two been doing with yourselves?"

"We've done work for the Neys. We planned to leave after the wedding."

"I'm sure you did."

"So where did you get the cash?"

"We had it when we got here!" Tyler insisted.

"You're sure you didn't rob any banks to get it?"

"No more questions. I want to talk to a lawyer."

47

For the rest of the morning, Victoria fielded comments from co-workers who expressed surprise and happiness at her impending nuptials. Victoria was polite and thanked them for their good wishes. But she was starting to feel the pressure build. If anyone found out about her and Jeffrey . . .

I'm going to have to call Alfred and ask how my name got out, she thought. I told Regan Reilly that I didn't want publicity. When it was almost time for her to go home, a young, earnest reporter with a microphone in his hand approached the front desk. He looked about twelve.

"Victoria Beardsley?"

"Yes."

"I'm Evan Charlton with *The Big Apple Sunday Morning* radio program. I understand you are one of the April Brides. Could I have a few words with you?"

Victoria stiffened. "I really can't talk now. I have work to do."

"I understand. But our listeners would just love to hear your reaction to the stolen dresses."

"I'm sorry it happened," Victoria said, "but I won't let it ruin this happy time in my life."

"Have you heard the news about what happened in Central Park?"

"What?" Victoria asked quickly.

"One of your fellow April Brides is a *thief!*" He told the story succinctly but with great excitement. "What do you think about that, Victoria?"

"It's a shame," Victoria answered. "I'm just glad they didn't get away with it."

"Not as glad as that Fifth Avenue couple! For a quiet Sunday morning, this really gives us something to talk about. We want to know what's going on with all the other April Brides!" With a twinkle in his eye, the zealous young reporter asked, "Victoria Beardsley, do you have any secrets you want to share with me?"

Victoria tried to laugh. "None. Now, if you don't mind . . ."

"Would you be willing to come to the studio when you get off work and sit down for a chat with us?"

Victoria shook her head, but tried to remain charming. "My fiancé and I are private people. I didn't do anything to deserve this attention. All I did was order a wedding dress from two very talented designers. That's it. I want to stay out of the limelight." She turned and disappeared into the back office.

Evan spoke into his mike. "There you have it, ladies and gentlemen. Another of the April Brides. We'll do our best to get statements from them all. Back to you in the studio."

In the office Daisy looked up when Victoria walked in. She could see that Victoria was upset. "Are you all right?"

"I think that this wedding dress business is finally getting to me," Victoria said. "Do you think you can handle the front desk alone until Kelly gets here? I want to go home."

"Of course!" Daisy walked over to her co-worker and grabbed Victoria's hand. "It will be okay."

"I don't want Frederick to get angry with me. There was just a reporter at the front desk asking me questions. He's trying to dig up dirt on people."

"It's not your fault."

"I know."

Daisy smiled. "Maybe the publicity will get people interested in Frederick's paintings! Your mom would be happy about that!"

Victoria waved her hand. "One of the April Brides was just arrested in Central Park for stealing jewelry," she said, her voice a little shaky.

Daisy's eyes widened. "You're kidding! Whew! Did you ever meet her?"

"No," Victoria answered honestly. "I didn't."

"Well you go home, honey, and get yourself some rest. You have the next couple of days off, don't you?"

"Yes, I do."

"Are you going to go see Frederick?"

Victoria nodded. "I suppose it will be good to get away."

"Get going!" Daisy said. "And I don't care what you say, I'm planning you a party!"

When Victoria was out on the street, she picked up her cell phone and called Jeffrey. "Darling," she said. "What a fiasco!"

"I know. I was dying to call you but I knew

you couldn't talk at work. I've been watching the news and I have the *New York Post* in my hands."

"A reporter just stuck a microphone in my face at the front desk and started asking obnoxious questions."

Jeffrey inhaled nervously. "My phone has been ringing off the hook. People I barely know, who saw that Tracy is one of the brides whose dress was stolen. I have to tell them I'm not getting married. They're asking a million questions."

"Jeffrey, I think we should get away for a couple of days. We should leave town."

"Call me when you get home. We'll figure it out."

"Okay. But I want to get away. In case Frederick decides to pay an unexpected visit."

"I thought you said he wouldn't bother us."

"I don't think he will. But all this publicity might stir him up."

"Call me when you get home, darling. Be careful. I'll get you out of there today. I don't want Frederick to come near you."

Victoria smiled. "I'll go home and pack my bags."

48

Up in Connecticut, Ellen and Montgomery Timber were relieved that Tracy was not awake for the *Patrick and Jeannie* show. And they'd hidden their copy of the *New York Post* under the kitchen sink.

Tracy and her friends had been out until four in the morning, playing darts until Jeffrey's face was full of holes. Then they'd all come back to the house and crashed. The four of them had pulled the mattress from the guest room and dragged it down the hall and onto the floor at the foot of Tracy's double bed. Tracy and Catherine slept in Tracy's bed, Claire and Linda slumbered on the mattress. They all wanted to sleep in the same room, like the nights in college when they had stayed up late discussing their lives and attempting to solve each others' problems. Most of the chatfests involved their love lives.

Not much had changed in twelve years.

When they awoke, Catherine volunteered to rustle up a pot of coffee. She knew that it was going to be a tough day for Tracy no matter how many holes they'd pierced in Jeffrey's face.

Down in the kitchen, Tracy's parents were having breakfast. Ellen was perfectly dressed and made-up. She wouldn't be caught dead lounging around in an old bathrobe. As usual, she greeted Catherine with a big smile. "Did you girls have fun last night?"

"We tried. I'm on a caffeine patrol," Catherine answered. "We'll help Tracy ease into the day with a cup of coffee."

"Catherine Heaney, Tracy couldn't have a better friend than you," Montgomery proclaimed. He loved to call people by their first and last names.

"She's my best friend and doesn't deserve to be treated like this by that creep."

"She doesn't," Ellen agreed. "But I'm afraid we have a new problem."

"What?" Catherine asked with alarm.

Ellen opened the cabinet under the kitchen

sink, pulled out the *New York Post,* and held it up. "They printed Tracy's name. And it's been announced on television. Several reporters have already called the house asking for a comment. We've told them the truth—Tracy's asleep."

Catherine's mouth nearly hit the floor. "This is exactly what Tracy was afraid of."

"We know," Tracy's parents said in unison.

Catherine took a deep breath. Then another. Finally she said, "Mr. and Mrs. Timber, the four of us upstairs have been together for twelve years. During that time we've been through thick and thin. I'll break it to Tracy for you. Between us, we'll come up with a graceful way for Tracy to handle this. She'll be fine."

Ellen hugged Catherine. They assembled a tray with a coffeepot filled to the brim with steaming fresh java, four mugs, milk, sugar, and Tracy's favorite croissants, which her father had run out and bought early in the morning.

Catherine put both hands around the tray. The copy of the *New York Post* was under her arm. "Tracy's a big girl," she said as she headed out of the room. "She'll be just fine."

"She's a Timber," Montgomery agreed.

About a minute and a half later, Tracy's bloodcurdling scream echoed through the house. "I'll sue him!" she cried.

Tracy's parents looked at each other.

"That's our daughter," Montgomery said matter-of-factly.

Ellen nodded. "Would you like another cup of coffee, dear?"

49

The Reillys' family room in Summit, New Jersey, was an extension of their large open kitchen. Nora and Luke were relaxing on one of the overstuffed couches, the Sunday newspapers in front of them. They'd watched Regan on the morning show and then turned on a classical music station.

They knew that they'd hear from Regan when she had a chance to call.

"I somehow didn't think this was the way we'd be spending the Sunday morning before Regan's wedding," Nora said. "Watching our daughter on television talking about her stolen wedding dress."

Luke smiled. "Shouldn't you have learned by now to expect the unexpected?" He leaned over and broke off a piece of a crumb bun sitting on a plate on the coffee table.

"I suppose."

The phone rang. When Nora answered, the caller hung up. "I don't know what that was about," she said with a shrug.

"I got a strange call yesterday," Luke said. "Someone asking exactly when Regan was getting married. Something about sending a gift. It didn't sound legit."

The phone rang again. Nora looked at the caller ID. "Unavailable," she said.

Luke grabbed it. "Hello."

"Mr. Reilly?"

"Who's calling?"

"I'm Georgie, the leader of the band that's supposed to sing at your daughter's wedding this Saturday."

"Supposed to sing?" Luke repeated.

"I'm really sorry. But it doesn't look good."

"Doesn't look good?" Luke asked, astonished. "What do you mean?"

"We were playing at a wedding last night when a brawl broke out. The crowd knocked over a lot of our equipment. Most of it has to be replaced. You should see my guitar. It's toast. One of my guys has a broken wrist and another is in jail for throwing punches. I've told him a hundred times he needs to go to anger management classes."

Luke was silent for a moment. Finally he said, "You have a contract."

"What do you want me to do, get out there with a harmonica?"

"Certainly not."

Georgie sighed. "It looks like our band is going to break up for good."

"I'm sure the public won't be as heartbroken as when the Beatles called it a day."

"You don't have to be sarcastic, Mr. Reilly. I'm trying to give you plenty of notice."

"You call six days plenty of notice? Who do you suggest I get to play at my daughter's wedding? A bunch of high school kids?"

"They're probably already booked. Some of the kids' bands out there are not bad."

Luke's voice was icy. "We gave you a deposit."

"I'm sending it right back."

"You'd better."

"I know, I know. I'm returning your check and I'm getting out of the wedding business. Too many problems with emotional people who complain if you don't sing their first song at the exact pace they rehearsed it in the one dance class they took in their lives. It's not my fault if they've got two left feet. Or the bride's mother complains the music is too loud. The young generation wants one kind of music, Uncle Harry wants another. I've had it. I need a rest."

"I hope you get a nice long one," Luke said and hung up the phone. He turned to Nora who looked as dismayed as he did. "As you have gathered, the band canceled. There was a brawl last night."

Nora sighed with frustration. "I tried to convince Regan to hire one of those lovely twelve-piece orchestras, but she and Jack had heard this group at a wedding. She said they really got the crowd going."

"Apparently they have that talent."

"I can't believe it. First Regan's dress is stolen. Now she's without a band. What are we going to do?"

Luke managed a smile. "Your cousins all love to sing. Eamonn never met a microphone he didn't like. Maybe he could fill in."

The very thought of it propelled Nora out of her seat. "God forbid! I'll start making phone calls and see who we can find."

50

On the way out to Joyce's home, Regan gave her parents a call. When her mother answered the phone, she could tell something was wrong.

"What's the matter?" Regan asked Nora.

"Don't you say hello? You're always asking me what's the matter."

"Because I can tell there's a matter."

"So there's a matter."

"I'll ask again then. What's the matter?"

"Your band can't make it to the wedding. There was a big fight last night. Their equipment is destroyed. It's a darn shame."

"What?"

"You heard me, Regan."

Regan turned to Jack. "Our band canceled."

Jack made a face and shrugged.

"The only reason I'm telling you at this

moment," Nora said, "is because if you or Jack have any ideas . . ."

"Jack," Regan said. "Do you know anyone who just happens to be free next Saturday night and can play 'Till There Was You?' "

Jack smiled. "I'll sing it to you, baby."

"Don't worry, Mom," Regan said. "We'll figure it out. Right now there are a few other things we're worried about." First she filled her in on their adventure with Shauna and Tyler.

"I told your father we shouldn't have shut off the TV! Luke, turn it back on."

Then Regan told her mother about Joyce.

Nora was silent for a moment. "Well, that is what really matters, isn't it?"

"That's right, Mom. We're going to her house to pick up her picture. We'll run off copies and tack them up downtown."

"Where's Kit?"

"I called her a few minutes ago. She's just getting up. She slept through the show. We're going to pick her up at the apartment."

"Well, Regan, let me know what happens," Nora said quietly.

"I will."

When Regan and Jack arrived at Joyce's, Cindy had the pictures of Joyce she'd picked out ready to go. One was of her alone. The other was one taken at the pet shop. Joyce had a big smile and was holding a dalmatian puppy in her arms. Cindy had disregarded the pictures of Joyce and Francis that were in the bedroom. By now Cindy couldn't stand the sight of him. If he hadn't left her alone last night, this never would have happened, she thought. And why hadn't he called back?

She'd also rallied all the girls who had been with them the night before. "We're going to hang pictures of Joyce downtown," she told them. "We've got to find her."

They had all agreed to meet outside the club where Joyce was last seen. They'd fan out in all directions and tack her image on every telephone pole, tuck it under the windshield wipers of every parked car.

Brianne had gone to Pauly's apartment after the morning show. "We'll both be there," she said when Cindy called her.

Now, Regan and Jack rang the bell of Joyce's house. Cindy answered and let them both inside. "Here are the photos," she said and told them of the search party she'd organized.

"That's wonderful," Regan said. "What a good idea to meet down at the club." They were standing in the entryway of Joyce's living room. Once again Regan got a feeling for the girl she had never met, a girl who kept a cozy home. "Before we leave I'd like to call Joyce's boyfriend," Regan said.

"He hung up on me before."

"What?"

"I told him what happened and the line went dead."

Regan and Jack looked at each other.

"I looked at the caller ID and called the number back, but it was his friend Marco's cell phone. No one picked up."

"Joyce's purse was found on the street," Jack said. "That's not likely something that her boyfriend would have anything to do with."

"Could he have been in New York City and called her on her cell phone and said to meet him outside the club?" Cindy asked.

"Anything's possible," Jack said. "I'll tell my guys to check her cell phone for received calls. They'll be able to tell if she received a call last night at around the time she disappeared. We'd better get going."

"If you don't mind, I'll ride with you."

"Of course. We're going to stop first at Tiger News and leave a copy of Joyce's picture. Hopefully they'll run it." Regan paused. "Maybe we should try to get in touch with her mother."

"I just tried," Cindy said. "It's impossible to get through right now. She's out in the middle of the ocean somewhere."

"As upsetting as it might be if she finds out about this before you can tell her," Jack said, "I'm sure she'd want us to do everything possible to get Joyce back."

Cindy nodded.

"Hello!" Romeo called from the kitchen. "Hello!"

"Goodbye," Cindy called to him.

"Lazy bums!"

"That's his favorite expression," Cindy told Jack. "I think it applies to Joyce's boyfriend and his buddy who's been making himself at home around here for too long." She glanced around the living room. Knowing that Marco's belongings were hidden behind the couch filled her with disgust.

"All set," she said. They walked out of Joyce's house and shut the door behind them. As Cindy locked the door, she could hear Romeo calling out for Joyce.

51

On the way back to the city from Joyce's, Regan called the producer at Tiger News and told her about Joyce.

"You mean she was at Brianne's bachelorette party last night?" Dana asked, surprise in her voice.

"Joyce's group met up with Brianne's group, at Club Zee, that hot new club on Fourteenth Street. Then Joyce disappeared. Now that her purse has turned up, it appears certain that she must have run into serious trouble."

"This is unbelievable! We'd be happy to run her picture, but I'd like to show it in relation to the April Brides story. I'd like to have Brianne on to talk about their last moments together. I'd like you to be on again as well. We'll have a camera crew cover your search downtown."

"I'm sure Brianne would agree to being

on the show again," Regan said. "I appreciate you bringing attention to this story."

"We have some great footage of you and your handsome fiancé tackling those two thieves in Central Park. It's getting a great response from our viewers."

"How did you get it?" Regan asked.

"There are always tourists in Central Park with video cameras. They caught the 'Dynamic Duo' in action."

Regan smiled. "I'm just glad the Neys got their jewelry back. I'll call Brianne, and we'll see you in a little while."

"Sounds good."

As expected, Brianne was more than pleased to go back on the air. But she sounded serious. "I'm so happy right now about getting married, Regan. I hate the thought of Joyce being in danger."

"I know."

Regan and Jack swung by to pick up Kit. "I knew there was something about that Shauna," she said. "I just wish I had seen you two in action."

"You can see it on tape," Regan muttered.

Regan's cell phone rang again. This time it was Alfred, but he didn't sound as happy.

"I heard from Tracy," he moaned.

"Is she suing you?" Regan asked.

"I'm not sure. She was screaming so much I'm not very clear about it. She hung up on me. Would you call her?"

"What do you want me to say?"

"I don't know, Regan. Think of something."

"Give me her number." Regan jotted it down, ended the conversation with Alfred, and then called the Timber household. Tracy's mother answered.

"Oh, good morning, Regan!" she said, sounding as if she didn't have a care in the world. The old stiff upper lip, Regan thought.

"Hi, Mrs. Timber, may I speak to Tracy?"

"Sure. Tracy's here with her friends having a lovely breakfast."

Regan blinked. I'd have thought Tracy would be suffering from indigestion.

"Regan," Tracy said abruptly as she grabbed the phone from her mother.

"Yes, Tracy. I know what you're upset about. Alfred is very sorry."

"What good does that do me?"

"I understand. But you're just going to have to put a good face on it."

"That's what my friends say. I have to say I'm glad I missed the show this morning."

"We're going back to the studio now."

"What?! Don't you dare mention my name!"

"Tracy!" Regan said impatiently. "We're dealing with something else. A girl is missing and her purse was just found on the street. Brianne Barth was out with her last night. We've gotten a search party together of all the girls who were with her to canvass downtown and distribute her picture. This girl's life could be at stake, and her friends are most anxious to find her before it's too late. That is my concern right now. Not stolen wedding dresses or embarrassing news items. I can assure you your name won't come up in this conversation."

The kick in the pants was just what Tracy needed. Her grip tightened around the phone. She looked out at the three friends who'd been there for her, who would never betray her, the friends who would do anything for her. They wanted to spend the day with Tracy doing whatever she wanted. They'd even joked about driving into the city and stalking Jeffrey, planning his demise. "I've got my three best friends in the world with me, Regan," Tracy said quietly. "We'll drive in and help you."

Regan was shocked. "You will?"

"Yes. I know I'm lucky to have such a great family and wonderful friends. I've been dumped but I'm grateful for what I have. Where can we meet you?"

"There might be cameras there. This story is gaining a lot of attention."

"It's okay. I don't want to sit here and feel sorry for myself. We'll leave right now."

Regan smiled and gave her the address of Club Zee. She could hear a man in the background cheering, "Tracy, my dear, you've got that Timber spirit!"

52

When Joyce woke up again, her mouth was dry and her body felt like rubber. She opened her eyes slowly, afraid of what she might see. I don't believe it, she thought. I really am in this crazy place. She attempted to turn on her side to get a better look at her surroundings but groaned as a sharp stab of pain shot through her right foot.

The old woman was sitting at the tiny kitchen table with her head down.

Joyce felt so weak. A wave of nausea swept over her entire being, and she started to cough.

Hattie jumped up. One of the dogs started to bark and was soon joined by the other three as Hattie hurried over to the couch. She leaned over Joyce, violating the seventeen inches of space that normal human beings like to keep between themselves and anyone who isn't a contender to be their valentine.

"You want some more tea?" Hattie breathed, her scraggly hair perilously close to brushing against Joyce's cheek.

"No. I have to go to the bathroom."

"Okay." She turned to the barking dogs. "Quiet, fellas!"

Joyce pulled back the ratty blanket, swung her legs around, and attempted to stand. But her right foot gave way under her. "Oh!" she cried. "My ankle. It hurts so much. I can't put any weight on it." She lay back down.

Hattie's eyes darted about. "Do you want me to help you to the bathroom?"

"No!" Joyce said, not wanting to be touched, then quickly added, "Thank you. I'm all right. I can wait." Will I ever get out of here? she wondered.

"I'll go get us some breakfast. And a bandage for your foot. You must have hurt it when you fell down the steps." Hattie hurried for the door and reached for an old coat that was hanging on a lone hook. "I'm making us a nice stew for supper tonight. My friend Edie and I used to have dinner together every Sunday night. Since she died I didn't have anyone to eat with. Now I have you. You like jelly donuts?"

Joyce felt herself falling back asleep. "Can you make a phone call for me?"

Hattie didn't answer. When she closed the door, the dog in the bedroom started to bark and throw himself against the door.

The four little dogs all jumped up on the couch and cuddled with Joyce.

They're afraid, she thought, as the barking and thumping continued—just like I am. They know that the mutt behind that door is vicious. I have to get out of here.

But she was so groggy she couldn't move. She put her head down and drifted off.

53

Regan called Alfred and told him that Tracy had turned over a new leaf.

"So she's not going to sue me?"

"We didn't discuss that. She's coming down to help us look for Joyce."

"That's wonderful. We'd love to help you out hanging those posters and whatever, but it's so busy here! The phone is ringing off the hook with reporters wanting the scoop, and at the same time we're trying to hunt down fabric for both your dress and Brianne's."

"You don't have fabric?" Regan asked. "I thought you said you were already working on the gowns."

"We don't have enough fabric in the salon, Regan! The fabric that was supposed to be expressed yesterday from one of our suppliers didn't arrive this morning. It is Sunday you know."

"Okay, Alfred," Regan interrupted. "I have to go. Brianne and I are going back on the *Patrick and Jeannie* show. Because your April Brides are now the talk of the town, the producer is willing to cover the story of the missing girl who was out with Brianne last night."

"Do you think my presence on the show could be helpful in some way?"

"I thought you were busy," Regan said flatly.

"We are, but . . ."

"Alfred, this segment is about trying to find Joyce. It's not about the stolen dresses."

"I understand." Alfred paused. "It's just that so many reporters seem to be so very interested in what I have to say. They are all asking if Charisse and I had any idea that Shauna was a crook, and they what to know what I think about the rest of my April Brides."

"And what are you telling them?"

"Charisse and I have prepared a statement."

Regan rolled her eyes. "I'm all ears."

Alfred cleared his throat. "In our eyes, every bride is beautiful. We regret that one of our April Brides turned out to be someone who we would never want to darken the doors of our lovely salon. But we would stake our lives on the integrity of the other four."

"Gee thanks," Regan muttered.

"—we love them dearly and are sure that they will feel like princesses on their wedding days, bedecked in one of our gorgeous gowns."

"I'm all choked up, Alfred."

"Don't you think it's all right?"

"It's fine. Four of your April Brides are accounted for. Have you heard from Victoria? She didn't want her name in the paper, either."

"No, I haven't," Alfred answered meekly.

"Okay. I'll talk to you later."

In the greenroom at the studio, Regan, Jack, Cindy, and Kit were greeted by the same young assistant who'd been there earlier. "Thanks for coming back," he said, looking at Regan and Jack with admiration. "We have the most awesome video of you tackling those two weasels. You wouldn't believe all the phone calls we're getting about this story."

"Thanks to your show we caught them," Regan said and handed him Joyce's picture. "Hopefully with your help we'll find her."

The assistant nodded enthusiastically. "We'll put her picture right up there on-screen. My producer also wanted to know if you'd like us to make up the flyers. If you just tell us what you'd like them to say, we can do it right now."

"That'd be great. Thank you," Regan answered, as she pulled a piece of paper out of her notebook in her purse. She wrote out the information, gave it to him, and he hurried out the door.

Jack handed her a cup of coffee.

"Thanks." Something tells me I'm going to be drinking a lot of this today, she thought.

"I'm so grateful they're willing to talk about Joyce," Cindy said anxiously, looking up at the television screen on the wall. "So many people go missing who never get any publicity."

"We are lucky," Regan agreed. "And all it takes is one person watching the show who saw something . . ."

When Brianne and Pauly arrived a few minutes later, they were all immediately ushered into the studio. Regan and Brianne joined Patrick and Jeannie in the same area of the studio where they'd had their earlier

chat. The two seats Alfred and Charisse oc-
cupied had been removed.

Like musical chairs, Regan thought.

This time the interview had a different
tone. Jeannie introduced the segment, re-
capping the whole story for the audience.
They showed a clip of the earlier interview,
then they replayed the video of Regan tackling one of the April Brides. "Thanks to one
of our viewers who called in this morning after our interview with Regan and Brianne,
she was caught," Jeannie said with a smile.
"Regan and Brianne have joined us again,
but unfortunately it's because of another
twist in the story of these brides." She
turned to Patrick who explained to the audience Brianne's connection to the missing
Joyce.

"The fact that she didn't make it home
last night was a worry to her friends. But
when her purse was found this morning on
a street downtown, the situation became
much more serious." Patrick sighed and
turned to Brianne. "When did you last see
Joyce?"

"We were all at Club Zee downtown.
Joyce got up from the table, presumably to
go to the ladies' room. It was about 11

o'clock. She hadn't been there that long. The deejay had just played Julio Iglesias's 'To All the Girls I've Loved Before.' We all sang along and then started joking around about loser ex-boyfriends."

Jeannie made a face. "Now there's a topic we could spend hours on."

Patrick looked at her. "Heyyyy—I feel as if I should defend the guys out there in our viewing audience."

"It was just in fun," Brianne explained. "It was my bachelorette party. I had finally found the right one to marry, my wonderful Pauly Sanders, and my friends were teasing me about a couple guys I'd gone out with." Brianne smiled. "Listen, I know Pauly has had some horrible relationships. He told me about every one of them in great detail. He said he never went out with anyone who wasn't a loser until he met me."

In the corner of the studio, Pauly almost fainted.

"Do you think this discussion about bad relationships might have upset Joyce?" Patrick asked.

"I don't know," Brianne said. "She got up from the table and that was the last any of us saw of her."

They showed Joyce's smiling face on the screen. She looked so happy holding the black-and-white puppy.

Jeannie looked at Regan. "We understand that Joyce's boyfriend is out of town. He must be upset."

"Apparently so," Regan said evasively.

"And you have a search party that's meeting down at Club Zee."

"Right after this interview, we're going straight there. We'll put up Joyce's picture all over the neighborhood. We'll talk to people and ask if anyone saw Joyce or noticed anything unusual last night. I can't stress enough that we need help in finding her. People should call in with any information they have, no matter how insignificant it seems."

"Okay, then," Jeannie said. She turned to the camera. "If anyone in the New York area would like to join the search party, I'm sure you'd be most welcome. And if you do have any information, please call this number. . . ."

When the interview was over, Regan and Brianne walked over to rejoin the rest of their group.

"Where did Pauly go?" Brianne asked.

"He said he'd meet you down in the lobby," Jack answered. "He was sweating and said he needed some air."

Brianne was out the door in a shot.

"Cindy, you don't look so well either," Regan said.

Cindy shook her head. "I'm just thinking about Joyce. I'm not surprised if talk of loser ex-boyfriends upset Joyce. Her problem is that she is still with someone who should be her ex. And he hasn't even had the decency to call me back. Where could he be? I'm beginning to think maybe he did have something to do with this."

"We'll find out," Regan assured her.

"They're checking Joyce's cell phone records," Jack told Cindy. "But even if he isn't involved, he doesn't sound like such a swell guy."

"He's not. He let his unemployed friend park himself on Joyce's couch for the last three months. When we get Joyce back . . ." Cindy's mouth started to tremble, "when we get Joyce back, I'm going to help her throw both of those losers' belongings out into the street."

54

A tired and bored Phoebe Muller was baby-sitting at her next-door neighbor's apart-ment on the Upper East Side of Manhattan. Sixteen years old, she'd been out late with a bunch of kids the night before and was grateful that the rambunctious two-year-old in her care had just gone down for a nap.

Settling on the couch, she pulled her school books out of her all-purpose bag. Al-ways a multitasker, she then picked up the remote control and flicked on the television. Phoebe wanted to watch that new weekend cable show while she did her homework. Patrick and Jeannie were cool.

As she watched the segment about the missing Joyce, she started to come to life. Her eyes widened and her jaw dropped. Like . . . oh, my God! she thought. Could it be?

Last night her group had gone to the

movies and then to a diner. They'd walked past the popular Club Zee and looked longingly at the people being admitted.

"We've got to get some fake IDs, man," Dirk had said as they ambled along. "I don't want to wait another five years to go to Club Zee!" A few blocks later, on a small side street, he had spotted a little black purse on the ground and picked it up. He fished out the eighty dollars cash, stuck it in his pocket, then looked at the driver's license inside.

"Thanks, Joyce," he'd said, before dropping the license back inside.

"We should turn the purse and money in to the police," Phoebe had said.

"Goody Two-shoes," Dirk had said derisively, throwing the purse at one of his friends, and they'd run down the street playing catch with it. Several blocks later, Dirk tossed the small black bag on the ground between two cars.

Phoebe knew there was no fighting with Dirk. And she didn't want to give the purse to the police with the money gone. She hoped Joyce would somehow get the purse back anyway.

But now someone named Joyce was

missing. It must be the same person, Phoebe thought, and it might help the police if they knew where her purse had been before Dirk moved it. Phoebe realized she couldn't call the police from her cell phone or from the Darbers' phone. They'd be able to trace the call easily, and she didn't want to give her name. The baby was asleep, so she couldn't go out and use a pay phone.

Maybe I should just forget it, she thought. Chances are it won't make a difference. But as she tried to concentrate on her homework, Phoebe couldn't stop thinking about the missing Joyce.

55

Hattie hurried down her little, tree-lined street, turned the corner, and darted into a bakery where she purchased jelly donuts and orange juice. Then she went into the small pharmacy where she'd been a customer forever.

Jay Stone, the handsome young owner, peered down from his pharmacist's perch. He was working on a Sunday because one of his employees was on vacation. He was also ambitious and prided himself on getting to know his customers and their needs. "Good morning, Hattie," he called out, surprised that she was in again. She'd refilled her prescriptions the day before.

"Morning," she said, giving a quick wave with her gnarled hand. Her eyes were darting around as they usually were.

"I don't see your dogs outside," Jay said conversationally. He got a kick out of Hattie.

She was one of those neighborhood characters who had been around for the whole ten years he'd worked in the store. He actually got a kick out of a lot of people. Being in the business of dispensing meds, he'd seen all kinds. Hattie was the type who came into the store and never stopped talking until she was out the door. It was as if a dam had burst. Clearly she was lonely and grabbed the chance for conversation whenever she could. Even if it was one-sided.

"I left my dogs home."

"I don't think I've ever seen you in here without at least a couple of them sitting outside waiting."

Hattie shrugged.

"Is Mugsy staying out of trouble?"

"Yes, he is!" Hattie answered with an edge to her voice he had never heard before.

Jay knew that Hattie's best friend had recently died and left Hattie with her mixed-breed mutt who had a bad temper. Residents in the area were terrified when Hattie took him out for a walk. Hattie had had to restrain him numerous times when he charged at other dogs or people who had the nerve to walk on the same sidewalk he did. In Jay's opinion, Hattie was the last person on earth who should have inherited such an aggressive animal. She was a little off and didn't have the strength to handle him.

"You should let me find a nice home for Mugsy," Jay offered. "A place with a fenced-in backyard where he can run around. Those kind of dogs need exercise."

"I can't do that! I promised Edie I'd take good care of him. And I am. Mugsy has the bedroom to himself."

"Lucky Mugsy."

"He and the other dogs still don't get along so good. But they'll get used to each other."

Jay raised his eyebrows. "What can I do for you today, Hattie?"

"I need one of them Ace bandages."

"Right there at the end of the aisle."

Hattie stared at the display. She pulled one off the rack. "This looks all right," she muttered.

"What do you need it for?" Jay asked.

"Nothing," Hattie answered.

She'll probably wrap it around one of the dogs, Jay thought, watching as she walked over and picked up a pair of crutches that were hanging on the wall. She looked at the price tag and put them back. No matter how hard she tries, the dogs can't use those, he thought.

A moment later she tossed an ankle support bandage onto the counter.

"Anything else?" he asked.

"Nope."

He rang it up. "It looks like a nice day. Are you taking your little guys up to Central Park? I know you like to do that on Sundays."

Hattie handed over her money. "I have to. They get mad at me if I don't. I promised them."

Jay counted out the change into her hand. "Have fun today, Hattie. And think about what I said to you—"

But she was out the door before he could finish.

What's up with her today? he wondered as he went back to his perch. She's not acting herself at all. He smiled. Not that that's such a bad thing . . .

———◆———

"Welcome to Nebraska," Marco read aloud as they sped along the highway. "You think the guy who made that sign really cares whether we feel welcome?" He laughed, knowing Francis wouldn't bother to answer. "By my calculations, we're halfway to Vegas."

"With the way you drive, I'm surprised we're not there already," Francis answered. "Let's stop at that gas station ahead. I want to get a soda and see if they have anything to eat."

"A pit stop is in order," Marco agreed, getting into the right lane. At the station he pulled up to the pumps. "I'll fill up."

"Want anything?" Francis asked.

"Surprise me," Marco answered.

Francis used the bathroom, then headed inside the minimart. Newspapers were lined up on the floor inside the front door. The *New York Post* was among them.

Francis gasped at the headlines. He picked up a copy, hurried through the store collecting sodas and hot dogs, paid the cashier, and raced back to the car. "Look at this!" he hissed. "It's made the national news. We're never going to sell those dresses."

Marco waved his hand at him. "I just talked to my buddy in Vegas. He's already been down at the courthouse where all those couples in love line up to get their marriage licenses. Owners of all the wedding chapels compete with each other for the lovebirds' business on the steps of that courthouse. I hear that can get nasty. But not too many people there are selling designer gowns at great prices. My buddy says if they're really nice we'll sell them in about five minutes. He's already got people interested. He told me to get there as fast as possible. No one has a prolonged engagement in Vegas." Marco laughed. "Marriages happen so fast they even have drive-through wedding chapels!"

Francis bit into his hot dog. "Let me use your cell phone. I want to check my messages and see if Joyce called."

Marco handed it over. Francis quickly

pushed in his number, then his secret code, and waited. The only message was from his mother.

"Francis! Call me! I just saw on the television that Joyce is missing! What's wrong with you? Why didn't you let me know? *Where are you?*"

In the fight-or-flight state that the human body produces in times of extreme stress, Francis opted for flight. He opened the door, jumped out, and started to run. But with his injured leg, he didn't get very far. He turned around and headed back to the car.

"I guess it was a bad message," Marco said as Francis fastened his seat belt.

"My mother heard that Joyce was missing. It's on television!"

"What? Already?"

"Yes! Already!"

Marco sped out of the gas station. Sweat broke out on his forehead. He started to curse.

"What?" Francis asked, bewildered.

"I left a lot of my stuff at her house."

"I'll send it to you."

"If the cops start snooping around—"

"Marco, you don't have any drugs in your bag there do you? Because if you do, that could really be trouble. I told you I don't want to get involved with that—"

"No!" Marco snapped impatiently. "But when you were sleeping before, I was doing a lot of thinking. It occurred to me that I might have left those designers' keys back at Joyce's house."

"You didn't get rid of them?"

"No, I didn't get rid of them! I was going to. But I didn't know we were going to take a road trip! And I also didn't plan on Joyce being missing!"

"It looks like you made the one stupid mistake that Regan Reilly was talking about on television."

"This is your fault!" Marco yelled. "If we get in trouble it's because of Joyce."

Francis stared straight ahead as they crossed the state of Nebraska.

57

When Victoria was safely back in her apartment, she called Jeffrey.

"Are you all right?" he asked solicitiously.

"Yes, sweetie. But I want to get out of here."

"I know. I'll come pick you up."

"I need some time to get ready."

"I can't wait to see you again—I'm leaving now. As soon as you're packed, we'll drive out to the country."

Victoria smiled. "Just be careful. I have the feeling that everyone is watching."

Twenty minutes later Jeffrey was hurrying up the first flight of steps inside Victoria's building. He was reminded of a quote by Guy de Maupassant, who wrote: "The best part of love is walking up the stairs." How true, he thought. With Victoria it is so true.

He rang the bell and waited while Victoria unlocked all the locks. Finally she opened the door. The apartment was a mess. Victoria grabbed his hand, pulled him inside, and melted into his arms. When they finally let go of each other, Jeffrey looked around.

He smiled and made a joke. "You didn't have to clean up because I was coming over."

"You should see the bedroom," she answered gaily. "But you really shouldn't! Whenever I pack I have a hard time deciding what to bring. I end up throwing things all over!"

When she disappeared into her boudoir, Jeffrey sat on the couch. He felt restless. He didn't want to turn on the television in case there were more stories about the wedding dresses. And he didn't like to sit in such an untidy room. He looked around and noticed that dirty dishes were piled in the sink. A thought occurred to him. He stood and walked to the doorway toward the tiny bedroom. "Victoria, have you talked to your parents about...?" he said as he pushed open the door.

Victoria turned to him and gasped. "I told you I'd be right out, honey."

Jeffrey looked down at the floor, then

back up at Victoria. Nervously, he asked, "What are you doing with that?"

Victoria giggled. "Jeffrey, I told you I love costume parties!"

As she leaned over to give him a kiss, Jeffrey felt a pit growing in his stomach. A very large pit.

58

Outside Club Zee, a crowd of about fifty people had gathered. Many of them had seen the story about Joyce on Patrick and Jeannie's show.

"When I saw the picture of Joyce hugging that little dog, I knew I wanted to help," one woman said as she snuggled with her little Yorkshire terrier. "Dog lovers are kindred spirits."

Also in the crowd was the group Joyce had been with the night before and many of her customers from the pet store. Television cameras from several of the local stations as well as the cable news stations were there to cover the continuing story. As Regan was about to address the group, the door of the club opened. A husky man with a shaved head, tattooed arms, and rings dangling from his nose, ears, and lips emerged. He had on jeans and a tight black shirt.

"Hello, everyone. My name is Wally. I own Club Zee. Please come inside and use my place as your base of operations. I feel terrible that Joyce disappeared from here. I can't understand why she wasn't having a good time. Come on in." He turned and started to go back inside.

"What about our dogs?" one of the crowd called out.

"They're welcome, too," Wally replied with a wave of his hand.

Once inside, Regan and Jack thanked him.

"No problem," he answered gruffly. "The place is yours. But I'll have to open the doors at ten tonight for my customers." He went behind the bar and turned on the big-screen television.

Regan and Jack looked at each other. They both had the same thought. If they were still here at ten tonight, things would be very bleak.

Jack's cell phone rang. "It's the office," he said. While Jack went off to take the call, Regan got up on a chair to address the crowd.

"Thank you all for coming," she began. "In missing persons cases, the first twenty-four hours are crucial. I have maps of downtown that we've divided into six sections. So we'll form six different groups that will fan out from here. Each group should cover the streets marked off on the map I give them. Put the flyers up everywhere. Don't be afraid to talk to people. Ask them if they saw Joyce or anything out of the ordinary. Call my cell phone or the police if you have anything urgent to report."

"You can call here, too," Wally grunted.

"You heard that," Regan told the volunteers. "You can call here. Please be careful. Don't put yourself in danger. Call 911 if you have to. Okay, folks. We'll meet back here at three o'clock. That's in two hours. Good luck. Let's form the first group."

As the groups drifted out the door, Jack returned to Regan's side. "They checked Joyce's phone records and listened to her messages. Her cell phone showed no calls made or received at around the time she disappeared. Her boyfriend called earlier last night and told her to call him on his friend's phone because his battery had died."

"But he hasn't called Cindy back since she talked to him this morning."

"He might have called the house. We don't know. They've been trying his friend's number, but no one is picking up."

Tracy Timber hurried over to them. "My friends and I just got here, Regan. We're ready to go."

Regan smiled. "Thanks, Tracy."

Cindy was nearby, handing out the flyers and assigning newcomers to the last group. Tracy took a stack and turned to her buddies. With determination on their faces, the sorority sisters headed out the door.

Jack put his hand on Regan's shoulder. "Regan, I have to run over to the office. The police chief from Philadelphia is in town unexpectedly. We have a couple things to go over."

"Go ahead, Jack. Kit and I will be walking around together. I have my cell phone."

Jack leaned down and kissed Regan good-bye. "Be careful. I'll be back as soon as I can."

After he left, Regan and Kit started out the door. A young man was hurrying down the street toward them. He was walking an Irish setter. "Excuse me, I just saw you on television. My name is Tom Belfiore. I'm the guy who found Joyce's purse this morning. I'd like to help."

"You already have," Regan told him. "If it weren't for you, we wouldn't be doing this now." She smiled at him. "I'd like to take a look at the location where you found the purse. Why don't we start there?"

Tom nodded. "It's this way," he said. The three of them fell into step as they headed down the sidewalk.

It was in the opposite direction from Hattie's apartment.

Hattie came bursting back into the small apartment. The dog in the bedroom, who had quieted down, resumed his barking and thumping against the wall. Within seconds all the dogs started barking again. Joyce was terrified.

"Hello," Hattie said. "Quiet, fellas! Joyce, I got you a lovely donut and some fresh juice." She set the bag down on the coffee table.

"Thank you. I think I'd like to go home."

"Not yet!" Hattie cried. "You have to stay for Sunday dinner. I'm making stew. It's delicious." She turned to the barking dogs. "I said quiet or we don't go to Central Park!"

"I'd love to go to Central Park," Joyce said hopefully.

"You can't walk around with that foot of yours," Hattie said dismissively as she pulled the donuts out of the bag and opened up the carton of OJ. "I bought you an Ace bandage but I'll help you with it later. Now eat! I'll be back soon. First I have to walk my doggie that's in the bedroom. He's what you call antisocial. But he'll guard you while I'm gone with the others."

"What?" Joyce asked. She watched in dismay as Hattie scooped up the four little dogs, put them in the bathroom, shut the door, then opened the door to the bedroom.

"Hello, lovey!" Hattie cried. "Time for your walk." She led a ferocious-looking mutt from the bedroom.

Oh dear God, Joyce thought. At least it's on a leash.

Hattie and "lovey" went out the door and were back in two minutes.

As Hattie led him past the couch, the dog stared hatefully at Joyce.

"There you go, Mugsy," Hattie said as she shut him in the bedroom. "You're so lucky. You have a bedroom all to yourself." Hattie then rescued the other dogs from the bathroom, put them on their leashes, and took them outside.

Joyce sat up. Thank God! If I move fast, I can crawl out of here. Or maybe if I start screaming someone will hear me.

But a moment later Hattie was back. "Okay, the fellas are waiting for me outside. I'm sorry I'm so busy with the dogs, but when I get back we'll have a nice dinner and talk. I want to hear all about you."

"Why don't we go to my place?" Joyce suggested. "I can make you dinner."

"*I told you I made beef stew!* It's Edie's recipe. She wants us to have it!" With an annoyed sigh, Hattie scurried back to the bedroom and brought Mugsy back out. "Mugsy here guards my apartment when I'm gone. He'll take good care of you. We both miss Edie very much."

"You're going to leave him out?" Joyce asked, fear gripping her throat.

"I'll tie him up by the front door."

"Please let me leave," Joyce pleaded, her drowsy state a distant memory. Every nerve in her body was on full alert.

"You're irritating me!" Hattie cried, coming toward her. She leaned over Joyce. "All I want to do is take care of you, and you won't let me. I don't like that."

"I'm sorry," Joyce said. "I'm nervous around certain dogs. Why don't you take him with you?"

"He's not so well-behaved when he goes

out. But you couldn't ask for a better watch-dog."

"Please put him in the bedroom," Joyce begged.

"What good is he going to do in the bed-room if someone breaks in here? Can you tell me that? Don't worry. He's tied up. He won't hurt you. He'll protect you!" Hattie tied the dog's leash to the leg of a heavy chair by the door. A leash that looked like it could almost reach the couch. "Get some rest, you two."

"Hattie, please!" Joyce begged.

But she was out the door.

The room was silent.

Joyce glanced over at Mugsy, afraid to make eye contact. He didn't look too thrilled with the plans either. She lay back down, afraid to move a muscle. Maybe if I stay still he'll forget that I'm here.

She was too afraid to scream for help.

60

Jack hated leaving Regan. He had an uncomfortable feeling and wanted to get back
to her as quickly as possible. After his meeting with the police chief from Philadelphia,
he stopped by his office briefly to check in.

One of his detectives was poring over the
surveillance tape from the previous day's
bank robbery. "Take a look at this, boss," he
said to Jack as he rewound the tape and
played it again.

The bank robber came into the bank,
closed his umbrella, and headed for a teller.
His face was pretty well covered by his rain
gear, beard, mustache, and glasses. He
handed the teller the note and then glanced
around. He reached back and massaged his
neck quickly, then rested his gloved right
hand on his right cheek, with his index finger pointing up. Then he let his hand drop.
It all took just a few seconds.

"I've been studying all the tapes," the detective said. "This little mannerism is on all of them."

"No surprise The Drip's got tension in his neck," Jack said. "Anything new on Dan's Discount Den or the stolen credit card?"

"We're going over the card owner's charges for the last couple of months, checking out where he's been. Unfortunately he's a big spender. He's been everywhere with that card. Any number of sales clerks have had their hands on it."

"Okay, I'm heading back to Club Zee."

"Nothing new on the missing girl?"

"Regan hasn't contacted me, so I guess not."

"Those situations usually don't end up so well."

"I know," Jack said somberly as he strode out the door.

61

Joyce felt as if she had been lying there in the dark apartment for an eternity. Perspiration had broken out all over her body. I shouldn't be so terrifed, she thought. But even though Mugsy was tied up and had stretched out on the floor, his very presence was threatening. Joyce couldn't believe that she was actually hoping that crazy Hattie would return home soon.

I've never felt afraid around animals, Joyce thought. Taking care of them is what makes me happy. But this dog is different. He scares me to death. He looks as if he could tear me apart in about ten seconds.

Suddenly Joyce felt a sneeze coming on. She tried to stifle it but that only made the eruption stronger and louder. Her whole body shuddered as she sneezed three times.

Mugsy stood up and glared at her.

Oh, no, she thought.

He started walking toward the coffee table.

His leash is too long, she thought desperately. He is going to reach me. But he was staring at the donuts, not at Joyce. He was just a few feet away from the couch when his leash wouldn't allow him to go any farther.

He started snarling.

Maybe he's hungry, she thought. Hattie said he hadn't been eating. She leaned over, picked up a donut, and tossed it in his direction. "Here, Mugsy," she said in her friendliest tone.

But it hit him in the face.

The dog went berserk.

He charged toward her, his whole body in a frenzy. Growling and barking, he bared his killer teeth. They were perilously close to the end of the couch.

Joyce swung her legs around so she could get off the couch and attempt to make her way over to the safety of the bathroom. I've got to get away from him! she thought frantically. But her every movement enraged him even more.

A wave of nausea swept over Joyce, and the room started to spin.

She pushed herself up on one foot and started hopping, her eye on the bathroom door several feet away.

Behind her, Mugsy was barking furiously, straining his leash as he tried to charge in her direction.

Joyce felt as though she was going to be sick. She was passing the kitchen counter when she heard the most terrifying sound of her life. The leash snapped. Out of the corner of her eye, she saw Mugsy bolting toward her. With a strength she never knew she possessed, she threw herself in the direction of the sink, pushed herself up onto the counter, stood on her left foot, and grabbed the handle of the kitchen cabinet. Her whole body was trembling.

Mugsy charged over and tried to throw his front paws onto the counter. But they weren't long enough to reach, and he slipped down. He jumped up again, then started running around in circles. He threw himself again and again up against the counter, trying to reach Joyce, his mouth of killer teeth just inches from her left foot.

If I slip, Joyce thought desperately as she pressed herself as far as she could against the cabinet, I'm going to die.

And I don't know how long I can stand here on one foot.

As tears slid down her cheeks, she started to pray.

———◆———

62

The search parties had all returned to Club Zee by three o'clock. Everyone reported the same thing. There were no leads. Several people had called the club to say they had seen Joyce walk out the door the night before but didn't know which way she'd gone.

Cindy was sitting in the corner, crying. Her friends were trying to console her.

"But it's my fault," she kept repeating.

Jack had rejoined Regan and was standing at her side.

"What do we do now, Regan?" Tracy called out.

"More of the same, Tracy. There might be someone out there who is just waking up and coming out of their apartment for the first time today. We've got to go back out and talk to more people. We have to stress to everyone that they should report anything unusual, no matter how insignificant it seems."

The image of smiling Joyce holding the black-and-white puppy flashed on the television screen behind Regan.

Outside the club, Jay Stone was walking past. The pharmacy closed early on Sundays. He stopped at the door of the club, paused, then resumed walking. It's silly, he thought. It's not enough to go on . . .

Joyce's life was passing before her eyes. Her left leg was about to give way. She couldn't kneel down and she couldn't put any weight on her right foot.

And the dog wasn't giving up. He was barking incessantly, and seemed more determined than ever to get himself up on the counter. Joyce glanced down at the pot of stew on the stove. If I could just push that over and hit him with it . . .

Jay walked a couple more blocks, then turned around. I'll just do it, he thought. It might be crazy, but that girl, Tracy, who came into his pharmacy kept stressing to him the importance of reporting anything unusual.

Joyce tried to scream but her voice was paralyzed. She took a deep breath, held onto the cabinet, crouched down, grabbed the handle of the enormous metal pot, and flung it toward the dog. Lukewarm liquid spewed all over the counter and all over the dog. The pot bounced off Mugsy and landed upside down on the floor.

The pot could now serve as a launching pad for the crazed animal to hop up on to reach her. Except it was slippery.

"Let's all go back out," Regan said. "We'll meet back here at—"

"Excuse me!" a male voice called from the doorway. Everyone fell silent as he made his way over to Regan. She looked at him and waited.

"My name is Jay Stone and I own the pharmacy a couple blocks from here. This girl here with the clipboard," he said, point-

ing at Tracy, "came into my pharmacy today. She kept asking if anything at all had
struck me as odd lately, anything at all that
had happened around the neighborhood. I
said no. But since she came back three
times, I thought I should come in and mention something that happened this morning.
It probably means nothing—"

"What is it?" Regan asked quickly.

"One of my customers is an eccentric
older woman who has five dogs, including a
dog she inherited from her friend who died
recently. Her friend's dog is very dangerous.
Anyway, today she came in and bought an
Ace bandage and then looked over a pair
of crutches. She obviously doesn't need
crutches so it got me to wondering. She's a
little eccentric to start with, but today she
really seemed different. When Tracy showed
me the picture of Joyce holding the dalmatian, it made me think of this woman again.
She has a dalmatian. Then this afternoon I
saw her go up the block with her four dogs.
On Sundays, she brings them to Central
Park but she always leaves her friend's dog
home because he is so hard to handle. It
occurred to me that if Joyce is in some way

injured and ended up in her apartment alone, that dog could be dangerous."

"Regan!" Wally called out.

Regan turned. "Yes?"

"A young girl just called here with an anonymous tip. Said she was with a group who found a purse last night belonging to a woman named Joyce. One of her friends took the money and ditched it on the street. She's not sure if it's the same Joyce."

"Where did she find it?" Regan asked quickly.

"Around the corner from here. On Maple, the little tree-lined street. She said they found it halfway down the block on the sidewalk. Next to a set of stairs."

Jay grabbed Regan's arm. "My customer lives on Maple."

As Cindy screamed, Regan tried to remain calm. "If she's trapped in there with the dog, we're going to need something to distract him."

"I'll grab a couple of steaks from the kitchen," Wally yelled. "I'll be right behind you."

Regan, Jack, Tom, and Jay raced out the door.

Followed by the entire search party.

"It's around the corner to the right," Jay instructed.

They all ran to the corner, turned right, ran down the block to Maple, and turned right again.

"She lives at number 10!" Jay shouted.

"Here it is," Regan cried. She and Jack raced up the steps of the building, Jay beside them. Jay quickly scanned the names next to the doorbells. "She's in the basement apartment." He started buzzing while Regan and Jack raced down the steps, turned, and hurried down more steps to Hattie's apartment.

Inside, when Joyce heard the buzzer, she was finally able to scream.

"Help me!" she sobbed. *"I'm going to die!"*

Joyce's left shoe was drenched, and she felt herself starting to slip. Mugsy was baring his fangs as he kept trying to jump on the slippery pot and hoist himself onto the counter. But Joyce had no strength left. Her left leg was giving way under her.

"She's in there!" Cindy screamed. "Break down the door!"

The sound of the dog's frenzied barking and growling was terrifying.

Jack, Regan, Tom, and Jay started to kick the warped wooden door. Finally, the wood started to snap. Jack and Tom threw their weight against it, and the door broke open.

Regan's heart stopped when she saw Joyce starting to slip off the counter.

Jack fired a shot in the air.

The dog turned toward them.

Jack fired again as Regan grabbed one of the steaks from Wally and threw it toward the bathroom. It landed inside the door. The dog turned his head in the direction of the steak.

"Oh my God!" Regan cried as Joyce started to fall.

Jack flung the other steak into the bathroom. It landed in the tub. The dog dove after it. With his gun drawn, Jack rushed over and slammed the bathroom door shut, as Joyce fell into Tom Belfiore's arms.

63

After Joyce stopped crying, she refused to go to the hospital. She insisted on going back to Club Zee to be with everyone who had searched for her.

"And I left there last night without saying good-bye," she said. "It's only right that I explain what happened."

"Allow me to carry you back," Tom said gently.

Joyce smiled up at him and nodded. He was so attentive and kind, she could barely speak. And good-looking, too! He scooped her up once again, and with his dog accompanying them, they sauntered back to Club Zee.

The television cameras were rolling.

At the club, Wally broke out the champagne. "Joyce, I don't want you to ever again leave my place unhappy."

They all raised their glasses to toast Joyce's safe return.

"Thank you, everyone," she said. "I never thought I'd make it out of there alive. I owe a debt of gratitude to each and every one of you."

Tom hovered over her protectively.

On the television behind the bar, a live shot of Victoria Beardsley coming out of her apartment building filled the screen.

"The missing April Bride!" Regan said, surprise in her voice. "No one's heard from her today."

A reporter called out to Victoria. "We'd like to ask you a few questions."

Victoria looked at the camera with a deer-caught-in-the-headlights expression. She started gesturing nervously.

The man who had followed her out of the building scurried out of camera range.

"That's Jeffrey!" Tracy screamed as something in Jack's eyes registered recognition and then disbelief.

"It couldn't be," Jack muttered as he stared at Victoria.

"Is he with her? Where does she live, Regan?" Tracy screamed. "Where? I've got to go find them!"

"I'll pull the car around," Catherine, her ever-faithful friend, cried.

"And, Regan," Jack said quickly as he continued to stare at the screen. "Do you know where she works?"

Regan looked from one to the other. "She lives on the Upper West Side and she works at the Queen's Court Hotel in Midtown." She knew why Tracy was reacting the way she was. But why was Jack so interested? He pulled out his cell phone and dialed his office.

"Where on the Upper West Side?" Tracy asked Regan. "I want her address."

Kit blurted it out.

Tracy turned to go.

"Wait just a minute!" Jack said to her. "I think I'm going to ride up there as well. You can come with me."

"What about my friends?"

"I can fit five people. The others will have to follow us."

"Jack, what's going on?" Regan asked as Jack finished his call.

Jack leaned over and whispered in Regan's ear. "That little lady up there," Jack said, pointing up at the frozen picture of Victoria on the screen, her index finger pointing upward as it rested on her cheek, "works at a hotel where the guy who owns the stolen credit card stayed. A receipt used by the thief of that stolen credit card was found on the floor of the bank that was robbed yesterday."

Regan's eyes widened. "You don't think . . . ?"

"I don't know, Regan."

"Kit and I are going with you."

Tracy, Kit, and Catherine jumped in the back of Jack's car. Regan and Jack were in the front. Claire and Linda were in a car right behind them.

"That idiot!" Tracy cried. "He must have met her at Alfred and Charisse's salon!"

Wait till Alfred hears this, Regan thought. And wait till he hears that he might have vouched for the integrity of someone who's been robbing banks for the past three months.

Two of his April Brides are criminals. And the third is in hysterics in the backseat.

Jack had ordered a police car to keep watch on Victoria's block. She had rushed back inside her apartment building after blowing off the reporter. Armed with her description, they were to contact Jack immediately if she came back out.

Now as they sped up the West Side Highway, Jack's mind was racing. If Victoria was the bank robber, she did a great job of passing herself off as a man. And if indeed she had stolen Tracy's fiancé, she knew how to make good use of her feminine wiles. But I can't prove anything, he thought. Not yet. He wasn't sure what he was going to do.

Of course, he hadn't revealed his suspicions to Tracy and her friends.

The car exited the highway at Seventy-second Street, headed over to Broadway, and turned left. When they got to Victoria's block, they turned right. A patrol car was parked on the corner. Jack stopped the car and called out to the patrolman in the driver's seat.

"All's quiet, Jack," the cop reported. "A woman came out with a couple of kids. That's about it."

"Okay."

"Someone's coming out of her building," Kit exclaimed as a car passed them on the left, pulled up to Victoria's building, and stopped.

"That's Jeffrey's car!" Tracy screeched.

"Oh my God!" Jack breathed.

"What?" Regan asked as they all watched a bearded, mustached man wearing a dark raincoat scurry over and open the door to Jeffrey's car.

"Is Jeffrey with a *man?*" Tracy cried.

"No, Tracy!" Jack said swiftly. "That's a woman behind that beard." He gave the signal to his patrolman, and they both turned on their sirens. At the end of the block, Jeffrey had no choice but to pull over. When Tracy got out of Jack's car, Jeffrey turned white as a ghost. Television cameras seemed to appear out of nowhere.

But when Jack announced that he wanted Victoria to answer a few questions about their investigation into a string of bank robberies, Jeffrey almost passed out, the first of many times in the coming days when he'd be in need of smelling salts: When the television stations repeatedly ran the videos of Jeffrey and a bearded Victoria getting out of the car. When Victoria was officially accused of robbing the banks. And the clincher: when Jeffrey found out that she didn't dump her fiancé to be with him.

Frederick never existed. Victoria had visualized a husband. That's why she bought the dress. She figured if she really felt like a bride, she'd end up one. And it had almost worked. She'd nabbed Jeffrey in the elevator at Alfred and Charisse's salon. Only problem was that she not only visualized herself as a bride, she visualized herself as a bank robber so she could afford Alfred and Charisse's prices. And she was a credit card thief to boot.

All in all, Victoria Beardsley was not the answer to Jeffrey's dreams.

She was the beginning of his downfall.

And Tracy Timber loved every minute of it.

64

The celebration at Club Zee started to die down at around five. They'd all watched the footage of Jeffrey and Victoria getting out of the car. The image of a bearded Victoria throwing her arms around Jeffrey was a sight to behold.

Joyce thanked Wally for his hospitality and everyone else for being part of the search party. "I'm going to have my foot checked out at the emergency room. But please. Come out to my house anytime after eight tonight. We're ordering pizzas. I feel like I have a new lease on life and I don't want to stop celebrating!"

At the hospital, Joyce was examined and her foot was X-rayed. Other than a bad sprain, she was given a clean bill of health.

Tom and Cindy were with her. "Let's go get my car," he said, "and I'll drive you home."

Joyce started to say something, then stopped.

"Is something wrong?" he asked.

Joyce smiled up at him. "Nothing at all."

Cindy decided it was time to interfere. "I think Joyce wants to warn you that her ex-boyfriend might show up. But we plan to pack up his things and throw them out on the street."

"Thanks, Cindy. You have a gift for getting straight to the point," Joyce said with a smile.

"Your ex doesn't worry me," Tom said with a strength that made Joyce feel tingly.

An hour later, Joyce was settled on the couch in the living room, her foot on the coffee table, her crutches leaning on the edge of the couch, and most important, Tom right next to her. Cindy called the pizzeria and placed a big order, then opened up a few bottles of red wine.

By 8:01, Joyce's house was bustling with activity. Romeo was going crazy.

"Hello!" he called from his cage. "Hello!"

Regan and Kit and Tracy and her friends arrived together. Like Joyce, Tracy was enjoying a new lease on life. "Let's turn on the

TV," she said, reveling in the images of Jeffrey's public humiliation.

Brianne was sitting on Pauly's lap, looking like a woman in love.

The mood was one of celebration.

Joyce's crutches fell to the floor. "Let me get them out of the way," Regan offered. She picked them up. "I'll stick them in the front closet." She opened the door, and there was another pair of crutches staring her in the face. "Joyce, it looks like you didn't need these."

Joyce waved her hand. "They're my ex's. He was hurt on the job and milked his injury for all it was worth."

"I personally think that limp of his is fake," Cindy stated as she sipped her wine.

Regan's cell phone rang. She looked at the caller ID but couldn't tell who it was. "You mind if I take this in the bedroom?" she asked Joyce. "It's a little noisy in here."

"Go ahead," Joyce said.

Regan walked down the hall, flicked the light on in the bedroom, and shut the door behind her.

Dana, the producer of the *Patrick and Jeannie* show, was on the phone. "Regan, I'm finally heading home but I thought you'd be interested in a call we received about the stolen dresses. An elderly woman says she found an antique-white lace button on the ground in a cemetery near Atlantic City. She was visiting her husband's grave. It reminded her of the button from her wedding dress sixty years ago. It has a tiny logo on the back with the initials *A* and *C.* She took a picture of it and e-mailed it to us. You might want to take a look at it."

"I don't know whether Alfred and Charisse have that logo on their buttons. But I can't imagine what the thieves would be doing in a cemetery with the wedding dresses."

"I can't either. But who knows?"

Regan frowned. "Can you do me a favor, Dana, and e-mail the picture to Alfred? If it is one of his buttons, he can call my cell phone."

"Sure, Regan. We also received a call earlier from a woman who wants to make trouble for Brianne and her fiancé, Pauly. She said she was with him yesterday and wants to talk to Brianne."

"Oh, great," Regan said. "Give me her name." When Regan hung up with Dana, she went back to the living room and signaled for Brianne and Pauly to join her down the hall.

"What is it, Regan?" Brianne asked as the three of them slipped into Joyce's bedroom.

"I hate to be the one to tell you this," Regan said with hesitation. "But the producer of the *Patrick and Jeannie* show said someone named Monica called the station. I guess she wants to stir up some trouble."

"I already took care of her, Regan," Brianne boasted as Pauly looked up in the air. "That's the reason we were late getting down to Club Zee. Pauly told me the whole story. Monica is Pauly's ex. She went out with him right before he met me. He lent her money, and she refused to pay him back, especially after he dumped her for me. Yesterday he went to her place to try and get it back because he didn't think we had enough cash for our honeymoon. He's been out of work and money is tight, but that idiot didn't care. She finally agreed to pay him. They went to the bank, and she withdrew the cash. Five thousand dollars, by the way. Pauly said she was threatening him, and then with all this publicity about the April Brides, he was afraid she was going to make trouble. She had thought they'd end up married. Then when I said on the show that all his ex's were losers, he was sure that she wouldn't keep her mouth shut."

Pauly was still looking up at the ceiling.

Brianne broke into a wide smile. "I told him that no matter how hard she tries, I'm not going to let that witch come between us."

"That's my Brianne," Pauly said with pride. "That's why I love her so much."

"And we're going to have a good time spending that money on the honeymoon!" Brianne added. "It was Pauly's right to get it back, and I'm glad he did. I can assure you, Regan, she won't be calling the show again. I called her up and gave her a piece of my mind this afternoon."

"Well, I'm glad that's settled," Regan said. "Let's rejoin the party, shall we?"

When they went back to the living room, Romeo had just been let out of his cage.

65

Jack was down at his office where there was also a celebratory atmosphere. The Drip had been caught. Jack looked through his notes and found the number he was looking for. Wait till that poor bank teller hears this news, he thought as he dialed.

Tara and Jamie were enjoying themselves in Las Vegas, trying to forget the trauma she'd been through the day before. When Tara's cell phone rang, she grabbed it. "Hello."

"Tara?"

"Yes."

"This is Jack Reilly."

Tara smiled. "Hello! Don't tell me another bank was robbed!"

Jack laughed. "No, Tara, I thought you'd be pleased to know that your bank robber has been caught. She even confessed."

"She?"

"Yes, she had us all fooled. Anyway, I hope you're doing okay."

"We're doing great. Right now we're sitting by the pool having a wonderful time. My man Jamie's taking good care of me. We almost got married last night."

"You did?" Jack asked, surprised.

"After what happened yesterday, Jamie didn't want to wait. We even went down to the courthouse to get a marriage license, but I decided I couldn't do it to my mother. She'd kill me! We've been planning the wedding for so long. Say, did they catch whoever stole your fiancée's dress?"

"No, they didn't."

"What's she going to do?"

"The designer is making a new one. I hope he gets it done on time."

"There was a guy on the courthouse steps handing out flyers last night. He said there'd be a special sale on a very limited number of designer wedding dresses, but they wouldn't be available until Monday." Tara laughed. "Maybe you should bring your fiancée out here and take a look!"

"He said they are going to be there Monday. That sounds odd."

"I know, but this is Vegas. They probably fell off the back of a truck."

"I might just have one of my contacts out there check them out. Do you still have the flyer?"

"It's in my purse. Hold on, I've got everything in there but the kitchen sink." Tara handed Jamie the phone, dug through her belongings, and emerged triumphant. She took back the phone and said, "There's no address. Just a phone number. Here it is . . ."

66

Regan sat on the floor of Joyce's living room next to Kit and looked around. Everyone seemed so happy. Joyce and Tom were really hitting it off, although Joyce's parrot was now sitting between the two of them. Romeo looked as if he would happily take a chunk out of Tom's hand if he got too close to Joyce.

Jay, the pharmacist, came in and made a beeline for Tracy. Her face lit up when he sat down next to her. Wouldn't that be nice? Regan thought.

The phone rang. Cindy came from the kitchen, carrying the portable phone, her hand covering the mouthpiece. "It's Francis's mother."

Joyce rolled her eyes. "Give it to me." She took it and said, "Hello."

On the other end, Janice was in a state of agitation. "Joyce, are you all right?"

"Yes. Thank God."

"Where's Francis?"

"I don't know. My friend Cindy talked to him this morning and told him I was missing. He hung up and never called back."

"Did you have a fight? Did you do something to upset him? Maybe he's . . ."

Joyce sat up. "We didn't have a fight. I have no idea what he's up to."

Regan's cell phone rang. She answered it quickly.

"Regan!" Alfred cried. "They e-mailed us the picture of the button. This is the button that was on your dress!"

"Are you sure?"

"Of course I'm sure. We ordered it specially from France. It's a beautiful unique button! You know I only use the best on my dresses! It's our logo on the back!"

"The woman found it in a cemetery near Atlantic City," Regan said.

"Which is where I lost my keys!"

"I know. Alfred, I'll figure out what to do next and call you back. I can't talk now."

"Me, neither!" he insisted. "Charisse and I are working our fingers to the bone."

"We'll talk later then," Regan said.

Joyce was ending her phone conversation as well. "I have to go," she said firmly. "If I hear from Francis, I'll tell him to call you."

"What's the matter, Regan?" Cindy asked.

"An elderly woman found an antique lace button that reminded her of the one on her wedding dress in a cemetery near Atlantic City. She e-mailed a picture of it to the cable station. Alfred says it's definitely the button he used on my dress."

"Atlantic City?" Cindy asked.

"Yes, and that's where Alfred lost his keys last week. We think that whoever robbed his salon used his keys to get in. We also think that two guys at the craps table he was playing at picked his keys off the ground when he dropped them. We saw the tapes. One of the guys has a limp."

As Joyce inhaled sharply, the whole room fell silent.

"Lazy bums!" Romeo cried. "Lazy bums!"

Cindy walked over and reached behind the couch. She picked up the set of keys she had pulled out of Romeo's mouth just this morning. This time she took a moment to look at them. A tiny wedding dress made out of sterling silver was attached to the key ring. "Oh, my God . . ." she said.

"What?" Regan asked.

Cindy turned to her. "Could these be Alfred's keys?"

Monday, April 4th–
Friday, April 8th

67

Francis and Marco had been driving for over forty hours. Neither of them had showered in two days. They were grubby, tired, and irritable.

Earlier, when they'd tuned in to the *Imus in the Morning* radio show, Imus had been talking about what complete losers the guys must be who stole the April Brides' wedding dresses.

Marco had snapped off the radio, and they'd ridden in silence. Just before noon, they finally reached Las Vegas.

"Where are we meeting your friend?" Francis asked.

"He's got a motel room. We'll drop off the dresses, check into a hotel, and hope he sells the dresses fast so we can collect the money and run."

"I'm flying home this afternoon."

"Suit yourself."

"Thank God Joyce is okay. I just want to see her. She sounded a little funny on the phone."

Marco shrugged.

They drove to a rundown neighborhood not far from the main strip of high-rise hotels. The directions they'd been given led them to an old, dilapidated motel. An outside set of stairs led to the second floor where Marco's friend had set up his temporary bridal shop.

Francis and Marco got out of the car, opened the trunk, and lifted out the dishwasher box. They dropped it onto the hot pavement. Everything was still and quiet.

The sun was beating down, and Francis already felt a little woozy and disoriented from being in the car for so long. That's why when he saw a car door open and a woman emerge with a killer expression on her face, he wasn't sure whether he was hallucinating. She looked like the woman on NY1 who'd said she'd tear whoever ruined her dress limb from limb. It couldn't be, he thought.

But when she started running toward them, like one of the bulls at Pamplona, there was no doubt that she was the raging bride.

"You ruined my dress!" Brianne screamed as she lunged at him.

He had no time to escape. Before he knew it, she had tackled him to the ground.

"I've got one of them!" Brianne cried out to Regan, Jack, Pauly, Tracy, Kit, Tracy's friends, and several Las Vegas policemen who emerged from several cars parked around the lot.

"You two stink!" Brianne screamed. *"You're going to rot in jail!"*

Marco had cursed and taken off across the lot, but he didn't get far. A couple of the cops chased him down, while three others hurried up to the room where Marco's friend was trying to escape through a back window.

"Brianne!" Pauly said with exasperation, "you were supposed to wait until they went upstairs!"

"I couldn't wait! These creeps destroyed my wedding gown!"

Francis lay on the ground in misery. Pauly pulled Brianne off him, and then a cop pulled him to his feet. He and Marco were quickly handcuffed.

"Ow!" Marco cried. "I've got a gash on my arm. It's probably infected."

"It must have been your blood, then, that was all over Brianne's dress," Regan said to him with disgust.

"I hope it hurts," Brianne sneered.

As Marco and Francis were escorted into the back of an unmarked police cruiser, the three April Brides ceremoniously opened the dishwasher box and pulled out the four dresses.

"My gown isn't in this box," Brianne said, "but I wouldn't have missed this trip for the world."

"Mine is here but it's going to charity," Tracy said. "I'm sending it to Haiti where women have to get married in a white dress but often can't afford it. But I wouldn't have missed this trip, either."

Regan made a quick inspection of her dress. Other than the missing button, it was in pretty good shape. All it needed was a good steam. "All right, everyone," Regan said. "Let's have a nice lunch at the Bellagio and then head back to New York."

"Thank your father for getting us the private plane," Brianne said. "I'm glad he had the connections to get one so fast. It was worth seeing the expression on those losers' faces."

"It certainly was," Tracy agreed.

Regan smiled. "My father said this dress had cost him so much already that he might as well go all out to see that I retrieved it personally."

"He's going to be telling this story for a long time to come," Kit said with a chuckle. "Just like the story of how he got kidnapped so you could find a husband."

Regan laughed and looked over at Jack. He was speaking with the police captain. She loved him so much. I don't care what else happens, she thought. Nothing in the world is going to stop us from getting married this Saturday. As she folded her wedding dress, she held it in her hands for a few extra moments before carefully returning it to the dishwasher box. It was beautiful. She couldn't wait to put it on in five days and walk down the aisle to join hands with the man she had waited for all her life. She smiled as their song started to run through her head—"Till There Was You."

68

Much to Nora's delight, Regan would now be able to keep her promise and devote the rest of the week to her wedding preparations. That is, after Regan finally woke up on Tuesday afternoon and caught up on all the newspaper stories and media coverage about the capture of the dress thieves.

The top priority was to procure a band. Tracy suggested they hire the band that she no longer needed.

"They're certainly free on Saturday night, Regan," she said. "But if you hire them, you have to invite me."

"Sounds like a plan."

"And I'd like to bring Jay."

Regan smiled. "There's nothing I'd like better than to see you two dancing at my wedding. I'm so glad you're doing well."

"I'm living with the satisfaction that Jeffrey is calling constantly, begging for forgiveness. Of course I would never go back to him, but I'm enjoying his misery." She sighed. "He wasn't the one. When I see you with Jack, I realize how I want it to be for me . . ."

Regan and Nora spent hours deciding who would sit at which table. When they finally finished, Nora sighed. "You know that someone's going to be unhappy with where we put them."

Regan laughed. "Mom, it wouldn't be a wedding otherwise. I bet it'll be Aunt Nahnah who complains. She got that nickname for a reason."

"Regan!" Nora protested.

"You're right, Regan," Luke said as he walked in the door. "I'm glad you didn't mention someone from my side of the family."

"Don't get me started!" Nora laughed, as her husband kissed the top of her head.

Luke was thrilled that the mystery of the strange phone calls was solved by the New Jersey police, who had raided an apartment for drugs. What they found on the dining table wasn't drugs but a pile of engagement announcements cut out of local newspapers. Regan's was on top. The Reilly home had indeed been targeted for a break-in on Saturday afternoon.

Nora and Regan checked and rechecked all the arrangements—the menu, the cake, the readings at the church, the flowers. There was an endless stream of phone calls and deliveries while Regan packed for her honeymoon. On Thursday, Regan went with her bridesmaids to a day spa in New York City where they were pampered with massages, facials, manicures, and pedicures. Lunch was served as they lounged in their terry-cloth bathrobes. They all emerged looking gorgeous and relaxed.

The rehearsal dinner was Friday night. In the afternoon, Regan received a special delivery from Pamela and Arnold. It was one of Pamela's antique bracelets. The card read, "We wish you the best tomorrow, Regan. Please accept this bracelet as a token of our affection and gratitude."

Regan called to thank them. Pamela was exuberant on the phone. "Regan, our son just called us. He and his wife were in the process of adopting a baby but didn't want to tell us until it went through. They didn't want to get our hopes up. So we will have a baby to spoil after all. You and Jack will have to come by when they're in town."

"We will," Regan promised.

Brianne called as well. She was about to head out to her rehearsal dinner. Her gown was hanging safely in her parents' house. Alfred and Charisse had worked for three days and nights getting it done.

"Regan," Brianne said, "I wish we could be at each other's weddings."

"Me, too, Brianne. When we get back from our honeymoons, we'll have a night comparing our videos and pictures."

"I'm so glad we're friends, Regan. I feel as if we really got to know each other."

"That we did!" Regan laughed.

"And I'm sorry if I acted like a jerk when you first met me."

"Hey—don't worry about it. Your dress was the one in shreds."

"Can you believe it?" Brianne asked, her voice becoming agitated. "I still wish I could have shown those two bums a thing or two."

"Brianne, I think they got your message," Regan chuckled. You can be comforted by the fact that they're suffering right now. Especially Francis. That guy is never going to recover."

"You're right, Regan. Can you believe we're the only two out of the five April Brides getting married? I think Alfred is a jinx."

"Brianne!"

"It's true, Regan."

"I don't think it's Alfred's fault that less than half of his April Brides are making it to the altar. You and I are lucky. And Tracy's better off without Jeffrey. Those other two, well, as Alfred would say, 'At least they have good taste in wedding dresses.' "

Brianne laughed. "All the best to you tomorrow, Regan. You're going to make a beautiful bride. And you're going to make someone very happy."

"So are you, Brianne," Regan said sincerely. "I'll see you in a few weeks."

Saturday, April 9th

69

At the back of St. Ignatius Loyola Church in Manhattan, Alfred and Charisse were making a final fuss over the train of Regan's dress when the processional music began.

"You look gorgeous," Alfred whispered.

"Fabulous," Charisse said as she blew a kiss. They hurried through a side door and up to their seats.

Kit handed Regan her bouquet. "It's really happening, Regan. You're getting hitched."

Regan smiled at her best friend. "I know. I'm glad I'm not just visualizing this."

Jack's three sisters were also Regan's bridesmaids. One of them started down the aisle, followed by the second, the third, and then Kit, Regan's maid of honor.

Regan looked up at Luke, her arm tucked in his. "Are you ready, Daddy?"

Luke's eyes were misty. "I never thought

I'd be ready for this moment. But the guy you're marrying makes it all seem right."

The music switched to the bridal processional. The congregation stood, and faced the back of the church, eagerly awaiting Regan's appearance.

Luke and Regan came around the corner of the vestibule and went up the steps.

On the altar, Jack's breath was taken away by the sight of his beautiful bride.

As Luke and Regan made their slow walk down the aisle, Regan savored every second. She was about to marry her soul mate, and the people she and Jack loved had come to share their joy.

Family, old friends, new friends. Some very new friends.

Tracy was with Jay, beaming. I've got to hand it to her, Regan thought. She's a survivor. Not many women could get out and celebrate someone else's wedding on the day she was supposed to be married, no matter how big a creep her fiancé turned out to be. Joyce and Tom were in the same pew. Tom had his arm firmly around Joyce's waist as she stood on one foot.

Regan smiled at them as well as at many of the other friends she'd met through her work. Lem and Viddy from Vermont, Thomas from the Settler's Club, the actress Whitney Weldon and her boyfriend, Whitney's aunt Lucretia Standish, Ellie Butternut, an aspiring actress from Los Angeles who Regan was sure would be a star, Louis, the restaurateur from Aspen, Lady Veronica from England, Will and his wife, Kim, from Hawaii . . .

Her dear friends Alvirah and Willy Meehan had a place of honor behind the family. Alvirah had helped them find Luke when he was kidnapped. She was wiping her eyes.

"I'm warning you," she'd told Regan. "I always cry at weddings."

Nora was in the front pew, her eyes shining with pride. Regan reached out and touched Nora's hand as she went by. Jack's parents were in the front pew on the other side. She couldn't ask for better in-laws.

Jack was standing at the altar waiting for her. He was so handsome. His groomsmen, including his two brothers, were lined up next to him. Everyone looked so happy.

Regan thought of the time Jack had shown up at her parents' house unexpectedly after her father was safely returned after being kidnapped. She would never forget the words he spoke to her when she opened the door . . .

Luke kissed her on the cheek, shook Jack's hand, and stepped away. As Jack reached for her, she leaned toward him and whispered, "Have you got room for another Reilly around here?"

Jack smiled broadly as he took her hand in his. "Like you had to ask . . ."